The Highlander's Curse
Legions of Fate

By

Katalyn Sage

Published by
Katalyn Sage
www.katalynsage.com
Copyright © 2013 Katalyn Sage
ISBN: 978-0-9910202-0-1

Dedication

To you.
You are my life, my heart, my universe.
I love you.

Acknowledgements

Thank you to everyone who has helped me put this together. I couldn't have done it without you.

And thank you to my fans.
Your support means everything to me.

CHAPTER ONE

"Is it true what they say, about what's under a Scot's kilt?" I waggled my eyebrows at a pair of spindly old legs as their owner loped past my table and joined a group of men.

Shannon glanced at the geriatric, a loud laugh escaping her as she took in the pastiness of his legs that were blinding between the bottom of his kilt and the top of his stretched argyle socks. After a lot of searching on my part, I'd found him to be the only man in the pub that wore a kilt. A fact that was more than slightly disappointing. On the upside though, the pub was exactly as I'd imagined a tavern in Scotland would be: lined wall-to-wall with Scottish men who were bantering in their awesome accents and having a good time. Many were packed with muscle, and somehow sported tans despite the fact that rain and clouds covered the skies nearly all the time—or so I'd been told—while others were small in stature and looked like they hadn't seen the sun in years.

Aside from Shannon and myself, there was only one other woman in the bar, and she was behind the mahogany and brass counter, serving up drinks as fast as they were ordered, in addition to handling food requests that were hollered at her from every direction. It was a wonder she could keep up, with as fast as these Highlanders were downing their liquor. There were also a few goth guys huddled over their drinks at the bar, one of which could have possibly been a woman—not that I could really tell, so I left that one clumped in with the more masculine sex.

As I looked around the pub, my gaze landed once more

1

on the creepy guy in the corner. I'd spotted him the minute we'd walked into the bar, the sight of him giving me the willies.

He still did, too.

Wearing a hooded cloak, the man slouched over his drink in the far corner of the room, as far as possible from any natural light that filtered in through the windows. No portion of his face could be seen, despite my multiple attempts at squinting in his direction. And, unless I'd missed any movement in that corner of the room, he'd been nursing that same drink since we'd walked through the door. I seriously doubted I'd missed anything going on there though, since one eye had been practically glued to his corner for the last ten minutes. Discreetly, of course.

"I can't really speak for every Scotsman," Shannon said, shaking her head at me. A small flush had worked across her cheeks, and I smiled. Like she didn't know that I live to embarrass her.

"Oh, come on. What about Sir William? Haven't gotten a look-see under his kilt yet?"

She studied the scuffed table, finding a single crumb to flick off the surface. "I've never even seen him in his kilt."

Well, well, I thought, leaning forward and folding my arms on the table. If there wasn't an undercurrent to the way she'd just said that, then I didn't know my bestie at all. "Don't tell me you two haven't had sex yet."

"*Oh my God. Shhh.*" Shannon blushed again as she sank down in her chair, glancing around to make sure no one heard. "Yes, we have. And the reason I haven't seen him in his kilt yet is because he wants me to wait and see it the day we get married."

That was...actually sweet. And totally something Shannon deserved. I leaned back against my chair. "Good. I think it's nice that he wants to surprise you. And I'm really

2

glad the two of you have done the nasty, because you know my stance on sex before marriage." Why anyone would want to attach themselves to someone else for the rest of their life without knowing what to expect in the sack made absolutely no sense to me. Shannon thought I'd lost my virginity years ago, and that was one thing I'd never corrected her on. It was probably the only secret between us. "It's not like I needed another maid of honor project, anyway. Glad I don't have to get you laid on top *everything* else I have to do."

"Me, too." She grinned, her expression morphing from mortification to appreciation. "I'm so glad you came."

"I am, too. I still can't believe you're getting married. *And to a Scot, no less,*" I added, trying my hand— terribly—at a Scottish accent.

We both laughed, my best friend holding her sides at the hilarity of my failed attempt. Shannon and I had known each other our entire lives. Being best friends and cousins, we knew almost every detail about each other. Shannon had always been the shy, sweet girl that kept to herself and had her nose firmly planted in whatever book she was engrossed in at the moment.

I went to parties and waited for the movies to come out.

When she'd told me eight months ago that she was going to Scotland to stay with some distant cousins, and to learn about their clan's history, I'd thought she was crazy, and was fairly certain—not that I'd ever, *ever* tell her—that she'd touch down in Scotland and turn right back. But that hadn't been the case. Apparently she'd fallen in love with the place during one of the many vacations her family had taken.

I'd spoken to Shannon on the phone every couple of weeks, and by the fourth call, my best friend had done a one-eighty. She'd actually started talking about guys instead of the incredible history that Scotland had to offer; and then just three months ago, she'd called me up and asked me to be her maid-of-honor. I had accepted right off the bat, and had the pleasure of informing my dad that his baby girl would be flying to Scotland before he did to help out with the wedding.

In reality, life at home just hadn't been the same without my Shanny Panny there. And since she'd left mere weeks after graduation, my post high school life hadn't been nearly as party-centric as I'd imagined. With missing one of my two best friends, I just hadn't found going out to be quite as fun. We'd had another bestie, Tory, until right before graduation, but that bitch had gone off her rocker. She'd been a major topic of my phone conversations with Shannon over the last few months, and had grown to be a big pain in my ass. As for our third amigo…

"Oh, Carrie changed flights, so she isn't flying in until next Tuesday. And I guess she doesn't need you to pick her up," I said, recalling my last conversation with our other best friend. "She also said she hopes that doesn't mess with your plans on her helping out with the wedding, since apparently the two of us will pretty much have handled it anyway."

"Oh?"

I shrugged. She probably didn't find this all that surprising. Not with the carefree way Carrie lived her life. "I guess she found a date that actually has a passport and could afford the ticket over here, so she wants to spend a night in Glasgow with him first."

"I wonder if he knows that." Shannon laughed, nodding in thanks as the waitress set our burgers and drinks on the table. I didn't even have to lean forward to smell the alcohol permeating from my glass. Then again, the whole place smelled like an alcoholic sponge. She brought the glass to her lips and took a sip, smiling. "You should try it. This is a lot stronger than anything back home."

I gawked at her, mocking offense. "Shannon Perry, are you suggesting that I, who am not even legally able to drink yet, have tasted *alcohol*?"

Her eyes bugged, and I threw my hands up, shielding my face as her drink sprayed from her lips. "Of course not," she teased grabbing her phone and hastily scrolling to whatever she was looking for. "You couldn't *possibly* be the one responsible for giving me my first taste of Jack and Coke, or," she flashed her cell's screen at me, "the one in this picture sucking Jell-O shots off Jimmy Alder's chest."

I grabbed her phone and stared at the picture, taking a few extra seconds to admire Jimmy. He looked that good up close, too. "I can't believe you still have that."

"*Pfft*. Like I would ever get rid of it? I planned to use it against you if you refused to come out for the wedding."

I shook my head, smiling as I handed her phone back. "Those were good shots. You should have tried some." I reached for my glass and threw back some whiskey, instantly realizing my mistake. My throat closed up and I had to force out a cough as the burn of alcohol rushed through my chest. After a helpful slug to my back, I sputtered a quick "thanks" to the guy behind me as I regained breath. "That's strong." Eyes tearing up at the burn, it came out no more than a wheeze.

"Stronger proof than we get in Utah."

I nodded. *Stronger than we probably get in the States.* Damn, I wish I could have said that out loud. I pounded my fist against my chest twice, trying to dislodge whatever still had me gasping.

"Probably better than Jimmy's Jell-O shots." Shannon waggled her brows.

"Debatable." My throat got with the program and

opened up again, and sweet, maybe-not-so-fresh-air seeped into my lungs. "So, what can I help with that's *weddingy*?"

A flicker of excitement washed over Shannon's face, and she picked up a binder, opened it on the table and scrolled her finger over a checklist. "I still need to go through the RSVPs and see who's coming and who isn't, and make a spreadsheet of who wants which entrée. Oh, and I need to figure out the seating arrangements. After that, I need to call the caterer and give them the final count."

Seemed like a good place to begin, some of which probably should have been started weeks ago. "Alright, where are the cards?"

"They're at Will's. Oh, I should call and see if I can catch him before he leaves. He *so* can't wait to meet you." Shannon speed-dialed on her Scotland cell and held the phone to her ear, peering up at the ceiling as she waited. "Hi sweetie."

I turned and pulled my tablet out of my purse, letting it power up as I attached my mini keyboard. By the time Shannon hung up—after too many kissy sounds to count—I had already opened Excel, entered column headers, and had started entering details below the headers. "...Pan-seared chicken, additional guests: none, and honorary table, yes?" At Shannon's nod, I saved the spreadsheet. "There. One down. Scarlett Michaelson, check."

The man in the corner shifted violently, making me jump as he lurched to his feet. He was covered from head to toe, and I peered at him openly, wondering just how much he'd had to drink, and exactly why he wore a cloak. Must be a Scottish thing. As he lumbered his way toward me, I suddenly got the vision of Monty Python's *The Holy Grail* and hoped he'd begin to chant: *"Pie Iesu domine."* *Whack.* *"Dona eis requiem."* *Whack.*

Like that would really happen. I smiled to myself at the thought just before the guy bumped heavily into our table.

"Whoa. You alright there?" I stood, holding my hands out to brace one of his arms. He was already facing me, and as his hood fell back from his face, panic-stricken, dark blue eyes bore into mine.

He wasn't drunk at all. He was terrified.

"What's yer name?" he demanded, gripping my arms.

I shook my head, still trying to figure out exactly what was happening. "Wha—"

"What is yer name?" he pleaded, his thick Scottish brogue rushing from his lips.

"Scarlett."

"Scarlett what?"

What the hell did my name matter? "Listen, I don't—"

"*Please*, lass!"

There was something deep in his voice, deep in that dark gaze that made me pause. I didn't have a clue what knowing my name would help, but if it could help this guy in some small way, I'd tell him. "Michaelson," I stammered.

He drew back, blinking in shock as his eyes lit on me and then stared off into whatever void he was dealing with. And then, almost as quickly as he'd stepped away from me, he rushed forward again, grasping my forearms hard enough that I squeaked in alarm. "I didnae think it was true. I didnae ken…but it is. And God, lass, ye must go. Ye must set it right."

"Hey!" Shannon yelled, wrenching on his shoulder. He brushed her off easily—though that was no wonder with his size—and even ignored the other men who stepped in to separate him from me.

I couldn't look away from him, no matter how hard I tried. No matter how hard my heart beat or the way my mind screamed at me to run, I was somehow compelled by this lunatic.

"Here," he said, suddenly yanking his gaze from mine. He reached into his cloak and pulled something out before pressing it into my hands: Coins and an old-fashioned pocket watch.

Holding the coins in one hand, I lifted the other to inspect the watch, wondering what the hell this guy was going on about as he mumbled hurriedly. As I peered at the face, the secondhand ticked backwards. And did it again. The next two ticks went in time with my heart beat, the twin thumps somehow echoing loudly in my ears.

Tick-tick, thump-thump. Tick-tick, thump-thump, TICK-TICK, POUND-POUND. HAMMER, HAMMER, HAMMER.

Now the minutes were going backwards as well. It whipped counterclockwise faster and faster, my heart beat no longer recognizable. My head grew dizzy as I stared, now unable to avert my eyes from the phenomenon. Red-hot fire singed my palm and I yelped, trying to drop it from my hand. It wouldn't go though, no matter what I did. My hand refused to unclasp it's tight hold, even as I tried to pry it free with my fingers.

"...Please dinna fail. Dae ye kin what I've said? Please, *ye mustn'ae fail.*"

His words reached me through my disorientation, but they were like an echo, dancing all around me as though they hadn't come from one mouth—or from one direction. The burn in my hand intensified, traveling up my arm like waves of lava, and crashing into my heart. I screamed—or I thought I did—the sound of it rushing around me like the echo of that pleading voice.

And then, the ground was no longer there; the people, the bar, all gone. A black pit surrounded me, crushing me in its oblivion.

I fell away, screaming as I reached for everything that had just surrounded me. Shannon, the pub, the cloaked guy, even the other patrons. It was all distorted as it shrunk farther away from me, and then disappeared into the black distance.

⌒◇◇⌒

I sat up, bracing my arms on my knees as I glanced around, certain I wasn't really seeing what I thought I was.

I was out in the middle of nowhere, where nothing was in sight other than the green grass that rippled in waves until it met up with the murky water of the lake. There wasn't a single house. Not even a freakin' sheep, and I'd seen *thousands* of those since I'd touched down in Scotland.

Alright Scar, what have you gotten yourself into now?

Feeling grateful I hadn't removed it at the bar, I reached into my purse and rummaged through everything inside until I finally felt the unmistakable smoothness of my cell phone. The screen was lit up before I even looked down.

It was 5:43 PM and not a single bar. No 4G. No 3G. Not even a stupid 1X. *Ugh.*

I pushed to my feet, wobbling as the heels of my stilettos sunk into the soft ground. Once I freed my shoes of their muddy prisons, I attempted facing different directions for a signal. I tried everything: holding it high, holding it low, holding it at an angle, dialing out, texting, and typing a quick SOS message on my social media handles. But after what felt like forever, I was forced to give up on trying to get even a blip of service.

For now.

Get me out of these damn fields, and I'll try again,

though.

I glared at the fields and the annoyingly pretty tall grass that swayed in the wind, and at the dark clouds that rolled in, pushing the lighter gray ones out of their way as though their rainy purpose was far more important.

Okay, something happened at the bar. But what? Had the whiskey been too strong for me? I wasn't that much of a lightweight, and most of it hadn't even made it down my throat. But I had grown dizzy. What if I'd been poisoned?

As I surveyed my surroundings again, a chill started at the top of my spine and coursed through my body. That lake looked really familiar. The shape of it, and the slope of the hills on the other side. I powered on my phone again and scrolled through the pictures I'd taken on my trip so far. I passed the one I'd been searching for and quickly recalled it.

Yes, it looked the same. Minus the city, streets, cars, people, docks, and boats. The shape of the lake and land on the other side was nearly identical. But, there was no way could I be staring at the same one I'd seen in Oban, could I? They might have been identical, but where were the buildings and the roads, the docks and the boats? Where were the *people*?

No, I can't still be in Oban, I thought as I slid my phone into my purse. Or at least not in the part I'd been to. So where was I, and how had I ended up here? Shannon would have never put up with that crazy guy running off with me.

Unless something happened to her, too.

My heart lurched at the thought. What if Shannon had tried to stop him and he hurt her? Or *killed* her? What if she was out here somewhere, unconscious in the tall grass? I had no idea how long I'd been out, and the thought of Shannon being anywhere out here—or worse, with that guy—had my entire body strung with panic.

"Breathe Scar, breathe," I muttered to myself, taking a long, slow breath. I had to find Shannon. And I doubted that would happen if I just stayed here.

I took a step and stopped when my heels caused something underfoot to *clink*. Lying in the tall grass was the small pile of change and the gold pocket that had burned me in the pub. Turning my hand up, I glanced down and gasped. A light red scar raised the skin in my palm; a sort of round, haphazard design that looked mean and ugly. What the hell happened?

I gingerly picked them up—careful not to touch the watch other than by the chain—and shoved them into my purse. That bastard must have kidnapped me and dropped me in the middle of freakin' nowhere. Asshole.

Shaking my head and mentally kicking him in the balls, I picked a direction and went with it, stepping through the wet grass as thunder rolled in the cloudy sky above. I didn't even have my stupid jacket and had to yank off my shoes since my heels succeeded in sinking into the damp ground with every step.

Heaving myself up and over the first rock fence I came to—which wasn't all that easy in a short skirt—I felt a raindrop land on the back of my thigh. To my left were some trees, maybe the edge of a forest. I didn't feel safe walking through the woods during a lightning storm, but as I glanced between that and the open, rolling fields, I opted for the protection the forest might provide. At least in there, I wouldn't be the tallest thing around to act as a lightning rod.

Four more drops landed on me, and I ran toward the trees. My purse collided against my hip with every jar and my heels banged together as I held them looped over my finger. I made it under the shelter of the leaves just as the sky opened up, dropping sheets of rain. Some misty drops still hit me, so I went farther into the forest and found a nice big tree to sit under.

Freakin' great, I thought as I hugged my knees to my chest. I was cold, damp, had no service, and my high heels were gunked with mud. *Thanks a lot, asshole.* If I ever saw that guy again, it'd be more than just a mental ball-kicking. With any luck, his voice would permanently go up a few octaves.

Drumming my fingers on my knees, and trying to force myself to calm, I did the only thing I could think to do: I waited for the rain to die down. Although, if rumors of Scotland were true, then any likelihood of that happening was pretty much nil. It could be days, or even weeks. Okay, so waiting was out. Would I have any luck trekking it through the forest? I'd have to eventually stumble on people. What kinds of animals lurked in the forests of Scotland, anyway? Probably nothing nearly as scary as what prowled the mountains at home. And with any luck, I'd pull a Lara Croft and find random weapons, medi-packs and food lying around. I smiled to myself. Yeah, who else would hope a shitstorm like this could turn into a real-life video game?

I stood and headed in the direction I'd been going before. Trekking it was the best plan to get me warmed up and at least gain some ground in the search for civilization. As soon as I found a house or a town, I could call the Scottish police and find a way back to Oban, and to Shannon. Hopefully she was home. If not...well, then I'd go back to Lorne's Pub if I had to to get some answers. I'd call the damn U.S. Embassy and light a fire under their asses until she was found, and until Captain Cloak was locked away for life.

My skirt caught on the rough, dry bark of a large fallen tree I'd just crawled over, snagging just before my feet landed on the ground. "Son of a..." I sighed. *Dammit.*

Focus, Scar. You can take it out on his ass as soon as you find him. There were more important things to do first.

I'd learned over the past hour or so that as I'd meandered through the forest, there were only a few spots where raindrops actually landed on me through the thick covering above. I continued on, focusing on the *pitter-pat* of raindrops hitting the leaves, until I picked up on another sound. Not the pounding of the rain all around me, but a rhythmic, muffled *thudding* that had me stopping to listen better.

There was definitely something there.

I ran toward the sound, dodging around trees, lifting my feet higher as I rushed through the grass and vines that threatened to take me down with every step. My feet throbbed as every few steps landed on something sharp, and I feared looking down, knowing that they were probably bleeding. I was getting closer to the lake, the clouded sunlight reflecting off of it in shimmering patterns that danced through the trees.

An old-fashioned horse and carriage came into view, and I had to stop and catch my breath from all the running. I found some soft leaves to stand on, giving my feet a break since they needed rest even more than my aching muscles and lungs. The horse was pulling the buggy at a leisurely pace, and I knew I'd catch it after another minute of running. The carriage was nothing fancy, but it looked old. What was interesting, though, was the driver on top, dressed to the nines in old-world clothes I'd only seen in movies. I'd heard that Scots took their history seriously, but jeez. Who still went for rides in horse-drawn carriages?

That distraction was what I'd needed, my aches and pains fading as I focused on the taboo of Scottish life. The horse stopped suddenly, forcing the carriage to lurch to a halt and drawing my full attention. Had they seen me? Stopped to help? I squinted, trying to focus through the rain and saw the driver's hands up in the air, the reins still dangling from them.

What the hell?

I took another step forward and two more fully-kilted men came into view, only these two were holding rifles pointed directly at the driver. One fired off his weapon—a warning shot that couldn't have buzzed very far past me. I gasped and a hand shot around me, a large palm covering my mouth as an arm pulled me to a hard body. I screamed, but it hardly made any sound.

Holy Jesus, holy shit, holy Jesus, holy shit, oh my God, oh my God, ohhhhh my God.

My personal defense training kicked in, and I lifted my hand and shoved it backward. Contact. The man groaned and released me with a curse, but as I shot forward, he grabbed me again.

"*Christ*, that hurt," he mumbled against me as I struggled.

I threw elbows and even my head back, trying to get free again, but he was too strong.

More gently, he added, "Shhh. Shh, lass. I'm no' here tae hurt ye. Be still."

I did still, though that was more his doing than my own. My heart threatened to leap from my chest as my heart hammered, and I could feel that his did, too. I had to keep reminding myself to breath, even though doing so from behind his hand made it more difficult. I shivered, the chill of the cold seeping into my bones at the same time as did the heat of his body. He didn't loosen his hold on my mouth, or around my waist. The man was holding me subdued, his breath fanning over my cheek and neck as I looked out at the horse and carriage, and at the people who

I'd hoped would rescue me.

One of the kilted gunmen slid the barrel of his rifle into his kilt as the driver and passengers—a man and a woman, both decked out in full Scottish regalia—stood on the muddy road, their clothes already soaked from the pouring rain. He had begun pulling luggage from the racks on top of the carriage, opening them and ransacking their things. I squinted at the whole scene unfolding in front of me, a million thoughts filling my mind at once: One being that I wondered just what the man holding me was wearing. I had a feeling I knew. My second thought: What did he want with me?

Kilts and violence. You ended up in the wrong part of Scotland, Scar.

"These will fetch a hefty price," the pillaging gunman grunted, holding up a gown for his partner to see. "Look at the quality."

"Aye. And where are ye travelin' tae, then?" the other asked, regaining everyone's attention, though it was hard for me to hear over the sound of the pounding rain, the beat of my heart, and the man's breath in my ear. Not to mention the fast way they talked. I'd had a hard time understanding them even when they'd dumbed it down for me at the airport and spoke slowly. In all honesty, I didn't know what to do at this point: Get the attention of the people on the road, including the rifle-wielding Scotsmen; or stay with the lunatic holding me?

What if he was the one who'd kidnapped me?

The gunman who'd rummaged through the couple's things carelessly tossed the luggage on top of the coach, and approached them again with his rifle in hand. "Get in the carriage," he ordered, flicking the barrel in that direction.

The man and woman did as he'd demanded and were

shut inside with one of the gunmen. The other bandit kept his gun trained on the driver as he stepped up onto the coach and took the reins.

"Now wait a minute," the driver huffed indignantly. "That's *ma* carriage."

"Nae longer." The one that held the reins pulled his trigger, the blast deafening as the coachman fell to the ground.

I screamed behind the man's palm, pushing away from him with all my strength as the horses lurched forward, and the coach disappeared around the bend. He pulled me back toward him, stopping me from making any movement at all, let alone race down to the road to check on the driver.

"Woman, be quiet," he growled. "Nae doubt there are more o' those bloody heathens nearby. Dae ye want us tae all be deed?"

"*Muwenededonthe*," I mumbled from behind his palm.

"I said be silent, woman. I'll nae let ye get either o' us killed, aye?"

I stopped fighting and slumped, still tight against his body. I only recognized the sound of my own breathing and the feeling of my limbs shaking. Oh, and the tears that trailed down my cheeks.

I couldn't have just seen that. A coldblooded shooting? Let alone by people who looked like they were taking a trip down Ye Olde History Lane a little too seriously? I mumbled against the man's palm again, only slightly calmer than I'd been minutes before.

"Ye're goin' tae be quiet?"

I nodded, and he hesitantly peeled his fingers and palm from my face. I might have felt safer had he not just moved his arm down to brace my chest and shoulders.

"We have to get down there," I repeated, this time without the muffling of his hand.

"Nae."

Of course. Why would he care if the driver was still alive or not? "Why didn't you do anything?"

"There's naethin' I could hae done. We're on MacDougall land."

"What does that matter?" I asked, shifting against him. The man tightened his arms and I let out an irritated breath. "Oh *let go*."

"Ye're nae goin' tae try and run, woman," he warned, his rough Scottish brogue making it sound more like *wooman*. "Nor make a peep louder than we're speakin' now."

A single nod, and my captor's arms loosened before he backed away a single step. I turned, facing him, but my eyes landed on a taught chest, which was barely concealed by a strip of plaid cloth running from his waist up to one shoulder. I'd known he was huge from when he'd held me against him, but imagining his size and seeing it were two different things. I forced my gaze upward, startled to see a scowling face with piercing blue eyes narrowed on me; a swollen, bloody nose; brown hair so dark it almost looked black, and a square jaw that was heavily dusted with at least a few days' stubble. I took a step back, getting him the hell out of my personal bubble—or getting out of his. The guy tensed at my movement, his broad chest and shoulders appearing even bigger as he folded his arms. This was not the man I'd seen in Lorne's Pub, but that didn't make him any less threatening. Probably more so. Was that a freakin' sword at his side?

"Dinna run," he barked, his r's rolling heavily as he glared at me in warning.

I folded my arms in response, giving him a scowling every bit as much as he was giving me. "Why didn't you do anything to help them?"

"No' ma clan lands." He shrugged.

"What does that matter?"

"What does that matt—where are ye from?" he demanded, his brows drawn low. He looked me up and down, his face taking on a look of horror at my Juicy t-shirt, short skirt, and legs. "And what in Christ's name are ye wearing?"

"I'm an American. And what the hell does it matter what I'm wearing?"

He made a Scottish grunt. "An *American*, is it? Aye, ye're definitely no' a Scot." He turned away then and rubbed his hands over his face. "And where are yer clothes, woman?"

Zero time was wasted at his turned back. I whirled around, bolting toward the road, hopping over brush and anything else that got in my way. I made it out of the trees and onto the downward slope. And then, I wasn't running anymore. I was tackled to the ground, with a heavy body on top of me. I barely had time to register that twigs and leaves were slapping me in the face before I was rolled onto my back, and the Scot's body pressed me to the ground. I screamed and brought my hand up, intending to shove it into his already bleeding nose, but he cupped his hand over my mouth and halted my hand with a tight grip that instantly numbed my entire arm.

"Be *quiet*, lass. Did ye nae hear what I said?"

I shook my head back and forth until his hand left my mouth. "*Get off of me!*"

"Nae. Ye said ye wouldn'ae run, and ye did."

"I didn't say I wouldn't run, you just told me not to."

"And. Ye. Nodded," he said slowly.

"Of course I ran, ass wipe. Do you really expect me to remain in the presence of a…a…barbarian?"

He laid on top of me for a few seconds more, his scowl

increasing before he pushed off of me, and stood to his feet. "Barbarian, is it? So I should'ae left ye tae the bastards that killed the driver down there? Left ye for deed rather than savin' yer pretty little arse?" He stabbed his fingers through his hair and flicked his gaze at me. "And what does what I wipe ma arse wi'hae tae dae wi'anythin'?"

I sat up, picking leaves and twigs out of my hair. My butt and back were freezing now, soaked through from being thrown onto the wet ground by this monstrous brute. I got to my feet and stared him down—or up, rather—as I brushed at my skirt.

"Ye move fast for a lass." He brought his hands up to his nose. "And I think ye broke ma nose. Verra lucky I didnae kill ye."

Holy shit. I gaped and stepped back from him again, trying to remember any other tricks I'd learned in defense training.

"Nae, no' from the nose. I was hunting," he added, evidently seeing my shock. "I was trackin' animals, but I had nae idea what was coming when ye crashed through the forest." A smirk formed across his face and his eyes lit up. "I thought ye were a *boar*."

And what the crap was he saying about me there? "Well, as I'm sure you can see, I'm not. Now, are you going to keep me here or can I go?"

The Scotsman's eyebrows rose into his hairline. "Go? And where would ye be headin' then? The only town nearby is where those dirty bast…" He rubbed a hand over his neck. "Uh, where those men live. Ye're no' a Scot, so I dinna imagine ye're part o' their clan."

"Where is the next town then? Where is Oban?"

He blinked. "Oban? Ne'er heard o' it."

"How have you never heard of it? It's like a big city. Have you maybe heard of Lorne's Pub?" Scots liked to drink.

"Big city?" he said quietly. "Lorne's Pub? I dinna ken the foolishness ye speak o'. Now, where are yer clothes?"

I peered down at my Juicy t-shirt and skirt, and popped my eyebrows. "What does it look like I'm wearing?"

"Och, those are no' proper clothes for a lady. I've ne'er seen such..." His voice died away as he frowned at my shirt and mouthed the word "Juicy". "It's just no' right."

"Oh you have got to be kidding me!" I stomped my foot and took a step toward him, pointing my forefinger toward his chest. "I've been kidnapped and abandoned, saw someone get shot—*right over there*—and witnessed two more people get snatched; I've been personally attacked and tackled to the ground like I'm a *freakin' quarterback*, lost my shoes somewhere in this godforsaken forest because I was trying to get away from *you*, and you're worried about me wearing a skirt? News flash buddy: Women have been dressing like this for-like-ever, so get the hell over it."

He eyed my pointed finger with a lift of his brow, and I dropped it. "Surely *Americans* dinna allow their women tae run around in such attire, nor tae speak so rash."

"Well, I could really care less what you think of my clothes or how I talk. I'm. Not. Scottish."

"Nae, ye're no'," he agreed. "But ye are on Scot's land, lass, and unless ye want tae start somethin' o' a scandal, ye'd be wise tae find a proper dress."

I was physically unable to keep my mouth from gaping open. "You know what, I'm done with you." Turning on my heels, I started yet again toward the slope that led to the dirt road, and the body of the driver. I couldn't just leave him there without at least making sure he was really dead, even though there wasn't much chance of him still being alive after so much time had passed.

I heard footsteps right behind me. "I said, I'm done with you. Finished. *Whoa!*" The Scot scooped me up, throwing me over his shoulder. "*What the hell are you doing?*" My breath huffed out in a rush as my stomach crushed against his shoulder. His hand covered my skirt, but I felt the heat of his skin as his palm cupped my ass. "*Let me down!*"

"Och, ye need tae be makin' up yer mind, lass. '*Get off o' me*', '*Let me doon*'. Which will it be, then?"

"I want you to put me down." It ended up coming out in grunts as every step took a little more breath out of me.

"No."

"I'll scream."

"Try it, woman. If the MacDougalls e'en think ye might hae seen what some o' their clansmen hae done, they'd likely kill ye on the spot. Or worse."

It was the "or worse" that kept me from actually crying out. And after some time, I eventually forced my breathing to slow. "Will you please just put me down?"

"I'll consider it. If ye promise nae tae run again."

"Fine."

"Fine," he repeated, and hefted me off his shoulder before settling me on my feet.

It took a few minutes for blood to rush back into my head. Once the dizziness finally ebbed, I ran my fingers through my hair, looping some behind my ears before I straightened my skirt, pulling the bottom hem down as far as it would go.

I really hadn't paid much attention to how far the Scot had taken me, but when I finally peered up at him, I could have sworn he didn't look worn out at all. Even after carrying me all that way. He seemed a lot more alert than I felt, and that just pissed me off.

He returned my gaze, eyeing me for a few seconds

before nodding once. "Now there's a good lass. Come wi'me, I've got a fire tae keep ye warm." He turned, taking a few steps before looking at me from over his shoulder. "I said, come."

Thought he could force me into it, huh? Treat me like a dog he could order around?

I folded my arms and raised my chin, meeting his steely gaze with one of my own. I may have promised that I wouldn't run. But I hadn't said that I would go with him. "No."

He faced me fully now, his eyebrows lowering as he glared. "And why no'?"

"I'm not going with you," I insisted. "Like I should trust some creepy guy who hangs out in the forest all alone, kidnapping unsuspecting women? I'll take my chances with the woods."

"Oh, aye," he said, nodding, his face lighting with humor. He folded his arms the same way I did and spread his feet apart. I had a feeling that out of the two of us, he was a lot more intimidating. Damn him. "And I bet ye'll take yer chances wi'the bears too, then?"

Bears? I blinked.

"That's what I thought. Now, come wi'me lass, and I'll keep ye safe from the wee beasties."

Face dangerous animals on my own, or go with this guy who hasn't given me any reason to trust him in the slightest. My breath slowly leaked out of me, but still I didn't move. "I think I'll take my chances with the '*wee beasties*'."

"Nae, ye will no'," he replied gruffly, slowly. He stepped toward me and I stepped backward, my bare, stinging feet sinking into the moist earth with each step I took. "I dinna want tae keep chasing ye, lass. But make nae mistake, I will if ye run again." He gained, and I turned, propelling myself away from him. In seconds, his arms wrapped around me, and I shrieked. He hastily clamped his hand over my mouth, but on I screamed, not caring that my voice was now muted.

"Shh," he hissed. "Just exactly who are ye trying tae attract? Bears or murderous fiends?"

I opened my lips slightly, allowing a single finger of his to slip far enough inside. I bit down hard, and he groaned and ripped his hand away.

"Anyone," I spat, already bolting away.

"*Are ye mad, woman?*"

I ran and ran, rushing over small bushes and under low branches. I made it…about six seconds before he caught me.

"Dinna make me take ye doon lass, I'm nae afraid tae dae it."

He held me tighter than he had before, so hard that I couldn't make another attempt at escape. Not that I thought I could anyway. I'd grown exhausted, my body giving out from everything that had happened today.

"Ye're coming wi'me, whether ye like it or no'," he breathed. "We'll figure out what tae dae wi'ye in the morn." He lifted me over his shoulder once more, hauling me away as I slammed my fists against his back.

CHAPTER TWO

The big, highland brute sat across from me as a fire roared in a small pit between us. He watched the flames lick up into the air, seemingly entranced as they danced around the body of a rabbit he'd caught in one of his traps. I'd been lost in my own thoughts as I watched the blaze, but that wasn't the first time since my abduction.

After he'd manhandled me into his tiny camp, I'd been immediately introduced to his two hounds: Broch and Duff, which now rested at his side. They looked relaxed enough, but I got the sense they were always watching. Always listening. Whenever I moved in the slightest, both dogs' heads whipped up, and their dark, beady eyes settled on me. I liked dogs, but that was just unnerving.

The Scotsman was a minimalist. He camped there without the protection of a motor home or a tent, and as far as I could see, there wasn't even a sleeping bag or pillow. So it came to no surprise that I couldn't see a car anywhere nearby, which would have come in handy in my attempt to get away from him and find civilization. Outside of checking my surroundings, I'd spent my time sneakily checking my cell phone for the time, and to see if I was lucky enough to score any bars. Still nothing. Even more depressing, I was already down to half-battery, so I didn't dare check my phone for a while. I shut it down and zipped my purse shut again.

We hadn't spoken in hours. I hadn't made any attempt to talk to him, and he seemed more than comfortable pretending I wasn't there. I had caught him looking at me every once in a while, but he quickly glanced away when he saw that I'd noticed. The man hadn't smiled once in all the time we'd sat there, keeping that angry expression on his face. I had no idea what was going through his mind, and that glower scared me.

I bit the inside of my cheek and tapped my fingers as I eyed the Scot. The firelight played over his features, making him appear even darker and bigger. I probably should say something to him. He had provided a fire which, as promised, had warmed me and dried my clothes. But he didn't look happy about it.

"You know, you really could act like I actually exist, since you went through all the trouble of dragging and carrying me here."

His gaze jumped to mine, but then he looked into the fire without a word.

"Do you live on your own?" I still couldn't decide if I was glad no one was in his camp or not. No telling what sort of people this guy hung out with. The Scot certainly knew how to pick a good camping spot. The trees and bushes crowded each other tightly, completely encompassing this area. If he'd aimed for privacy, he'd definitely nailed the location.

The Highlander cut off a piece of the rabbit and popped it into his mouth. "Mmm-hmm."

"How long?"

He cocked his jaw to the side, considering. "Two years, maybe. It's hard tae keep track o' time out here, so I only learn what day it is when I must travel tae town."

Two years on his own? Had he spent all that time out here? No. No way would someone live like this for two whole years.

"You don't even have a cell phone?" I would die without mine.

He scowled. "What's a *cell phone*?"

What the crap? Seriously? I cleared my throat, wondering how I got stuck with the only person in the world that didn't know what cell phones were. "Nevermind. Is there a town nearby?"

"No' far. And before ye ask, nae, I dinna ken which town I'll take ye tae. Since ye dinna belong tae a clan, 'tis verra likely ye could be turned out."

I blinked and rubbed my hands over my arms despite the warmth that radiated from the fire. "I have my credit card. I can pay for a room."

The Highlander's eyes narrowed. "Ye speak verra strange, lass. I dare say ye dinna make any sense a'tall."

Okay, so make that stuck with the only person in the world who didn't know what cell phones *and* credit cards were. I closed my eyes and let out one long, slow breath. "I mean that I have money to pay for a room somewhere, so if you can just point me in the direction of a town, I'll be on my way. I've just got to get ahold of my dad."

He brightened, almost excited. "Ye didnae tell me yer da' was near. When was the last time ye saw him?"

"Two days ago." I shrugged.

"Where was he?"

"In Utah."

"I dinna ken where *Utah* is, but I can guarantee it isn'ae anywhere near here. Are ye sure it's been only two days since? Ye may be a little…shaken, aye?"

I groaned and dropped my head into my hands before peering at him through gaps between my fingers. "Utah is in America—in the U.S. Of course it's not near here."

"*America*? Ye mean, the Colonies? Far more than two days then lass, it must hae been *weeks* since ye last saw him, and it'll be weeks if no' months before ye could get word tae him."

I opened my mouth to argue, but his expression changed to one of concern as he knelt forward, rolling his elbows onto his knees.

"Did ye no' hae an escort when ye traveled here? Surely yer da' didnae allow ye tae travel all this way wi'out protection?"

"Protection? What the hell time warp are you stuck in? I wouldn't have needed any protection if it weren't for that creep in the pub, and then waking up in the middle of freakin' B.F.E."

The Scot blinked, narrowing his eyes on me as he seemed to be hung up on some of my words. I felt some small satisfaction that he was having just as hard of time discerning what I said, as what I did with his accent.

"What's B.F.E?"

"Bum Fu...You know, nevermind." If he didn't know, he wasn't learning it from me. "You missed the point anyway: Nobody travels with protection, unless you mean people who travel with their parents or with like the CIA or something. Not that parents offer any real protection except for having the knack for taking all the fun out of everything."

"Och, aye. Yer mam and da couldn'ae possibly hae kept ye from endin' up here. Is that what yer tellin' me then?"

Actually, my dad probably could have. If he'd come to Scotland, then I wouldn't have even been in that bar. Probably wouldn't have met Captain Cloak at all. My face must have betrayed my thoughts because the Scot gave me a very satisfied smirk.

"Like I said. He couldn't offer any real protection except for keeping me locked up in a hotel room."

"And I take it ye dinna think that's protection?"

"No. It isn't."

He handed me a chunk of meat he'd cut from the rabbit. "And yet, if ye'd stayed locked in a room wi'yer mam and da' ye'd nae be here wi'me."

Ooh, damned Scot. I scowled at him and averted my eyes, instead focusing on the sizzling meat in my hands as I took a bite. The Highlander had me there, and he knew it.

Game. Set. Match.

"Where did ye get such ridiculous clothing anyway?"

I glared at him through the pops and whizzes of the flames as the savory rabbit meat practically melted on my tongue. Swallowing, I said, "They're not ridiculous. If anyone here looks like an idiot, it would be you." I glanced over him, taking in the sight of his red and green kilt and bare shins, weird-looking shoes, and the part of his kilt that he'd thrown over his shoulder. That strip of cloth had been one of the first things I'd noticed about him. That, and the fact that it hardly covered the tan, taught skin of his chest and stomach. "I mean, come on…where's your shirt?"

He snorted. "I only wear it if I'm goin' intae town. Why would I risk ruinin' a perfectly good shirt just tae sit alone in the forest?"

"Why do you live in the forest?"

"Why dae ye wear such improper clothing?"

"Well, if you'd help me get back to Oban I could change my clothes."

"I canna take ye tae a town or village I've ne'er heard o'."

I shook my head, barely able to bite my tongue from what I really wanted to say. In the hours since he grabbed me, I'd listened to the woods around us, and had come to a very scary conclusion: There was no one around us. I hadn't heard a single car pass in all this time. I hadn't even heard a jet fly overhead, and that was something I could always hear from anywhere if I listened hard enough.

"Ye're cold, lass," the Scot said suddenly.

I was cold. Or rather, half of my body was. The front half was warmed by the fire, but my entire backside was chilled from the night air. Not that I'd tell him.

"I dinna ken why ye're bein' so stubborn. I've done nae harm tae ye."

"Oh? Tackling me to the ground doesn't count as harm?"

"Well." He shrugged, and I could have sworn an embarrassed flush warmed his face. "Ye brought that on yerself, lass. Ye're a feisty wee thing, are ye no'?"

He had no idea.

"Hae ye nae cloak then?"

Great, we were talking about my clothes again. I gestured to myself with my hands. "Does it look like I have a cloak?"

"Watch the fire, aye?" He waited for my nod and stood, stepping away from the flames and disappearing around a tree. I sat there, staring into the fire and then at the surrounding darkness, wondering just how far I could get if I tried to make a play for escape. Probably not far, I decided. My best bet was to wait until he fell asleep. Maybe if I played nice for now, he'd trust me enough to sleep without keeping one eye on me.

The Highlander returned a minute later with a bundle of white cloth in his hands, holding it out for me to take. "Here, maybe this will help tae keep ye warm."

I took the proffered item and unwadded it before raising my brows. "Your shirt?"

"Aye. Be careful wi'it, mind. 'Tis the only one I've tae ma name."

I stood and held it out to him. "I think you need this more than I do. Out of the two of us, I'm the only one actually wearing a shirt."

He waved it away. "Nae need. I've ma tartan tae keep me warm." In illustration, he fanned out the cloth that had been looped over his shoulder and wrapped it more securely around himself. "Now, put it on before ye freeze tae death."

I sat back down on the log and drummed my fingers on my knee. I didn't want to wear his shirt. My clothes were perfectly fine. I'd worn this outfit probably twenty times and not once had anyone had anything negative to say about it. But oh, get kidnapped and tossed out into the middle of nowhere, and suddenly my clothes warrant a reaction so negative that I'm forced to cover them up....

Finally, I yanked on his shirt and cinched closed the wide opening just below the neck, tying the strings together. I was swimming in the thing, but could immediately feel the bubble of warmth around me. Biting my lip, I peered across the fire at him. "Thanks."

"Ye're welcome." He drew himself closer to the fire and cut off another chunk of meat, carefully handing it to me.

"So, uh...should I just call you Scot, or what?"

"Eh?"

"I don't even know your name. I guess since you're Scottish, I could just call you Scot."

"Och, aye. O' course, if that's how it works then ye'll be callin' a fair number o' us Highlanders 'Scot'." He eyed me for a minute before he stepped around the fire and stopped by my side. Reaching down, he took my right hand in his and bowed. "Ye can call me Cailen. At yer service, mum."

I coughed and quickly chewed the meat that was in my mouth before swallowing. "I'm umm..." I faked another cough. The last time a Scotsman had asked my name and I'd given my real one, I'd ended up alone in the empty, rolling fields of Scotland without any knowledge of where I was or how I'd gotten there. So should I offer my real name, or a fake one? On one hand, I didn't trust him. On the other, he might be the only chance I had to get back to Shannon and any form of civilization. Then again, I planned to sneak away as soon as he was asleep, so any knowledge of my real name could only hurt. "I'm Elizabeth," I answered finally. It wasn't a complete lie. There'd be no harm in giving him my middle name.

Cailen pressed a gentle kiss to my knuckles and released my hand. "'Tis verra nice tae meet ye Elizabeth…?" He drew it out, waiting for my last name.

"It's nice to meet you too, Cailen…?" Yep, two could play at this game.

A small smile flickered across the Scot's face. "Verra well. Ye better eat up lass, we should be headin' tae bed if we want a good start in the morn."

I nodded, meeting his eyes as he sat once again on the log opposite from me and took a big bite of meat. I definitely wanted a good start in the morning. Preferably long before he got his.

I laid there for hours, with my back toward the fire, and toward Cailen. Lost in my own daydreams, I'd imagined I was camping with my family again, letting the scent of fire lull me into thoughts of home. I could almost believe it too, with the pine trees surrounding me, pointing up to the starry sky as their familiar scent lulled me.

I wasn't sure how much time had passed exactly, with only the sights and sounds of the forest to gauge the time by. After I'd shimmied out of my clothes from under shirt, I'd listened to the Highlander and his dogs shuffle around the camp until they'd finally settled down. And in all that time, I hadn't moved an inch since I'd found my spot on the ground—not even when he'd laid something over me to keep me warm. I was afraid that any movement would alert the Scot or his dogs that I was awake, and I wanted them as far away from consciousness as possible. It was hard to lay there. To not just jump up and make a run for it. But I knew making an escape attempt too early would only result in failure.

And so I waited. Waited until the fire died down, and only the hum of the red-hot embers made any sound at all. Waited until the hounds were snoring away, dreaming about chasing cats or whatever it was they dreamed. It was probably about boars.

Finally, I rolled, glancing over the barely lit embers at Cailen. It was dark out, and with the fire having long since burned out, I couldn't see him very well. He was facing in my direction with one arm pillowing his head. I squinted, barely making out his strong jaw and cheekbones, and the thick lashes of his closed eyes. His brown hair fell loosely around his face, a few strands lying across his cheek. It took me another minute to see the steady rise and fall of his chest, and I watched him for some time, both to make sure he was sleeping, and also to admire him in a way I hadn't dared when he'd been awake. Cailen was just as handsome in his sleep. Only now he didn't seem as fierce, as primal. As barbaric.

Had I really called him that to his face? What was *wrong* with me? Watching him now, the way he'd tackled me to the ground had seemed a distant memory. Now he seemed as innocent as a child, his features relaxed as though he hadn't a care in the world. How had I called him a barbarian? He'd chased me, yes. Had tackled me as well as any football player, but he hadn't actually harmed me.

He could have done anything to me. Could have touched me against my will—or worse. But he hadn't.

He just hadn't wanted me to leave him.

And that was the problem. He'd meant to keep me here. Who knew what his real intentions were? He said that he planned to take me to town tomorrow, but that didn't mean he'd meant it. I wondered what his definition of town was, considering he hadn't even heard of Oban. Pulling my gaze away from the dreaming Highlander, I peered at the star-filled sky above.

It was time.

I silently pushed to my feet and grabbed my shoes, which Cailen had somehow grabbed without my seeing it during our trek to his camp. My purse was already slung across my body, and I'd been using my clothes as a pillow, so at least I didn't have to waste time searching for those. I took one step farther away from the fire pit, and then another, and another, making sure that my feet didn't land on anything loud as I snuck out of his campsite. I'd just rounded a tree when I realized I still had his shirt. His only shirt.

I couldn't just take it.

Setting my heels and purse on the ground, I untied the laces near my neck.

"What dae ye think ye're daein', lass?"

"*Holy freakin' hell!*" I gasped, whirling around to find Cailen leaning against a tree. My eyes had already somewhat adjusted to what little moonlight filtered in through the trees, so I could see he'd folded his arms. "God, you scared me! Can't a girl go to the bathroom in peace?"

It was by far the most reasonable excuse I could think of during my hours of lying on the ground, and I was grateful that I'd had the forethought to think of one in the event I got caught.

In the very likely event, as it turned out. Damn him.

The Scot's eyes wandered down to my bare shoulders and the open gap of his shirt over my chest. They lingered there, and my heart began to pound as his breath grew heavy and his eyes lidded; his desire evident enough that I could see it in the moonlight. I'd never seen such longing in a man's eyes.

I forced myself to cinch his shirt closed, and shrug the cloth back onto my shoulders, which effectively broke whatever spell he was under.

"Dae ye make it a habit tae undress each time?"

"Well," I replied, a little breathless from his stare. "I wouldn't want to pee all over your shirt accidentally, now would I?"

His brows twitched and he pushed himself off the tree. "Dinna wander too far," he warned, giving me a glare as he bent and snatched up my high heels. "If ye run, I'll find ye and drag ye back myself. And I think I've made it verra clear about ma thoughts on that." He stepped away then, and I was left standing there with my heart in my throat.

"Broch," he called after a short whistle. "Watch our guest. Oh, and Elizabeth? Be careful, aye? There's somethin' in the forest, circlin' our camp."

Holy crap. Was he serious? Or just trying to scare me?

Broch, the lighter brown of the two hounds, trotted over to my tree and plopped his butt on the ground, his dark eyes settling on me.

I dinna want tae keep chasing ye, lass, Cailen had said. *But make nae mistake, I will if ye run again.*

And if there was something else out here, it might not be him that caught me.

Great. Now what was I supposed to do?

CHAPTER THREE

"Elizabeth. Elizabeth, wake up."

I squeezed my eyes shut and groaned, rolling over to ignore whoever was talking to me. I wasn't done sleeping yet. Or, I wasn't until my face landed in something damp. I leaned up on my elbows and blinked, focusing on whatever plant was in my face.

"Oh no," I groaned, falling against the ground again. That rough, Scottish voice had called me Elizabeth, and I was sleeping outside, which meant one thing: yesterday wasn't a dream.

I had ended up peeing in some bushes last night, under the watchful eye of Broch the Hound, afraid that if I didn't, I wouldn't get another chance to sneak away again. There hadn't been any toilet paper in sight, and the Highlander hadn't offered any—not that I was under any assumption that he even owned a roll. Thank God I had sanitizer in my purse.

After Cailen had ordered Broch to keep an eye on me, I'd stood there, arguing with the damn thing for a few minutes, telling him to turn his back and at least give me some privacy. But the dog wouldn't have any of it—just kept his eyes trained on me as his master had ordered. And to make it more humiliating, I could have sworn I'd heard the Highlander chuckling from somewhere in the distance. At my expense, no doubt.

When I'd finally returned to Cailen, with his dog trailing closely behind, I'd sat down on the ground next to the newly rebuilt fire, folded my clothes up once more as a makeshift pillow, and threw his blanket at him.

He'd tossed it back. "Cover yerself. I'll no' hae ye catchin' a chill on ma watch because ye dinna ken how tae dress yerself."

"No." I'd chucked it to him, this time narrowly missing dumping it right into the fire. "I'm already wearing your shirt. I really don't think I could handle any more *hospitality.*"

"Fine," he'd barked, checking the blanket for any sign of damage. "But ye canna say I didnae warn ye."

I'd rolled away from him, wondering exactly what he'd meant by that. It was a while later when I'd finally peered over my shoulder to see if my captor had fallen asleep yet, only to find him watching me, his eyes dark and angry, sinister as the firelight cascaded over his features. I'd laid my head down again, angry at him for keeping me there against my will. I'd planned to wait until I heard him snoring away before I made another play for escape.

Apparently I'd fallen asleep instead.

"How much longer dae ye plan tae sleep?"

"'Til I'm dead." I groaned again and eyed the Scot with as much sleepy anger as I could. His chest rose and fell in a silent snort and he turned away.

"If we're goin' tae get a good start, ye'll need tae wake up. Dae ye no' want tae go tae town?"

I bolted into a sitting position. "Town? You're really taking me?"

"Aye. I told ye I would. But first, we must buy ye a proper gown. We canna hae ye wanderin' the countryside in those clothes, and I dinna think folk will take kindly tae ye wearing ma shirt."

Reminded of what I was wearing, I picked up my clothes and ducked my head into the tent I currently had on.

Cailen sputtered. "What are ye *daein'*?"

"What do you think I'm doing? I'm getting dressed." I spat back as I yanked on my bra from under his shirt. I stood and shimmied into my skirt and shirt before pulling off my makeshift nightgown. "I've seen plenty of women since I got here and only one was wearing a dress." *And a lot of luck she had with it—she'd gotten kidnapped in a horse-drawn carriage*, I thought with a shudder.

I hated Scotland.

"I dinna care what ye think ye've seen. We need tae get ye dressed proper. I willn'ae be responsible if somethin' happens tae ye because o' yer...*attire*."

I sighed, exasperated. "Can we just drop my clothes?"

His eyes widened and a deep flush covered his face.

Realizing how he must have understood that, I added, "I mean, can we just let it go? These are my clothes and they're just fine."

"I'll only *'drop it'* once ye're in a proper gown."

I slid my purse over my shoulder. "Oh my gosh, *fine*."

"Good," he said, looking and sounding a little too smug. It irritated the crap out of me. "Now, how much money hae ye?" He stood and stepped toward me, offering his hand, palm up.

I handed him his shirt before swiping at the dirt on my legs. "As long as they have a credit card machine, I'm golden."

The Scot scowled and reached for my purse, yanking it off over my head even as I tugged back.

"Hey!"

"Ye speak verra strange. Can ye no' just answer a simple question?" He stepped back from me, purse in hand, and hesitantly zipped it open with a confused expression on his face. "Look at that, nae buttons, nae hooks. Where did ye find such a tidy wee fastener?"

"Oh my gosh, it's just a zipper. Now give it back." I

made an attempt to get my purse, but he dodged me, a little too easily.

"Ye've a nice stash o' money," he said, even more surprised after he spent time zipping and unzipping my bag. "Ye can purchase a new dress and hae plenty left o'er."

"Great," I replied monotonously. I couldn't help my irritation at Cailen playing keep away with the only thing I had left to my name. "Can you give me my purse back now?"

He looked as though he were about to nod when his eyes narrowed and he peered once more into my bag. "Another compartment?"

No, no, no! Not that one! I surged forward again, trying to keep him from opening my purse, but he unzipped the inner pocket. "Stop Cailen. Don't. Just leave it alo—"

My voice died away as he pulled out the tiny silver bullet I'd stashed in my hidden pocket before coming to Scotland. Heat flamed across my face, chest and ears.

"Dammit, can't you just leave my stuff alone?" I felt more embarrassed than I ever had in my entire life. Leave it to this infuriating Scot to find my toy. "Give it to me." I held out my hand, demanding him to place it in my palm.

He didn't of course, and instead, handed me my purse before inspecting the bullet-shaped vibrator. "Shiny wee thing, is it no'?" He blinked, looking up at me questioningly. "What is it?"

Oh my God. I rubbed my hands over my forehead, still feeling the heat on my own skin. "You know what? It doesn't matter what it is. I'm not going to use it ever again now anyway." Not now that he'd had his dirty paws on it. I turned away and zipped up my purse, slinging it across my body and grabbing my heels before I stomped out of his camp.

"Elizabeth," Cailen called out, catching up to me in

seconds. "I've no' meant tae anger ye."

"You didn't *mean* to anger me?" I stopped walking and faced him, feeling like a midget compared to his damnable size. "Are you kidding? Excluding everything that happened yesterday and the fact that you sent your dog to watch me pee, what part of you going through my personal belongings *shouldn't* have pissed me off?"

"I wouldn'ae've had tae go through yer belongings if ye'd just gi'en me a straight answer, woman," he said, his voice taking on a low growl.

"It's my choice what kind of answer I give you. That doesn't give you the right to go through my shit."

He blinked in surprise before his brows lowered. "Proper lassies dinna speak that way."

"*Ugh!* Proper, proper, proper! Proper dress, proper speak, blah, blah, blah," I ranted, not caring that my hands went flying. "Seriously. What's your deal?"

Cailen eyed me until my hands returned to their normal, probably not-so-violent position. He looked uncomfortable then, and held my toy out to me. "I apologize if I've offended ye, Elizabeth."

Well, he could just stew on it. I sure as hell was.

He walked by my side, steering me through the forest toward what was, hopefully, a nearby town. I let him, hoping that my irritation would keep him from doing any other pig-headed moves.

"So, what was that?"

I froze, gaping up at him. "Oh my gosh. Really? Do you really want me to say it? Fine, women use it to pleasure themselves, okay? Happy?" *Asshole!*

He remained silent for a while, and as we gained ground through the thick forest, I kept an ear out, hoping that I'd hear a car or, even better, a highway. At least then I could flag someone down and find my way back to Oban, or at least get some sort of cell service and call Shannon and my dad. At this point though, I'd even gratefully take one of those stupid carriages if I had to.

"Is the town we're going to close?"

"Nae," Cailen replied quietly. This was the first time since his apology that we'd spoken. "Nearby is too dangerous. We're far too close tae Dunollie Castle. The MacDougalls dinna take verra kindly tae havin' squatters on their clan lands, especially no' so close tae where their chieftain is." He peered at me then, a small smile forming at his lips. "Nae matter how bonny that squatter may be."

Really? Was he actually trying to flirt with me? After everything?

My heart *didn't* just skip a beat. It didn't.

The Scot stepped up onto a trunk and turned, holding out a hand toward me.

I glared at Cailen and his proffered hand before finally giving him mine. The warmth of his hand enveloped mine and he gently pulled, helping me up onto the fallen tree, before he dropped down on the other side. Without my heels, I felt everything I stepped on, and the rough bark scraped at my feet. Before realizing what he was doing, Cailen turned and grabbed my waist, slowly lowering me back down toward the ground. Our eyes met, and I gripped his arms, steadying myself until my feet touched the damp earth. My heart hadn't sped up at the feel of his hands on me. It probably just sped up because my feet hurt.

I cleared my throat as we started walking once more. "Where are we going then?"

"Kilchrenan. I ken a seamstress there. Let's just say she's proven tae be discreet when certain folk dinna want the entire town tae ken who's been tae her. Besides, I could dae wi'a new shirt."

"Great."

"I'm sure we could bribe her tae get ye a new pair o' shoes as well."

"What's wrong with these?"

He flicked his gaze at the heels dangling from my fingers and gave me a shake of his head. "Correct me if I'm wrong, lass, but I've yet tae see ye actually wear yer 'shoes'. And they shouldn'ae be so revealing."

"Wow, everything about me is too revealing for you. Gotta watch out for this chick, her toes peek out from the tips of her shoes."

He shrugged. "Glad we kin each other then. Oh, careful o' the midge, there."

I looked down to where he gestured and slapped at a humongous mosquito, squashing it. "Holy crap. What is that thing?"

"A midge. Let's hope ye dinna swell up tae twice yer size."

"*What?*" I gaped just before my foot landed on something hard. I pitched forward, stubbing my toes on something, and fell to the ground as my foot erupted in pain.

Cailen's hands were on me in the next instant, pulling me to my feet. "Are ye all right?"

I nearly replied that I was, but couldn't as pure agony shot up my leg.

He must have seen the shock in my face because he stepped back and looked down. "Ye're bleeding." The Highlander's hands left my shoulders before one looped behind my back and the other went behind my legs. And then I was up in his arms, unable to squeak any type of protest. "Elizabeth, ye're turnin' red. And ye're no' breathing. Ye need tae breathe."

I fixated on his swollen nose and inhaled, not realizing I'd been holding my breath. Growing up, whenever I'd gotten hurt or scared, I'd stopped breathing until I either passed out or someone reminded me. I couldn't count how many times I'd terrified the bejesus out of my parents and friends, only to find out when I came to sometime later. No matter how much I tried to overcome it, apparently it still stuck with me.

"Sorry," I said. "I sorta do that without knowing."

Cailen carried me to a large boulder and planted me firmly on it. I closed my eyes, too stunned to look at what was wrong, and instead, concentrated on the cold rock that instantly chilled my thighs. I braced my hands on the Scot's shoulders as he lifted my foot with his warm hands.

"Does it hurt still?"

"Mmm hmm."

"We'll need tae get it cleaned up. I canna see how bad it is wi'all this blood."

Oh, God. I squeezed his shoulders as panic shot through me. "Is there a lot?"

The Highlander stood, and my hands slipped from his shoulders as he rose to his full height. "It's probably no' as bad as it looks," he said gently. "Ye're no' afraid o' a wee bit o' blood, are ye?"

"I don't like seeing blood, no." The pain that was palpitating from my toes upward was unbearable, and I'd barely been able to keep myself from crying.

"Elizabeth, look at me."

I clenched my jaw and shook my head as I felt his breath fan lightly across my face.

"Look at me, woman."

He was even closer now. Closer than I thought he'd be, and my eyes flashed open, meeting his piercing blue gaze.

"There's a good lass," he soothed. "I will'nae hurt ye if I can help it. But I need ye tae dae one thing for me."

"Okay," I said quietly.

"Just breathe." Cailen reached into the pouch that hung from his waist.

"What's in the bag?" I asked, hoping to distract myself from the throbbing in my foot and leg.

He cocked an eyebrow. "Ma bag? *Oh*, this…it's called a sporran." He withdrew a small bottle and bit off the cork. "Now, ye dinna hae tae watch what I'm daein', but ye dae need tae concentrate on yer breathing, aye?"

"Aye. I mean yes…Okay."

"Right." The Highlander dropped to his haunches and carefully gripped my foot. I didn't focus on what held his attention, fearing what I'd see—or rather, what I wouldn't. I sat there, wondering if I'd lost toes or filleted my foot wide open, and tried to console myself. If there was anything missing, the Scot would have undoubtedly reacted differently. I focused on the bushes and trees behind him, keeping the expressions on his face in my direct view.

"This may sting." He poured liquid from the bottle, dousing my foot with alcohol as my foot erupted once more in a new rush of pain. I screamed as the first drop hit my skin, feeling my entire body shake. Cailen didn't even look up as I tried to wrench my foot from his grasp, and he muttered a quick, "Breathe."

Air seeped in through clenched teeth, and I dug my fingernails into the Highlander's shoulders as he patted my foot dry with his kilt.

"Och. Ye've a splinter. I must ge'it out if ye want tae walk." He pulled a dagger from his sporran, the blade glinting in the sunlight.

I scrambled backward at the sight of his knife, yanking my foot away from him and tumbling off the boulder, falling flat on my back.

"Elizabeth. *Elizabeth!*" Cailen shot forward as well, keeping me from going far as I crab-walked in the dirt.

"Calm yerself. It'll no' be so bad once the splinter is out."

"It's not after I'm worried about," I stammered.

"Nae," he grumbled, his voice gritty as he drew it out. "Dinna move. This is only tae pry out the splinter."

"Says the guy with the deadly-looking knife!"

He rolled his eyes and gave my shoulders a shake. "Sghian dubh."

"*What the hell does that mean?*" I yelled, trying to break free of his hold.

"Jesus, woman. Ma wee knife is called a sghian dubh. Now, stop squirming. We must ge'it out." Still I continued to fight, and before I knew it, Cailen's entire body was covering mine as he pinned my wrists to the ground. I thought I ordered him to get off of me, but at this point, I could hardly do anything but fight and think about the agony pulsating from foot to knee.

"Dae ye want tae lose yer foot?"

I felt a tear slide down the side of my face. My lip trembled even though I'd tried to keep it from doing so, and soon, my stomach muscles did the same as I attempted to keep myself from a full-on wail. This was all too much. The pain. The knife. The bruting Highlander keeping me practically tethered to him since he'd found me in the forest. I laid there underneath him, breathing and shaking my head as more tears fell and settled in my ears. "No."

"Then ye must let me get the splinter out."

We were there for a while, just staring at each other. I hoped he would change his mind and let me go about my business. He was probably waiting for me to do the same. I had a hard time breathing, and not only from the throbbing the splinter caused, but also because of Cailen's weight. I had to force my breathing to slow, and as I did, I focused on his face. It was no longer strained from fighting me, or with the worry I'd seen as he'd peered at my foot. As I was calming, so was he. And his eyes were trained on mine. That radiant blue of his eyes had caught my attention from the very beginning, and so had the rest of his face. I'd thought before that he was nothing more than a real-life barbarian, catching glimpses here and there of something more. But now, seeing the way he looked at me, I couldn't see even a sliver of the savageness I'd come to know of the Highlander. He shifted suddenly, and held a lot of his weight on his hands as they continued to grip my wrists.

I felt so small against him; his body engulfing mine so much that I doubted anyone would know I existed if they stumbled upon us now. And yet, his weight was welcoming, somehow soothing. My eyes roamed away from his as I glanced at the rest of his features: his strong, square jaw was still stubbled with dark hair. It had grown out a little more since yesterday. His arms and shoulders were heavily muscled, flowing down to his tight chest and the ridges of his stomach that disappeared against the fabric of my skirt as his hips crushed mine. I drew my gaze back up to his as a very noticeable hardness pressed against my thighs.

Now there was only silence between us. Silence, and a surprising comfort I hadn't expected to glean from the rugged Highlander.

Cailen cleared his throat and looked away briefly before returning his gaze to mine. "Will ye remain still if I work on gettin' that splinter out?"

"I—I'll try."

"Verra well. Dinna move." He pushed himself off of me and settled next to my feet. I stared up at the towering trees, trying to focus on anything other than the fact that his warm fingers were wrapped around my foot and drawing it onto his lap.

"Are ye well, Elizabeth?"

I blinked hard, wishing for the first time that I'd given him my real name. Hearing my middle name come from the Scot's lips just didn't feel right, especially not since he was trying to help me. "Mmm hmm."

"Good. I'm goin' tae be as gentle as may be."

I pursed my lips and let out one long, slow breath as I felt the tip of his blade press against my skin. I flinched and Cailen's hand tightened, bracing my hand more firmly. "Sorry," I whispered.

My breath caught as immense pain radiated from my foot, and I cried out again. The knife pressed into my skin even more. I told myself to focus on anything else, to distract myself from what he was doing. *Gah, what had he called it? Skeen doo? Why couldn't he just call it a freakin' knife?* Breath hissed through my teeth and I squeaked, unable to keep myself from moving as he poked at my toe.

"There." He released my foot and then gripped it again. "Oh, hold on." More liquid doused my foot, the pungent smell of alcohol hitting me almost as fast as the sting. "Dinna ge'it dirty. I think I hae somethin' tae wrap it in." Cailen reached into his sporran and produced a swath of fabric. After ripping it into strips, he started wrapping my foot.

Once I felt the first wrap cover my toes, I dared to peek at what he was doing. His long fingers worked deftly, bandaging my foot with the thin shreds of cloth and creating a knot on top of my foot.

"Ye'll hae tae be careful, and I dinna think it's wise tae walk on it yet."

I sat up. "I can't walk on it?"

The Scot squinted doubtfully and rubbed his thumb and forefinger over his chin. "Ye can try. It might hurt, mind."

I drew my feet in and stood, putting the tiniest bit of pressure on my bad foot. I regretted it immediately as agony shot straight up my leg. "Dammit. What am I going to do now, hobble around the forest?"

"I'm no' sure ye're goin' tae like what I hae tae say." He shrugged. "I think we should go back tae camp until yer foot heals."

"What? *No!* I have to get back to my friend," I insisted. "How much farther do we have to go?" We had to be getting close to some sort of civilization. I refused to believe we were that far from other people. Reaching into my purse, I pulled out my cell phone and powered it on.

"What is that?" Cailen shuffled closer to me and peered at it as the welcome music and images flashed across the screen.

I looked up at him at the sound of the awe in his voice. "It's my cell phone."

He snatched it from me and weighed it in his palm, inspecting it at every angle. "I've ne'er seen anythin' like this before. Is it bewitched?"

"No." I laughed, taking it back from him. "You really haven't seen one before?" Flicking a quick peek at my phone, I deflated a little as the "No Signal" icon appeared in the top-right corner. I should have known.

"Nae, what is its purpose?"

"To call people."

"Tae call'em what?" His eyebrows lowered.

"No, you use it to dial people you know so you can talk to them. You've *got* to know what a phone is." Those have been around for-like-ever.

"Nae." He still looked amazed as I flipped through the screens. "Surely this is magic."

"'Fraid not." I powered it off to save the battery and handed it to Cailen again.

He gratefully took it and studied the phone again, carefully tracing the design of my phone's cover and running his thumb over the smooth surface. "Truly remarkable," he mused. "This is the technology they hae in the Colonies?"

"Yeah. Well, I mean, it's everywhere. When I landed in Scotland I saw just as many people on cell phones as I did back home." My stomach tightened at his obvious awe. How had he gone so long without seeing one? He was either yanking my chain, or he really lived in a part of Scotland that was lacking. Did Scotland have Amish communities? Whatever it was, something was seriously off here.

Cailen offered my phone back to me with a strange expression on his face. A boom of thunder sounded not far away, but he acted as though he hadn't heard it. "Landed? Ye mean when yer ship came tae port?"

"Uh no, I don't do boats. I hate huge bodies of water. I flew here on a plane." That niggling feeling I'd had in my gut intensified.

"Ye flew then? Oh aye," he scoffed. "Up in the sky wi'the wee birdies."

"Exactly."

Now he shook his head as he laughed. "Lass, are ye sure ye didnae bump yer head when ye fell? That's the daftest thing I've e'er heard." Cailen looked to the left, searching the bit of sky that could be seen from the heavy forest. "We should get back tae camp. I've got a bit o' whiskey that should make ye feel better."

The Highlander bent and picked me up, looping one arm behind my knees while the other cradled my back.

"Oh! You, uh…you really don't have to do that." How did he look like carrying me around was something he did all the time? He didn't even look strained. Our eyes met and held, and my face felt flushed.

"I dae. We'll ne'er make it back wi'ye 'hobblin' around

the forest'." He gave a teasing smirk and set off in the direction we'd come from, as I held him tightly around his neck.

"Ye're *eighteen*?"

"Yeah. Well, I mean, my birthday is in less than two weeks, so I'm basically nineteen. Why, how old did you think I was?"

"I thought ye may be younger. Ye seem verra…" His voice died away and he grinned. "Ye just seem young."

I blinked hard, focusing on the Highlander as I tried to glean what he'd really been about to say. "How about you? You haven't told me how old you are yet."

"Me? I'm two and twenty."

"Two and twenty?" I snorted. "You are *so* not twenty-two."

"I am, I assure ye."

I narrowed one eye on him before peering down at the bottle of amber liquid in my hand. He looked like he could be in his twenties, but no way did he act like it. I took a drink. "Mmm. Have I told you how good this is?"

Cailen smiled and took the whiskey bottle from me as the sounds of rain *pitter-pattered* on the leaves all around us. When we had finally reached his camp hours before, he'd built a fire and made sure I was comfortably near it without me having to put any weight on my foot. Of course, he'd rejected the idea of me going to see a doctor today, saying that I'd get soaked to the bone and would probably freeze to death on the way. Out of the two options, I would have chosen life and warm fire—if I'd even been given the choice.

I was a bit more grateful for his shirt when he handed it

to me this time. It had somehow stayed dry despite the rain—probably because he'd hidden it safely under a tree—while my clothes had been soaked through on the walk back to camp. The Highlander had dutifully excused himself, disappearing behind the trees so I could dress. I'd quickly hopped to my feet, careful to put the least amount of pressure on my bad one as possible, yanked off my wet shirt, bra, and skirt, and drew on his shirt. As damp as my thong was, I just couldn't make myself take that off. It was my last barrier between me and the forest.

And between Cailen and me.

However many hours later, I was still in his shirt. It was large enough that I was able to draw my knees to my chest and cover myself completely from my shoulders down.

I thought I'd seen a hint of a smile each time Cailen had seen me sitting that way.

At the moment, I couldn't seem to care how much time had passed today. I was warm, in dry clothes, had two dogs at my feet that seemed to warm up to me, I was with a guy who seemed to get more and more attractive by the minute, and my belly was full from the rich whiskey the Highlander had shared with me. The more whiskey I drank, the less my foot hurt.

I reached for the bottle and Cailen tightened his hold, pulling it just out of my reach.

"Feelin' better?"

Sweet Scot, I thought. *So caring. And so cute. Have his eyes always been so blue?* "Infinitely."

"Good." He re-sealed his bottle and stood, stuffing it into a small crevice in the tree trunk he'd gotten it out of earlier.

"Hey. I wasn't done with that."

"Aye, ye were. We dinna want tae drink it all. No' when ye might need a nip later for the pain." Cailen returned from the tree, sitting a bit closer than he had previously before eyeing me speculatively. "Can I see yer 'cell phone' again?"

I shrugged and reached for my purse, unzipping it and pulling out my cell. It was probably a good idea to power it on for a minute anyway, if only to see what time it was. After I saw that it was 3:48, I handed it to him.

Cailen carefully swiped his fingers across the screen until he reached the one that didn't have any apps on it. "Pure magic, isn'ae't," he mused, shaking his head. "Is this the hour?"

I nodded.

"And who is that?"

I didn't even need to glance down to know it was the picture of Shannon and me with our big cheesy grins during the all-night party we'd gone to after graduation. "That's Shannon. She's the reason I'm in Scotland."

"It's an incredible likeness o' ye. I canna believe the detail." He inched the phone closer to his face, his gaze wandering over the screen. "Who painted it, and how did ye ge'it on this wee thing?"

I sputtered. "That's just a picture. Here, let me show you." I grabbed the phone and touched the camera icon before pointing it at Cailen. I snapped the picture and then scowled at the results. Damn cloudy sky. "Hold on." Turning on the flash, I took another pic and his eyes bugged at the flashing light. I turned the screen toward him.

"Remarkable." He snatched it from me.

"Swipe your finger across the screen again like before—yeah, like that."

The Highlander saw the other picture of himself and a half-smile formed. "Ye're sure it's no' magic? I'm startin' tae believe ye're o' the *suire fem*."

"What does that mean?"

"Ye may ken them as fairies."

I laughed as he scrolled through more pictures. His eyes studied every detail and, sometimes, looked up at me to check my features before returning his gaze to the screen. I couldn't look away from him, the fascination in his features made my own heart beat with excitement. He looked so full of wonder and awe. I could have spent all day watching him like that.

And then his face reddened.

I flicked my eyes downward to see what caused that reaction, and my gaze landed on the picture of me in my hot pink bikini, tanning on a sunny day next to one of my friends' pools. Snatching the phone from him, I backed out of the pictures, and looked up at him. Oh jeez, his eyes were fastened on me. *Probably because I'm such a fat ass.* Why couldn't I have had one of those perfect model figures? "That was just, uh...I was tanning. I only took it for my boyfriend."

It was a while before he finally drew his eyes away from me, and I could feel my own embarrassment skitter through me, the heat of it flushing my face and ears. The Highlander cleared his throat and stabbed his fingers into his hair. "So ye're, uh..." Another small flush spread across his cheeks, barely adding color to his tan skin. "Ye're tae be wed then?"

"No." I shook my head emphatically. "I'm not engaged. I mean, he was just a boyfriend. He isn't anymore."

"Oh." He seemed on edge suddenly, his once calm demeanor turning to what reminded me of something like a caged animal. "We should check yer dressing, I think. Make sure yer wound is still clean, aye?" He scooted off the tree trunk and knelt in front of me as I placed my foot against his leg. With nimble fingers, he untied the cloth and carefully unwrapped my foot, revealing a whole lot of black and blue, and a bit of dried blood.

The Scot produced his flask from his sporran and poured alcohol over my foot before inspecting my big toe. "It' isn'ae much tae look at, but I think it'll heal fine."

"Will I be able to walk on it tomorrow?"

He prodded at the wound gently and I flinched. "I dinna ken. I'm no' so sure the bruises will'nae spread farther. That splinter went in fair deep. I'm nae doctor, but I fear it'll get worse wi'out proper care." He lowered my foot until it was on his leg once more and his hand rested on my shin.

My heart leapt at the feel of his warm hands on my chilled skin, and I drew my gaze upward, meeting his. I'd never had anyone put so much care into my comfort before, and not for the first time, I regretted the way I'd treated him up until now. Yesterday, Cailen had protected me from two other men who could have done so much more than just kidnap me. He'd built a fire to keep me warm, he'd cooked meat for me to keep me fed. Sure, he'd refused to leave me alone, but now that I thought about it, he'd meant to protect me then as well. And with my foot, he'd taken great care in trying not to hurt me even as he pulled out what had to have been the biggest splinter in history.

"Why do you carry around a lacy handkerchief anyway?" I asked, pointing to the shredded cloth he'd just removed from my foot.

"'Tis ma mither's. I like tae keep it wi'me."

"And you put it on my foot? You ripped it up?" He'd lived out here on his own for two years and had torn up the only thing he had of his mom's?

"It's naethin'. Here, I think ye might need a wee bit more." He offered me his flask, and I gratefully took a swig, savoring the feel and taste of the Highlander's whiskey rush down my throat as I thought of how hard that must have been for him. I know I couldn't give up anything of my mom's, and it had been a little over two years since I'd seen her last as well.

My opinion of the man skyrocketed.

I searched his face, feeling only the sensation of his touch on my skin and the thumping beat of my heart. "Thank you, Cailen."

"What happened tae callin' me 'barbarian'?"

I bent slowly, offering him a smile as I held his gaze. "You're not so barbaric right now." Closing the distance between us, I kissed him.

CHAPTER FOUR

I rolled over, drawing my legs and feet back up into Cailen's shirt. My back had warmed up a lot from the fire, but my entire front side felt like it'd turn to ice if I didn't do something to warm myself. The Highlander had stoked the fire again just before he'd lain down for bed, and it still burned brilliantly as I lay there. It was bright enough that I could see his sleeping form through the flames.

Oh, he wasn't asleep. Our eyes met and I saw that look of realization in his gaze as well.

"Canna sleep, lass?"

I shook my head.

"What's troublin' ye?"

I let my legs fall out of the comfort of his shirt and sat up, inching closer to the fire.

"Och, ye're cold then?" He moved to stand.

"Don't get up," I said, stopping him. "The fire's fine. I think I'm just chilled to the bone." Something that didn't seem to bother my Scottish companion in the slightest. He seemed perfectly comfortable in nothing but his kilt. He still hadn't donned a shirt—which made sense since I was currently occupying it—and the bit of plaid thrown over his shoulder seemed to be keeping him warm enough.

Cailen's head whipped to the right, and he lifted a hand, halting me from saying anything else. Extracting a black knife out from underneath the plaid that was thrown over his shoulder, he tossed it to my feet. "Take ma sghian dubh, and get doon. Use it only if ye must."

"*What?* What's going on?"

"Just dae it. Make yerself as small as ye can." The Highlander stood up, gripping a dagger in one hand as he held his sword in another. His gaze danced all around us, but kept landing on a certain location, eyes narrowing as he stared into the trees.

I was freakin' terrified. The look on his face, and the way he crouched—well, everything about him at the moment—made me feel like we were in serious danger. Even the dogs were shifting nervously, growling in the same direction Cailen was focused on. It wasn't only Broch and Duff growling though, there was definitely something else out there that was making even more noise than the two dogs combined.

"What is that?" I asked as I picked up the knife and laid parallel to the fallen tree.

"Boar."

A massive form launched itself into our camp. The Highlander dodged out of its way, narrowly missing getting stuck by one of its tusks. I'm pretty sure I was already screaming because I realized after just a few seconds that I'd drained myself of breath. Inhaling, I scrambled to my feet as the boar turned and rushed toward Cailen again.

"Get behind the tree and stay doon," he barked, slashing at the beast's side as he avoided getting stuck yet again.

The boar squealed a bone-chilling screech and let out another ferocious growl. I backed my way on top of the tree trunk, freezing as the creature focused on me.

"Oh, Jesus Christ," I breathed. Pure murderous intent seeped from the creature, and right now, I was its target. Blood dripped down the side of its face as it snarled and charged. I screamed, barely hearing as Cailen ordered me once more to get down. My ass hit the ground as the boar charged over the trunk, its enormous hooves pounding into the ground inches from me. I pulled my legs in and gaped up at the big-ass pig as it stopped, searching for…well, me I guessed.

I was about to bolt over to the other side of the tree when the beast whirled around, huffing out a big breath of air. Snot and blood flew from its nose in spurts, and I gasped. It was so close, there wasn't time to hide. It growled again as dug its hooves into the ground, its nose flaring and its eyes burning with malice. I cowered, holding the only weapon I had at my disposal toward it. If it was going to charge me, then I would die, I knew that, but at least the creature from the depths of hell might get injured in the process. Or who knew, maybe I'd get lucky and stick it right in its black heart.

It launched itself at me and I screamed, holding the knife's hilt with both of my hands and making myself as small as possible behind it. There was a crunch next to my ear as the log teetered, and Cailen leapt over my head, landing on the massive pig. It shrieked as his sword dug into its back, and it bucked and whirled, trying to throw the Scot free. He held tight though, and had somehow even managed to jab his dagger into it as well. The boar freaked, and the Highlander lost his hold with one of his hands. His body went flying before the other hand's grip whipped him back down to the creature's thrashing body, as blood gushed down his arm. He latched onto the beast once more though, and continued to fight it. Cailen was growling, the boar was growling, even Broch and Duff were growling and barking as they nipped at the boar's legs, and I…wasn't moving from my spot. The only thing I could even think to do was to maybe throw my knife at the demon pig, but decided that would help absolutely no one so I held onto it instead.

Cailen wrenched his dagger free of the pig's hide and

stuck it in once more, near the beast's neck. The boar took off like a bat out of hell, hauling the Highlander and his two dogs away. I stood up as they disappeared from my sight. What should I do? Should I follow? Should I stay? If I followed it and it came charging, I wouldn't have my log to hide behind. But what if Cailen needed my help?

Another shriek echoed through the trees and I gripped the knife harder. *Holy freakin' crap, holy freakin' crap...Breathe, just breathe. It's probably fine. Yeah, the Scot will be back any second. He—*

He did come back, with Broch and Duff trailing right behind.

"Oh my God." I ran to him and hugged him as tightly as I could. The man was sweaty, but that didn't bother me in the slightest. He'd just fought a boar and survived. One of his arms wrapped around me as well, just before I pulled away. "Are you okay? Oh my God, your arm. Sit down."

I had to do something, he'd just saved my life. Gripping the whiskey bottle in hand, I poured it over his arm, tuning out the grunt of pain coming from the Highlander. I ripped the bottom of his shirt and used half of the strip to wipe his gash before dousing it once more with whiskey.

"Och, woman. Can ye no' be more gentle?"

"I'm trying to hurry." Yes, I was panicking. Blood continued to seep from the cut that was at least four inches long, and was probably even deeper than I thought. I still had a clean strip of cloth in my hand and briskly wrapped his arm as tight as I could. "That'll have to do. It's all we've got for now."

"Lass, I'm fine," the Scot replied, his voice calm as he stepped away from me. "It isn'ae as though I've ne'er had tae dae that before."

"You've fought a boar before?"

"Aye." He shrugged. "It happens from time tae time.

They're no' so easy tae kill, mind, no' wi'their thick skins. Ye must ken just how tae kill'em tae make it quick." He studied my makeshift bandage, turning his arm to get as many angles as possible. "A fine job ye did. Thank ye."

Chills worked through me as I fought the tears that threatened to spill from my eyes. I'd never, in all my life, been as terrified as I'd just been, and the Highlander was acting like it was no big deal. "So it's like…dead?"

"Aye." Cailen's gaze wandered over me, and his gaze narrowed. "Och, ye must be chilled." He threw more logs onto the fire, stoking it by blowing on the embers. "Come, get close. Wi'out a cloak tae keep ye warm, ye're bound tae freeze."

I did get closer to the fire, numbly making my way to it and sitting down. I stared into the flames, feeling myself get almost mesmerized. It was probably far better to get lost in thought as I gazed into the fire than by ogling the way the flickering light played off Cailen's magnificent body. I picked up the black knife he'd given to me, and studied the design. It was actually beautiful, with swirling patterns that seemed to all connect to one another. This was more than a just a dagger, someone had gone through great lengths to carve the handle into a work of art.

"Here." I handed him the knife and gestured to his arm with my chin. "Does it hurt?"

"Naethin' a dram or two willn'ae fix." He was still breathing heavily and wiping at the sweat that slicked his skin. "Would ye mind terribly if I sit next tae ye? Tae keep ye warm, ye ken."

"No. I uh…I wouldn't mind."

Cailen stood and walked around the fire so he could sit by my side. I didn't dare watch him stride toward me, afraid that the sight of him would make my heart beat even faster. My thoughts were already wandering into dangerous territory as it was, and I didn't know where my imagination would take me when I felt him against me. Likely the same place I'd been when I'd felt him lying on top of me, pinning me to the ground. When had he become so damned alluring? What if he tried something once he was over here?

Would I stop him?

He sat next to me and we gave each other hurried, uncomfortable grins.

I had to think of something to say, this silence was too much, especially after what the two of us had just been through. "So, shouldn't the fire have scared off that boar?"

"Sometimes. Ye ne'er ken what lengths they'll go tae when they're enraged like that. But under normal circumstances, aye, they'd stay awa from the fire." He stretched out his legs, and leaned against the trunk before he opened the part of his kilt that was wrapping his torso and shoulders. "Here, there should be enough for the two o' us, aye?"

I glanced at his bared skin, getting my first real look at him without the plaid hindering my view. My breath left me at my first peek. The sudden loss was attributed to the bitter cold outside though, and because I was still affected by that boar. Not because of the very male, very enticing Highlander.

He must have misunderstood whatever expression on my face, because he said, "Dinna fash. It's safe now. I'll no' let anythin' harm ye."

I couldn't manage to say anything as I scooted toward him, a sigh escaping me as his body heat reached my skin through the fabric of the shirt. I drew my knees in and pulled his shirt down around them as Cailen wrapped the two of us in his plaid.

He was so warm that I dropped my head against his

chest, humming in contentment as my cheek began to warm. He chuckled, but I was too tired to look up at him.

"What's so funny?"

"Ye," he answered. "I think ye were only minutes from freezin' solid."

I smiled, staring out into the dark forest beyond the fire. "How do you keep so warm?"

"I'm used tae the cold. I've lived out here for two years, mind."

Yeah, who could forget something like that? I laid against him, closing my eyes as I ran through everything I'd learned of the Highlander: He talked funny, saying ken instead of know and mind instead of remember…I mean, who did that? He also slummed it out in the middle of nowhere with just knives and swords to keep himself alive, he was good at capturing and killing animals, and he battled boars to the death. Oh, and his lips were soft and warm, surprisingly perfect despite the scratchy stubble along his jawline and chin that sort of tickled—

I bolted upward, gaping at him. "Oh my God, I *kissed* you!"

"Ye did. Did ye no' mind that 'til now?"

"No I didn't. I'm so sorry. I can't believe I did—"

"Elizabeth, it's naethin'. Dinna fash yerself."

"Are you sure?"

He nodded and pulled me down so I laid against him again. We both laid there, silently listening to the forest, and to Broch and Duff snoring away.

"I'm still sorry. I don't normally go around kissing complete strangers."

He chuckled. "Ye prob'ly dinna usually drink like ye did earlier either. Whisky can make the most respectable person turn verra…friendly."

Ha. Friendly. That'd been me alright. That had to have

been the first time I'd gotten drunk enough to not even realize what I was doing. Usually it was the other way around: Guys at a party getting a little too frisky after downing a drink or two. Who knows what I would have done in that condition if the Scot had come on to me. "You know, I'm actually surprised you haven't tried to get me out of this shirt yet."

Cailen tensed and sat straight up, accidentally making the plaid fall. "Och, I'm sorry." He quickly grabbed the cloth and worked on re-wrapping us in it, shifting as he did. He laid down more this time, pulling me in so that I could lay closer to him as well. "I dinna ken what kind o' man ye're accustomed tae, but I wouldn'ae e'er suggest that ye—that a *lady*—should bare herself tae me."

I lifted my head so that I could look at him. "Are you telling me you've never tried to feel a girl up?" Yeah, right.

"Well," he said with a shrug. "I'm no' so sure what that means, but I gather from the way ye said it that it means tae umm…well, tae lie wi'a woman."

God, the way he said *wooman*. My pulse could slow down already. Really.

"More or less," I replied. "It's what leads up to it. It means to touch her, in the hopes of getting her into bed."

He shook his head, mortification plain on his face. From where I laid, I could feel that another part of him wasn't mortified at all, and that was growing increasingly obvious. "Elizabeth," he said, a little strained. "I've held many lassies, but ne'er for the hopes o' takin' her. I couldn'ae shame ye that way, and especially no' since ye're in ma care. I wouldn'ae dae that e'en tae a whore."

"A *whore*? I take it you know a lot of prostitutes?"

"Nae!" he stammered, his eyes widening. "I just meant that I couldn'ae dae that. Tae *any* woman."

"Are you telling me that you're never going to have

sex?"

Cailen's face flamed as red as I'd ever seen it, which wasn't nearly as much as mine did whenever I was embarrassed. "No' unless she's ma wife, and I dinna think that likely tae happen."

Something in his expression actually made me believe him. That this rugged Scot could honestly be telling me that he wasn't going to get laid until he was married. It made feel safer—*and not at all upset*—that this powerful man wouldn't even consider sex with me as a possibility.

I placed my cheek against his chest again, relaxing as his heartbeat slowed to a normal, steady thump. I cuddled as close as I could get to him, watching the fire lick into the air as I slowly dozed to sleep.

Och, that woman.

Cailen laid there with Elizabeth's tiny body against him, breathing in her delectable scent, and unable to ease the ache in his groin. She'd fallen asleep some time ago, but with her soft curves pressed against him, he'd never felt more awake. Nor more alive, for that matter. Even last night, watching her lay there in his shirt, he'd felt an inexplicable sense of pleasure at seeing the bonny lass wearing something that belonged to him. And tonight, seeing her pert arse poke out from under the cloth as she tucked her knees in close to her…

He'd never been so desperate to see more of a woman. Not even when he'd been a randy lad chasing the skirts of the lassies in his clan.

Elizabeth nestled in closer to him, straightening her legs as her wee body relaxed into slumber. Jesus God in heaven, the soft flesh of those legs tantalized him until his heart felt as though it would burst. It may still, before the night was through. He should cover them with his tartan, but it could wait a bit. It wouldn't hurt to admire her first. He'd never seen such a beauty, and it would be a shame to live the rest of his life through without memorizing every inch of her bonny wee body.

That brought Cailen to thinking of the painting of her in nothing but bits of fabric that barely covered her breasts and the patch between her legs. He nearly groaned at the mere thought of what lay beneath that cloth. Clenching his fists and jaw, he tried to force his thoughts from where they were. It wasn't his place to think such things about Elizabeth. She wasn't his, nor would she ever be. She deserved a gentleman to be her protector until she could be restored to her family.

And it had been long since he'd ever been thought a gentleman of any sort.

No, he couldn't let his thoughts wander over what he may have seen in Elizabeth's eyes. He'd thought that maybe she'd *desired* him. And when she'd kissed him, he was certain of her affections. At least for a time. It was likely just the whisky, affecting her the way it often had men that were once considered gentlemen. A great deal of him hoped it wasn't the alcohol driving the fire in her eyes, while part of him did. He could never do anything about it anyway. Not even when she'd glanced at him wantonly after he'd slain the boar. He didn't ken what he might have done had she kissed him again.

Och, the wee lass stretched against him, rolling over and sticking her arse against his side. Surely it wouldn't hurt if he just enjoyed this. She certainly seemed to.

Cailen turned, letting his aching cock settle against the warmth of her backside. God in heaven, could there be anything that felt better? He gently lifted her head, placing his arm as a cushion lest she get uncomfortable in her sleep. In doing so, he was brought much closer to her body, and wrapped his free arm over her, holding the lass to him tightly. She moaned in her sleep: a reverent, soft sound that went straight to his bollocks.

He laid there with her firmly against him, wishing for all the world that this night would never end. He wasn't sure what he'd do when he was back to being alone once more. Not with this feisty wee lassie keeping him on his toes.

A twig snapped somewhere in the surrounding forest, and as the dogs chuffed to attention. There were multiple sounds, all coming from the same direction, and they were far too clumsy to be from any animal.

He whistled quietly. Broch and Duff stood up and loped away, obeying his command. He'd found the two hounds in these woods when he'd first moved here, the two of them often took care of themselves and did so whenever he left. And it appeared it was time for him to leave once more. He was still recovering from slaying the boar, and there was no telling who was heading their way.

There was only one thing for certain: Someone was in the woods with them, and that meant his time with Elizabeth was coming to an end.

❧⊗❧

I woke sometime in the night, feeling Cailen's body stiffen against mine. "Hmm? What's going on?"

"Shhhh." He pulled his plaid from around the two of us. "We've got comp'ny."

I jolted awake and jumped to my feet at the same time he did. The fire was still burning, but the flames were only maybe an inch or two above the wood. Taking a cue from

65

him as he picked up his sword and sheathed it, I quickly bent and picked up my clothes, purse, and high heels.

"If I tell ye tae, run that way," he pointed to his left. "And dae it as quietly as ye can."

I nodded, my heart seeming to claw its way up into my throat as he packed his things. He didn't have much to speak of, but the few belongings I'd known he had were quickly placed into a satchel.

The Scot returned to me, getting very close as he leaned down and whispered, "They're comin' at us from that direction." He hitched his chin to the side. "I'd say there are three, if no' more."

"Do you think they're here to hurt us?" I breathed.

"Dae ye recall what I told ye about the MacDougalls?"

I nodded.

"Then aye, they're here tae hurt us."

What if it wasn't the MacDougalls at all? What if it was my dad or the Scottish police searching for me?

"How is yer foot?"

"It's okay, I think," I whispered back. "I'll go as far as I can." I'd deal with my foot as long as possible. Especially if it meant I could get away from the men who had probably killed the coach driver. "Are you sure it's not someone here to help?"

He nodded and gave my shoulder a gentle squeeze. "I ken it isn'ae. Anyone who means nae harm doesn'ae try tae sneak up on ye. Stay close."

Cailen turned and walked away, and I followed closely behind. The man moved silently even though he carried a bag full of whiskey bottles and the cooking utensils he used over the fire. I was surprisingly quiet too, even though every step on my right foot nearly made bite through my lip. So much for being okay.

We walked and walked, and he frequently turned to

check on me, making sure I stayed close. My heart pounded in my ears from fear, matching the rhythmic throbbing in my foot. How close were the others? Were they following us even now? I'd wanted to ask, but feared any sound I made could draw their attention.

"So, ye dae ken how tae follow orders."

"Hmm?" I asked, startled.

"Ye did verra braw back there, lass." He stopped and turned, smiling at me. "Ye didnae panic as I would hae expected."

"Can we actually talk? I mean, are we far enough away from them now?"

"Aye. We're almost tae the place where ye were injured yesterday."

I sighed in relief and found a place to sit down, giving my aching feet a break. As much as I'd wanted to ask him about the threat behind us, it was even more excruciating not to tell him I'd needed to take about a million breaks since the time we left. "Where are Broch and Duff? I wanted to ask a while ago, but I didn't really dare talk."

"I alerted them tae leave."

"But shouldn't they stay with you?"

"Nae," he drawled. "They've ne'er actually been ma hounds. We just found each other. They take care o' themselves mostly."

"So you just leave whenever you want?"

"Aye, and they dae too."

I pointed and flexed my feet, hoping to alleviate some of the pain from walking on them for so long.

Cailen set down his own bag and approached me before lowering to his haunches. "We must get yer foot seen tae when we reach Kilchrenan, I think." He eyed the bandage that was barely hanging on after all that walking. "Can ye walk farther?"

I bit my lip, considering as I rubbed my aching feet. "How much longer?"

"Two hours, maybe, so we haven'ae much farther now. If we hurry, we might find breakfast."

I smiled and pushed to my feet. "I could so handle breakfast. Let me get dressed first and we'll go." I moved to limp away, but Cailen put up a halting hand.

"I'll turn ma back. We must keep ye from walkin' as much as we can."

Ducking inside Cailen's shirt, I clasped my bra hooks together and looped the straps over my shoulders. Once that was in place I yanked on my skirt and replaced his shirt with my own.

"I'm done."

Cailen peeked over his shoulder. "That was fast."

"Try doing that in a locker room full of girls when you only have three minutes to get dressed *and* get across campus to your next class."

He blinked at me and shook his head. "Uh, well, let's see if we can fashion something for yer feet, aye? An idea occurred tae me while ma back was turned." He bent and plucked a leaf off of a bush and placed it on the ground, gesturing for me to step on it.

The Highlander grabbed more leaves, layering them on top of one another until there were two piles. He then removed the cloth strips that had been wrapped around my foot. "Here, step on these." When I did, he set to wrapping my feet with the cloth, binding the leaves to them. "There, that'll dae for now." He stood and smiled approvingly.

I guessed I couldn't complain. He'd provided a solution that would keep my bare feet from the elements, and keep me from having to wear my heels in the middle of the wet, grassy, bushy forest. "Thanks."

He shrugged uncomfortably. "Och, dinna mention it.

I'm only sorry I didnae think tae dae it before."

"Well, I don't think there was really a chance while running away from whoever was going to jump us in your camp." I shifted my feet, surprised that the leaves did actually provide some comfort. Looking up at Cailen, I smiled. "Okay, let's go. I'm starving. Whoa, *whoa*. What are you doing?" I pushed him away from me as he bent to pick me up.

He frowned. "I'm goin' tae carry ye."

"No you're not."

"Aye, I am. Ye dinna really think ye can walk the rest o' the way, dae ye?"

"I can try." Damn, why did my feet have to hurt so much?

"There's nae need tae be stubborn, lass."

"And there's no need for you to carry me unless I absolutely need it. Besides, I—*Whoa!*"

He flashed me a smile as he lifted me in his arms. "I'm tellin' ye, woman. Ye need tae be carried. I should'ae been daein' so this entire time, and it's ma fault ye're in pain now. So, I'll carry ye some o' the time and let ye walk others. And I dinna want ye tae argue wi'me."

I melted at the dark, heated gaze peering back at me as our eyes locked. "Why not?"

"Because ye dinna want tae find out what I'm like when I'm angry."

CHAPTER FIVE

"This is a *town?*" I hissed after the old woman disappeared through the door.

"Aye." Cailen looked down at me, his brows lowering in confusion. "What did ye expect?"

Seriously? What did I expect? I plopped down in a huge wooden chair in the woman's small parlor, shaking my head in my hands. I hadn't dared say anything until after she'd left—not with those untrusting glances she'd already thrown my way.

When we'd first strolled up to her house, I'd assumed it was a shack, or maybe a barn of some sort, until I'd seen a small sign stating that Mrs. Ferguson was a seamstress. It was even harder to believe when I walked inside, seeing dark wood walls and wooden furniture. It was like I was in one of those time-capsule cabins that were preserved exactly as they'd been so long ago.

The room wasn't very bright, with the only light coming through the window on the front of the house, and from the candles which didn't make the place smell all that pleasant. I realized with a shock that there weren't any lamps on end tables, or even lights on the ceiling. At least, not the lamps I was accustomed to. Other than the wooden chair I sat on, there were two benches and a table with needles and thread on it. On the floor, was what looked like a hand-made rug.

Freakin' time capsule.

Even Mrs. Ferguson was a bit surprising, in her red

plaid dress, and her brown and silver hair that was pulled up underneath a white cap.

Was the Highlander really just screwing with me here? Had he really known what a cell phone was the entire time and called ahead to pull off this prank? Unlikely. It's not like I'd known him for long, and unless Scots had really weird senses of humor, one probably wouldn't go through the trouble to mess with me.

And yet, that was the only explanation my mind would accept. Either that, or I really had stumbled on Amishville, Scotland.

"Whate'er happened tae yer clothes, ma'dearie?" Mrs. Ferguson stammered when we'd been welcomed into her home.

After getting over my irritation at yet another person gawking at my clothes, I'd explained some of the details of my kidnapping. Cailen had thrown in the bit about the gunmen—tactfully leaving out his involvement, or lack thereof, during that part—and Mrs. Ferguson had patted my hand sympathetically.

"Well," she'd said. "We'll get ye fixed up fine. I've got a brown dress that might fit, and some skirts tae go along wi'it. I was makin' it for ma granddaughter," she said pointedly at the Highlander, "but it should work just fine for ye."

"Hae ye any shoes we might purchase for her?" Cailen had asked.

"I dinna hae any here, but I can go doon tae the shoemaker's tae see what he has." Turning to me, she'd continued, "First, let me see what I've got tae get ye dressed. Ye're no' fit tae be in the comp'ny o' a gentleman."

"Thank you," we both said before she'd whirled around in her skirts and disappeared through her parlor doorway.

"I expected an actual town," I snapped. "This place looks like a ghost town. And what is with everybody's clothes?"

"What is wrong wi'our clothing?"

I glared and opened my mouth to tell him just what was wrong with everyone wearing kilts and dresses when Mrs. Ferguson whisked her way into the room again, carrying a brown dress and a whole lot of nearly white fabric. "I trust ye hae money tae pay for this?" she asked, sending a questioning glance toward Cailen.

"Oh aye, we've plenty."

"Good. Now, depairt so we may get the lass fitted and dressed. We'll call ye in presently."

Dismissed, Cailen left the house. Mrs. Ferguson disappeared through the door, returning a few minutes later with a bowl full of water, and a washcloth. "Here," she said, setting them down on the table. "Get cleaned up."

Not a request apparently.

I could have just used the sink in her bathroom, but the way she stared at me expectantly had me dunking the cloth in the cold water. It really didn't look all that clean. The water was brownish and not all that transparent, and the rag looked as though it'd been used countless times washing things I didn't even want to think about. I rung out the rag and brought it to my face, silently sniffing it, and hoping that Mrs. Ferguson hadn't seen me. At least it didn't smell bad. In fact, it smelled like it was infused with flowers. I scrubbed my hands, arms, neck, and face before Mrs. Ferguson helped me off with my shirt.

"Michty me!" she exclaimed, causing me to whirl around, gaping from her loud, surprised tone. "Whate'er are ye wearing?"

Jeez! What is wrong with these people? "That's my bra."

"I've ne'er seen somethin'…well, so revealing. Off wi'it." She looked at me like I was the spawn of Satan as she wrenched it off over my head and dropped it to the floor along with my Juicy shirt, forcing me to face away from her yet again. "Where are the ties for this…this…" Her voice died away as she pointed at my skirt.

I rolled my eyes and unzipped it, letting it pool at my feet. Mrs. Ferguson gasped and I turned to face her, backing away as I saw that look in her eyes. "No. Don't you even think about it. I'm *not* taking off my underwear, and I swear, if you try, you're not going to like what happens."

"I've ne'er—"

"You've never seen anything like it. Yeah, yeah, yeah," I groaned. "I'm not taking them off."

She glared. "Fine. Wash yerself and I'll set tae work on pinnin' the dress. I can see already that it's too long for ye." She turned and walked over to the chair that the dress and skirts were folded over.

I waited until I was reasonably sure she wasn't going to sneak up and force me out of my thong. When I saw that she really was busy with the dress, I dunked the cloth in the water and ran it up and down my legs until they were cold, but probably cleaner than they had been. The wraps around my feet were easily loosened, and I stepped off the leaves before I scrubbed them, careful not to put too much pressure on my right foot.

"All right," Mrs. Ferguson said a while later, obviously in a much better mood than she was before. "Stand right there. Aye, just that way." She slid whitish fabric over my head and shoulders, and then gave me a matching set of loose M.C. Hammer pants. I may have told her what they looked like, but Mrs. Ferguson seemed way too uptight and probably wouldn't know what I was talking about anyway.

Did people in Scotland even know who M.C. Hammer was?

Next came another slip and then a thick skirt, followed by the brown dress. "Holy crap. How much do you actually expect me to wear?"

"*Wheesht*," she shushed as she balanced pins between her lips. The old woman dropped to her knees and pulled pins out of the fabric. "I think this will fit just fine once ye get proper shoes. Gi'us a turn so I can see about the laces." She finished pulling out the last of the pins and stood up, yanking on the ties at the back of the dress. I nearly fell over three times and she chastised me about acting like I'd never done up a dress before.

"Exactly why do I have to wear all of this?" I asked, feeling like I was under a million layers of fabric. The dress was white and brown, with white lace that rimmed my neck and arms. "It's not like there's anything wrong with the clothes I've already got."

Other than the fact that they seemed to offend every single person I'd seen since my kidnapping.

"Why," she breathed. "Ye canna wander around the whole o' Scotland wearing naethin' but yer undergarments, dearie. I'm surprised naethin' has happened tae ye yet." She brushed through my hair, pinning it in random places and pulling it up before placing a hat on top of my head. "Ye're verra lucky yer laddie found ye before someone else. But e'en a gentleman like him could lose his head o'er a wee lassie in her underthings."

"Did you just call Cailen a gentleman?"

"Och, aye. Is that his name then? He's ne'er told me."

My ears felt heated suddenly. Why wouldn't the Highlander have told her his name? Was I supposed to keep my mouth shut?

"That young laddie has ne'er been anythin' but a

gentleman." Mrs. Ferguson's eyes met mine, her expression changing to inquisitiveness. "I think it's done him good tae hae ye tae take care o'."

"Why's that?"

"He's been comin' here for years now, and I've ne'er seen that spark in him."

Spark? I caused a spark?

"He's been on his own a long time, ken. Whene'er someone comes intae town and they've been awa from other folk for a long time, there's somethin'…different about them. That's how yer lad has been since he started comin' tae me for mendin' or for new clothes. He's always been cordial, but distant." Mrs. Ferguson's lips curled into a smile. "Aye, there's a spark in him now. Almost as though he's needed someone wi'him. Someone tae care for, maybe? Shouldn'ae come as a surprise," she added. "He's a fine young man. Any lass would be lucky tae call him hers."

I shook my head. "Oh no, no, no. He's not mine."

"I dinna ken, I think there's more between the two o' ye than either o' ye ken." She leaned in closer. "I've seen young lassies and laddies fall in love for forty years. I just may ken a thing or two," she teased.

I shook my head, ready to tell her yet again that Cailen and I were nothing more than acquaintances, but she cut off my reply.

"Now, ye just hae a seat. I'll send ma servant wi'some tea while I fetch ye a pair o' stockings and shoes. Oh, and I'll send the doctor tae come hae a look at ye."

She was gone before I even blinked, and the next thing I knew, Cailen was standing in the doorway, peering at me with an indescribable expression on his face.

He blinked and took a single step inside, ducking through the doorway before bowing. "Yer servant, mum."

He straightened, his gaze never leaving mine as he rose as close to his full height as he could in this house.

The way he stared caused a flush to work from my chest up to my face and ears, and I quickly glanced away.

"Ye look bonny, Elizabeth."

I flicked my gaze at him and smiled. "Thanks."

The Highlander nodded, but it looked more like a mini bow as he took a seat on the bench next to me. The servant bobbed her way into the room and set down a tray of tea and cookies, before she poured two glasses and handed them to us. She was gone as fast as she'd come.

"She has a way about her, aye?" Cailen said. "Mrs. Ferguson, I mean."

"Yeah. She sorta just makes you do what she wants." I sipped the tea and shuddered as the taste of weeds flooded my mouth. *Stupid tea. Sooo gross.* "Why did you make me get into a dress anyway? Isn't there like a mall or store around somewhere? I mean, I saw Glasgow and Oban, and a lot of cities and towns in between, so I know you all aren't that far behind the times." I stood and bent for my purse, finding it more than a little difficult to breathe in the garb I'd just been forced into. I turned on my cell and sat down. "Seriously? *Ugh.*" Still no bars.

"What's the matter?"

"I *still* don't have any service, and you seem to have brought me to a town that doesn't have anything. No cars, no phones, no freaking lights!" This was turning into a nightmare, and that rock in my gut just continued to get bigger and bigger.

The Scot was silent for a minute as I turned off my phone and shoved it angrily back into my purse. I threw it and it landed near my discarded clothes.

"I'm sorry," he said. "We mustn'ae hae certain comforts ye're accustomed tae in the Colonies."

I dropped my face into my hands, feeling even worse for causing that defeated tone in his voice. "Yes you do. I've seen them. Two days ago I was surrounded by people carrying cell phones and driving cars." I had just somehow ended up in the Twilight Zone.

Mrs. Ferguson's front door opened and a man walked in, followed by the lady of the house herself. "This is Mr. Docherty, our doctor," she said proudly, gesturing to the forty-something guy next to her.

Dr. Docherty dropped down to his knees and took my foot in his hands. "Och, aye. It looks like someone has already cleaned the wound. It's healin' up just fine. Just fine." He poked at it a few more times and then opened his black case. "Ye'll want tae rub this on it twice a day and be sure tae keep it clean. Mrs. Ferguson said ye've gone a while wi'out shoes. Ye canna dae that if ye want it tae heal. I dinna want tae hear that ye're runnin' around shoeless again, aye?" He smiled kindly and winked.

I couldn't help but laugh. "Alright. I'll be sure to wear shoes from now on." I took the small vial from him and he stood and left the room, nodding at everyone and speaking in a language I couldn't have understood if I'd tried.

Cailen excused himself as well, walking outside with the doctor and only returned after Mrs. Ferguson had my new socks and shoes done up. The stockings were basically what I'd thought they'd be, but the shoes were way different. They were practically the same as the leaf shoes Cailen had jerry-rigged for me, only these were made of some type of leather, with laces that wrapped around my feet and up past my ankles.

"Jeez, you guys go all out. I didn't even know you could still buy stuff this old."

Mrs. Ferguson blinked and her mouth dropped wide open. "Old?"

77

"Uh," Cailen stepped toward the woman. "She didnae mean *old*. She's just accustomed tae...other fashions in the Colonies."

"Oooh, so that's why she doesn'ae speak any Scots." She nodded to herself as if that had explained everything, but then she gave me another one of those looks. I was guessing I'd just lost a few more points in her eyes. Apparently the woman was only happy while she was sewing. "Well, that'll be four pounds for the lot."

I screwed up my face. "You're joking." Wasn't four pounds basically nothing? I didn't know squat about the exchange rate, but there was no way that was right.

Mrs. Ferguson's face turned to one of shock. "It looks like ye've taught yer lass well, lad. Fine, three pounds, six shillings."

"A fair price," Cailen agreed, nodding at me before shaking his head at the old woman. "But she isn'ae mine."

"So I've heard."

Ignoring the expressions crossing both the Scot and Scotett's faces, I reached into my purse and pulled out some coins, staring at them in my open palm, completely clueless as to what was what.

The Highlander reached over and plucked some coins from my hand before presenting them to the seamstress. I quickly snatched my clothes and shoes, shoving what I could into my bag.

"We're indebted for yer generosity, mum." He bowed formally to her as he held her hand and kissed her knuckles.

"Dinna fash." She smiled as a small flush worked across her cheeks.

Well well, apparently old Mrs. Ferguson has a wee crush on my Highlander. Whoa...The Highlander, not my Highlander.

"Ye can return in the morn," she continued. "I should

hae yer new shirt ready for ye then."

"Again, we thank ye." Cailen turned to look at me, a single brow raising in question.

"Uh, yeah…thanks."

He stepped by my side and guided me toward the door with a gentle hand to my back, and soon we were outside in the cool air. Not surprisingly, more than half of the sky was filled with dark clouds that looked like they were about to drop buckets on us at any minute, and a wind that had me shivering already.

"Looks like rain. Again," I muttered.

"Nae." He drew out the word, long and slow. "It looks like they're goin' awa from us. I think we may hae a good day."

"Sun?" I asked, feeling hopeful. God knew I could definitely use some vitamin D.

The Scot turned toward me, the corners of lips turning up in a small grin. "Aye. Does that please ye?"

"Heck yeah it does!" I nodded enthusiastically, nearly laughing at Cailen's shock, which turned into a wide grin at my excitement. Finally, *something* good.

As we walked away from Mrs. Ferguson's house, I could see that there were a few buildings spread out along the gentle hills of the tiny town, all of which were made of stone and wood, and with long, dry grass for their roofs. I wasn't sure how he'd accomplished it, but Cailen had managed to keep me away from any real towns, guiding me through the forest and open fields without me hearing a single car or airplane, and bringing me to this revived ghost town.

There wasn't a single sky scraper or car in sight, and not even a neon open sign lit any of their glassless windows. I knew Scotland had those too—windows and open signs—like the one I'd seen when Shannon and I had walked to Lorne's Pub. Even Mrs. Ferguson's place had one glass window, while the others had just been a square cut out of the wall covered by thick cloth.

The Highlander and I made our way farther from Mrs. Ferguson's house, walking the dirt road that led to the others. Not far from where we were, there were more buildings and shacks clumped closer together, which gave me hope of finding *some* sort of technology. I was determined to find *anything*. There were two horses grazing just to the side of the only two-story building in sight.

"I really just don't get what's going on," I admitted as Cailen and I entered what the old-looking sign outside had labeled as an "Inn".

There were men inside, sitting around wooden tables and throwing back alcohol as tiny flames flickered from candles and lanterns all around the room. There was a fireplace along one wall with a small fire crackling inside, and a wood stair case along the opposite wall, near where the woman tended the bar. The place smelled of alcohol, smoke, and stewing meat, and my stomach growled in response. A few of the drunks peered up as the door closed behind us; others didn't bother lifting their heads from the tables. Cailen led me to a table on the far side of the room, and hastily took the seat nearest the wall after pulling out a chair for me. It took me a bit to get comfortable with all the layers of fabric around me.

"This is all so weird. I mean, cool that you all value your history so much, but…yeah, it's weird."

"Two whiskys," he told the waitress, who wore something that looked like one of the layers of clothes I had on underneath this dress. She also wore a cap that didn't even attempt to conceal her wild brown hair.

"Weird? What's so weird?" He faced me.

"Everything. Ever since I met you, I've felt like I'm in

some crazy time-warp."

"Here ye are," the waitress said. She set two mugs of alcohol on the table before placing a lit lantern in the center. "Would ye like a bite tae eat as well?"

"No' just yet," Cailen replied. He waited until she scampered off before eyeing me again. "Time warp, is it? I haven'ae heard that term before, but I can imagine what ye mean by it."

"You're telling me that it doesn't feel like this town is stuck in the 1800's or something?"

He choked, spitting out a little of his whiskey before clapping his hand over his mouth. "1800's?" He laughed.

"Oh jeez. *Whatever*. You don't have to laugh. History's never been my strong suit." I narrowed my eyes, feeling my face blush with embarrassment. For the first time I actually wished I would have paid attention in Mr. Davis's history class. "Fine, what year do you think?"

"For someone believin' this town tae be old, I dinna ken how they managed tae get ahead o' the times." He lifted his glass in salute to the waitress who cocked an eyebrow at us. "Slange."

"Shut. Up," I muttered, shaking my head. I was getting more and more irritated by the minute. "What the crap are you talking about?"

"Well." Cailen returned my narrowed gaze, his brows lowering as though he thought I were slow or something. "I'd say that this inn fits right intae 1770, the year we're in presently."

My head whipped up and my eyes met his. "That's not funny."

"I didnae mean for it tae be."

He didn't laugh or even show a hint of a teasing smile. My mind scrambled as I hoped to hear the "just kidding" that had to be coming.

It didn't.

"You're on crack," I said. "I mean, you've got to be joking...right?"

"Oh? And what year is it then?"

"2013."

Now both of Cailen's eyebrows rose high onto his forehead. He stabbed his fingers through his hair and I could have sworn I'd heard him mumble, "*Daft*," under his breath.

"Excuse me," he said, before standing and walking toward the bar. He spoke to the waitress in a hushed voice, but it was still easy to hear the timbre of his voice through the loud drunks all around. After a minute he returned to the table and plopped a single-sheet newspaper down on the table, pointing at the date in the top corner.

July 14th, 1770

I felt as though my entire body was tingling as a chill crawled over my skin. I stared at the date before glancing over the news on the page. There wasn't much, not with a paper that consisted of smudged print that only filled one side of the sheet. I studied the date again, focusing on it in case I'd read it wrong the first time.

July 14th, 1770

"Is this a joke?" I looked up at the Scot again. "Did you have this made up while I was at Mrs. Ferguson's?" I hadn't seen or heard from him in a really long time, but now it made sense if he was in on a sick inside joke with the other people in town.

His eyes darkened and he leaned down close to the table, swiping up the newspaper. In a much louder voice than he'd spoken before, he faced the waitress. "I dinna think the lassie is feelin' well presently. We'll need a room for her, and a bottle o' whisky." He flicked his gaze at me for a second before returning it to the woman behind the old wooden bar. "Better make it two."

CHAPTER SIX

Cailen set the two bottles of whiskey and the newspaper on a small table, and gestured for me to take a seat on the bed as he plunked down in the only chair in the room. "What are ye playin' at?"

I sat, but didn't really know what to say. That chill that had worked through my body had taken a strong hold, and even my brain couldn't get past the date shown on that damned paper. "I'm not playing," I replied numbly. "Are you?"

The Highlander was already leaning his elbows on his knees, but his head quickly dropped down as though his energy had been sapped. "I dinna ken what tae make o' ye, Elizabeth. Dae ye really think it's 2013?"

I closed my eyes and took a deep breath before gazing at him once more. "That's the year I'm from."

"Ye truly believe it is the year 2013." He hadn't phrased it as a question.

"Yes. Because it is. Or, it was." I was numb and cold. And so very exhausted. So many things whirled through my mind: The clothing everyone had been wearing—and what I wore now—the lack of cars and lights, Cailen's awe at seeing my cell phone and pictures. "Can you please just tell me if you're messing with me?" I asked quietly, my voice barely more than a whisper. "There's just been way too much going on the last few days, and I can't handle any more pranks."

He was quiet for a while, so much so that the room felt oppressively silent. At the moment, I both wanted to be downstairs, and also despised the easy banter reaching my ears through the floorboards. I stood up, feeling an overwhelming need to do something. I walked to the window and pulled back the covering so that sunlight could brighten the dank room.

"I'd hae told ye by now if I was being dishonest."

I turned, meeting his eyes as he peered at me from over his shoulder. I crawled back onto the bed and placed my back against the wall. "I feel like I'm in some crazy dream. I mean, are you even real?"

My question stunned him and he blinked. "Aye, as far as I ken, lass. Ev'ra bit as real as ye."

"Yeah, yeah, that's probably what someone in a dream would say." Only one problem. People woke up from dreams, and I'd been living this one since Lorne's Pub.

My hands knotted together, and I peered down at them, a little shocked that they'd done that without me knowing. *1770...1770...1770.* Over two-hundred and forty years in the past.

"Elizabeth," Cailen said softly. "Can ye tell me what's happened tae ye? From the beginning? We'll sort it out."

I shifted on the bed and pulled the blanket over my lap. My mind wandered for a minute, wanting to focus on something—anything—else. The blanket didn't have much of a design, and the few colored patterns that were there were heavily faded. The room itself was nothing special. It was all wood with only a single, small window that had thick cloth flung to one side. And, as I'd seen of the other homes in town, there wasn't even glass in the window to separate us from the elements outside. Next to the whiskey and newspaper was a single yellowish candle that only had about two inches left to burn. Between the bed and the wall with the window, there was a single pot sitting on the floor. No pictures on the walls, no rugs, and no phone or alarm clock. It was basically a box with a bed, chair, and a small table that held a bowl of water and a folded rag.

And none of it was clean.

Or maybe it was, for 1770 standards.

The floorboards creaked as someone's footfalls pounded in the hall. I even felt the shift of boards under the bed, and used their passing to gather my thoughts as Cailen watched me. Another door down the hall opened and slammed shut.

"Well, I uh…" *Where to begin?* "I already told you that I came to Scotland because my best friend is getting married."

He nodded. "Ye said ye flew here."

"I did. On a plane."

Cailen looked interested at that and leaned forward. "And what is a plane?"

"It's like a bus that holds hundreds of people and flies through the air."

"A bus?"

I shook my head. Of course he wouldn't know what that was either. "A really long vehicle…Okay, imagine a carriage that could drive around without the horses. Now imagine that the coach couldn't just hold like four people, but it was really, really long and hundreds of people could sit in it." Was I really doing this?

"It isn'ae possible."

"It is. Buses are like that, only those just fit something like forty people. But planes are huge and carry a lot more."

Cailen reached for a whiskey bottle and pried it open, taking a long swig as the liquid *glugged* out of it.

"Anyway, that's what brought me here. I flew from Salt Lake to Glasgow. Salt Lake is in Utah. I don't think it *exists* yet." I know it didn't, not if I was really in 1770.

86

How in the hell could I be in 1770? Time travel wasn't real.

What if time travel really existed but no one knew because travelers never returned to their own time?

"Here," the Highlander said, handing me the bottle. "It looks like ye need this as much as I dae."

I took the whiskey and drank, setting the bottle on the blankets in the little nest between my legs. "I came here to see Shannon get married."

"Aye, ye mentioned her earlier. The one in the painting o' the two o' ye."

I nodded. "We met for drinks at a pub the day before yesterday, and this guy kinda attacked me."

Cailen's expression turned dark, but he kept his voice light. "The man who kidnapped ye?"

"Yeah. Only, now I don't know if he really kidnapped me or if..." *He sent me two-hundred years in the past.*

"Aye, I see. And what happened when he attacked ye?"

"I don't know." Goose bumps covered my arms, and I brought the blanket up to cover them. "I was really weirded out at first and then I was just scared. All I remember is that he gripped my shoulders and talked like he was crazy. And then he put change into my hand and handed me the pocket watch."

Which had burned me, and...

"What's wrong, Elizabeth?"

I reached into my purse and pulled the pocket watch out by its chain, placing it on the blanket. "This burned my hand. When he handed it to me, it started going backwards and then it burned me. I tried to drop it, but it wouldn't go, and then everything..." *Melted away.* "Went dark." I showed him my palm and the light pink scar the watch had left behind.

Cailen reached for the whiskey and poured some down his throat before handing it back. He sighed and rubbed a hand over his face. "What did the man say tae ye?"

"I don't know. All I caught was that I had to go back and 'set it right'."

"What did he look like?"

I shook my head and shrugged. "Light blue eyes, really scruffy face, dark hair, and he wore a dark cloak."

"Anythin' else?"

"No, that's it. The next thing I knew I was sitting out in the middle of nowhere, and then I met you." Had I landed exactly where Lorne's Pub was, only roughly two hundred and forty years earlier? The thought made me dizzy.

"Elizabeth, I've two questions for ye, and I expect the truth."

"Okay."

"Are ye lyin' tae me?"

I shook my head. "No." I couldn't blame him for asking, especially considering I'd assumed he'd been lying to me all along. A part of me still thought that he was really good at playing tricks on people. The longer this went, though, the less I could hope for that.

"All right. Then that leaves one question: Are ye a witch?"

My mouth fell open before I slammed it shut again. Had he really just asked me that? "Witches don't even exist."

A look of infuriation mingled with relief covered his face as he leaned back in his chair and pried open the other bottle. He must have assumed that I'd finish off the other one soon. And he was right. I had no intention of giving up the only thing that could muddle my mind from what was happening.

"Aye lass," he said after a moment. "They dae exist. I'm just tryin' tae figure out if ye are a witch, or if ye've been cursed by one."

Cursed by a witch?

My mind had lit on that more times than I could count ever since Cailen had spoken those words. Of course, that wasn't all I focused on. Time travel took up my foremost thoughts, second being that I had nowhere to go, no one who knew me, and no way of knowing how to get back to my own time; and thirdly, the existence of witches.

Cailen had left a while ago, needing to take a break from story time. I suspected that he'd gone down for more drinks, but he hadn't returned yet, and since he'd ordered me not to leave the room, I'd stayed put.

"Nae one else can hear what ye've told me," he'd warned. "I may believe ye're no' a witch, but others may no' gi'ye the chance tae explain." He'd exhaled slowly, and ran his fingers through his hair. "Quite a tale ye've got, though, aye?"

And so I'd stayed. I sat in the dark, square room, watching those last two inches of candle wax disappear as the flame slid lower and lower on the candlestick. Sunlight had crept across the floorboards as the sun made its arch over the sky, moving even slower than a tortoise. I checked my cell phone, though not to see if I had any service. Instead, I scrolled through the pictures, memorizing the faces I may never see again: Mom, Dad, my little brother, Jason, and my friends. I realized only then that I'd never again hear the recorded voicemail messages from Mom, the ones she'd left me before she died. I'd saved them repeatedly, refusing to delete them whenever my voicemail prompted me to. I'd never get to hug Dad again and smell the Old Spice he dashed on before heading to work every day; never get to tease Jason about his obsession with video games—that was completely my fault anyway—or buy him clothes so he'd dress somewhat decent and maybe actually get a girlfriend. I'd never get to go to the mall or hang out with my friends again, or get to talk about guys or make plans to rent a house together so we could have some privacy from our parents. I wouldn't see Shannon get married, or be able to tell her about this crazy, terrifying adventure and the man who was helping me through it.

All I had left of everyone I loved was in my hands. Pictures: some of them smiling, some from candid shots. And Mom's—a picture of the two of us, with my chin resting on her shoulder as we flashed cheesy grins at the camera.

I heard someone approach the door and quickly turned off my cell. I'd barely stuffed it into my purse when Cailen pushed the door open, his eyes meeting mine as he gave me a tight nod. The smell of food hit my nose and I looked down to see that he held two metal plates in his hands, piled high with meat, vegetables, and bread.

I scrambled off the bed and met him, grabbing the plates. "Thanks."

He shrugged a shoulder. "Dinna mention it. Someone should be up wi'drink shor—oh." He turned and stepped into the hall again and thanked whoever had just met him. A woman replied before he entered the room again and shut the door. Even from this side of the door, I picked up on the woman's flirtatious tone. It hadn't occurred to me until then that he might have been doing more than tossing back drinks.

The Highlander had told me he wouldn't have sex with anyone, but he hadn't said he wouldn't do anything else.

I set his plate on the table and turned to take one of the bottles from him. "I could have come down and helped," I said, crawling onto the bed and pulling the plate onto my lap. My stomach growled loudly and I glanced up at Cailen as my face flamed. "I guess I'm hungry."

He chuckled and placed his sword next to the door before sitting and taking a bite of his bread. Swallowing, he said, "I'm sorry, lass. I didnae meant tae be gone so long. I just needed some time tae think."

I finished chewing my bite of meat, not bothering to swallow it before saying, "What did you think about?" Probably trying to figure out how to dump the poor crazy girl who thinks she's from the future.

"Ye're situation. I ken by now ye've considered the fact that ye've nae family here, and nae friends tae speak o', no' tae mention nowhere tae call home—"

"I got that, thanks." I didn't need the reminder.

"Mmm hmm," he grunted. "And I suppose ye've noticed that what money ye've on ye will'nae last forever."

I nodded, chewing on a bite of bread. That had occurred to me while he was gone, too. Credit cards didn't exist in 1770, and any other little bit of money I had was U.S. dollars dated a lot later than the time I was in now. Other than the change Captain Cloak had tossed my way, I had absolutely no money. I met Cailen's eyes, noticing that he suddenly looked really uncomfortable. "What's wrong?"

"Well," he shrugged. "While I was out thinkin', I realized the only way I may be able tae help ye."

I set my plate down, sighing with relief as my gaze locked with his. Holy crap. He'd actually come up with a way to help me? "What?"

"Ye must get mairrit."

CHAPTER SEVEN

I sputtered, choking on the bread that I inhaled at Cailen's words. He quickly stood, setting his whiskey and plate on the table before pounding me on the back, dislodging the food. "Did you just say 'married'?" I said, blinking at the tears in my eyes. The man really was on crack!

He gave me another slap on the back and stepped away, still eyeing me. "I did."

"I tell you that I'm from more than two hundred years in the future, and your solution is to marry me off? No thoughts on how to get me back home or even point me in the direction of who could help me? Just *marriage*?" Pig-headed jerk!

He sat in the chair, bending to pick up his food and drink. "Aye."

I couldn't say anything as I gawked at him, my head shaking back and forth.

"Elizabeth," he said, his eyebrows lowering as he met my gaze head-on. "We're no' in yer time. And I've nae idea how tae get ye back tae yer own time."

"So you do believe me?"

"Kind o' hard no' tae, aye? Ye've spoken o' things I've ne'er heard o', and e'en yer '*cell phone*' is proof that ye're no' from here."

I set my plate down on the bed, no longer feeling the need to eat when marriage was being tossed around as a viable option. "What about a witch?" Cailen's face hardened so I hastily added, "You already told me they're

92

real. What if we found one? Maybe she could help me get home."

The Highlander was already shaking his head. "Nae. Witches are no' tae be messed wi', nor tae be trusted. I will'nae see ye put in danger for askin' for help from a witch."

I raised the whiskey bottle to my mouth and drank three big gulps before wiping a little off my lips. I only hoped he'd assume the tears in my eyes were from the burn of the alcohol. "I need to get back to my time, Cailen. How do you think my dad feels right now? And Shannon? As far as they're probably concerned I've been kidnapped. They might even think I'm dead. They're probably scouring Scotland looking for me and petrified of what they might find. I can't just sit by and do nothing if there is even a remote chance that I could go back home."

He still shook his head, more vehemently this time.

"So you're just saying that I have to get married? How is that a solution?"

"It's obvious, I should think. Yer a young lass o' proper age. Ye've a nice look about ye. There are plenty o' lads who would be o'erjoyed tae take ye as their wife."

"And I'm just supposed to let that happen?" I was so not going to let that happen.

"Aye. If ye mean tae survive, ye'll take any decent man who would hae ye."

He might have laughed if the alarm in Elizabeth's eyes wasn't from a very unfortunate set of circumstances. Aye, he truly felt sorry for the lass. To lose her family and all she'd kent in one fell swoop, only to end up in a time and place she didn't ken, nor did she even fit into.

Everything made sense now. The way she spoke and dressed, her casual yet impatient demeanor. He'd never met another woman like her. Not with the way she spoke her mind, nor how feisty she was, fighting him that first day. Certainly none in memory had compared to her beauty. Elizabeth was like a precious jewel: vibrant and lovely. Her blue eyes were the exact color of the sea on a sunny day, when he could stare at the rolling waves from dawn to dusk. She had lovely golden skin with wee freckles spotting her cheeks. She must have spent a good deal of time in the sun, not that that came to any surprise. He thought again of the painting of her wearing barely a stitch. Aye, she certainly was from a different time. Surely nothing like that came from present. Not with the way women dressed.

Elizabeth truly was special. Even her hair smelled different, as though every flower in the world scented her golden locks. Her glistening hair looked as though it had been kissed by the sun, almost as though every strand was the given the gift of its own shade of blonde. He'd oft wondered what it would feel like to run his fingers through those tresses. Oh, and those lips of hers. So soft and pink. For the last two days he'd dreamed day and night of seeing what they felt like.

Not that he'd ever get the chance.

Elizabeth was worth so much more than he could offer her. And his family meant far too much for him to give up on them. There was only one he could have, and it wasn't Elizabeth.

Maybe the lass's fear of marriage stemmed from a bad relationship, or perhaps her mam and da hadn't had the best of marriages. It was the best he could do for her though, to see her wed to an honest man. A clansman, maybe. Aye, that would make the best match. He kent quite a few laddies who'd yet to wed—or at least, he had before he'd left the clan. In any case, his da would ken everyone's current situations and be best to find a good man for Elizabeth.

God kent he could do nothing for her himself.

He looked at Elizabeth as she sat on the bed, her face and fists tense. She'd clearly exhausted every option she'd thought of, and wasn't pleased with whatever she came up with. Every once in a while, she mumble something under her breath, and he thought there were times he'd caught entire sentences that she spoke quietly.

The lass talked to herself.

He smiled again, but as her angry gaze landed on him, he dropped whatever grin had formed.

"What are you smiling about?" she barked.

"Naethin'. I just...I must go out for a bit. There are arrangements tae be made."

Och, it only riled her more.

"Like my *marriage*?"

"No' just yet. We've a little time before we must find ye a proper husband." He stood and walked to the door, pulling on the latch to open it. In truth, there wasn't much for him to do. He just couldn't sit there under her scrutiny. The lass was far from happy, and he feared it was only about to get worse over the coming days.

"I just can't believe you," Elizabeth muttered. "You make me confide in you and then you marry me off to the highest bidder."

He whirled around, still standing in the open doorway. "*What?* Ye dinna think I'm selling ye, dae ye?" Taking three steps into the room, he lowered himself so he was eye-level with her. "Elizabeth, marriage is the best thing I can think o' for ye. Wi'out a man tae provide for ye and keep ye warm and fed, there's nae chance ye'll survive. Marriage *is* the best I can dae for ye."

She looked away from him, focusing on the blankets that covered her bed. He'd never been one to deal with a crying woman. He needed to leave.

Standing, he walked to the door again. "I'll go now. Ye should get some rest. I'll be nearby if the need arises."

She didn't respond.

"I'll uh…I'll be sleepin' out here as well." That did earn him a reaction.

"You're not staying in here with me? You're leaving me *alone* now too? Why even stay, Cailen? Why not just go back to your life and let me deal with my own?"

Leave her? Surely she didn't think he would do such a thing? "Nae. I dinna ken what it's like in yer time, but here, it's just no' proper for a man and a woman tae share a room unless they're wed. I'm fine tae sleep in the adjoining room."

She'd shut down again, but kept her eyes on him until he'd finished talking. He backed out into the hall and shut the door as Elizabeth dropped her head onto her knees.

Emotions warred inside him. He'd never been able to do anything right. Not for his da, not for his family, and now, not for Elizabeth.

He didn't want to hurt the woman. But what else was he to do?

After a sleepless night, Cailen and I left the inn the next morning and, after picking up his new shirt, we followed the directions the innkeeper gave us to Mr. MacMillan's house, who may or may not have a horse or two he'd be willing to sell to us. No way was I on board with the Scot's plan to throw me at the first available bachelor we met, but I was grateful for his suggestion that we ride horseback to wherever it was we were going. For one, it got me off my foot that still throbbed like crazy, and as soon as the opportunity presented itself, I could escape Cailen and his harebrained scheme to make me some random Highlander's wife.

"I've only the one tae sell ye, mind," Mr. MacMillan said. The man had the blackest hair I'd ever seen, which was made all the darker by his wiry beard that covered half his face. He constantly stood with his arms folded, and he smelled like he'd been working with cows and horses all morning. "But she should be strong enough tae hold ye both."

We rested against the wooden fence that lined the horse's pen, and Cailen looked at me questioningly. "What dae ye think?"

"I don't know." I shrugged. "I've never ridden one."

Both men gaped. "How is that possible?" MacMillan said with a shake of his head. "I've ne'er met a lass who hasn'ae ridden a horse at least *once*."

"I just haven't. I've seen them in fields and stables and have petted a few on the nose, but that's the extent of it."

Mr. MacMillan shook his head and peered at Cailen. "Where did ye find such a ledy? Must be verra special indeed tae hae ne'er ridden a horse before."

"Ye hae nae idea," he mumbled. "How much dae ye want for the mare?"

MacMillan rubbed his chin with his thumb and forefinger, considering. "Oh, I'd say eight pounds ought tae cover her."

"Are we really only getting one?" I asked. How the crap was I supposed to get away from Mr. Matchmaker if I was on the same damn horse as he was?

"'Tis all we need," Cailen responded before returning his gaze to the horse master. "That's a fair price."

I reached into my purse to grab some coins, but the Highlander stopped me with his hand. Pulling change out of his sporran, he produced the money for Mr. MacMillan and entered the stable, carefully approaching a beautiful dark brown mare. She had a pitch black mane and a white nose, and long white hair adorned her legs just above her hooves. He tied her to the fence and bent on one knee. "Give me yer foot, Elizabeth."

"*What?*"

"Gi'me yer foot. I'll help ye up."

That's what I'd been afraid of, and I shook my head. "I don't know how to ride it."

"That's why I'll help ye," he said slowly as Mr. MacMillan smiled warmly. "Step intae ma hand and I'll help ye up. All ye must dae is swing yer leg o'er and hold onto her mane."

I stepped toward him and leaned down to his ear, whispering, "And what about all these skirts?"

"They'll go wi'ye, o' course. Step up wi'yer foot, Elizabeth. Now."

I let out one long, slow, shaky breath and gripped his shoulder as I plopped my left foot into his cupped hands and stepped up. I barely balanced myself on the horse's wide back before Cailen launched himself up as well, wrapping his arms around me as he untied the horse from the fence.

"Take good care o' her for me," MacMillan said, patting her up on the rump. "She's a good lass."

"We will," Cailen replied. "Good day tae ye." With a quick wave and a thank you to Mr. MacMillan, he steered the horse away from the stable and we trotted off with the sounds of the horse's hooves hitting dirt, leaving Kilchrenan far behind.

The Scot kept a tight hold on me for a long time,

pulling me close to his body as our horse strode just to the side of the winding dirt road. He'd informed me that it was easier to remain hidden from others if we kept off the path itself, making it more manageable to rush into nearby trees and brush. Of course, he wouldn't explain why we wanted to remain hidden other than the fact that we were on another clan's lands. For a while, we weren't in forestland at all, but riding through open fields of grass and heather, where we couldn't have remained hidden if we'd tried—at least, not on horseback. We'd passed two horse-and-buggies on the way, and neither of them had caused us any problems, so I wasn't sure why he was so cautious the rest of the time.

"Can we just stop?" I asked. "I'm exhausted."

He made a grunting sound and I turned to peer at him from over my shoulder.

"I didnae ken ye're the one who's been walkin' all this time."

"I didn't say I was. I just said that I'm exhausted. And how do you think this poor creature feels with the two of us on her back?"

He cocked his mouth to the side and raised a brow. "Aye, yer right. There's some water up the path a bit. We'll let our horse hae a bit o' rest while we find some food."

"Thank God," I breathed, relief spreading through my entire body. Before I'd realized it, I'd melted against him, and quickly straightened as his hard chest met my back. He'd been holding me tightly against him this whole time, but not once had I relaxed. "How much longer are we going to go today?"

"Shh." Cailen pulled on the horse's reins and it lurched to the side, taking us into the trees for probably the thirtieth time that day. "There's someone comin'."

"And again I ask, what does that matter?" I whispered

99

as the horse came to a stop and Cailen swung down to the ground.

"We dinna ken who it might be, nor their intentions if they come upon us. I've no' many friends, and no' one o' them are on these clan lands." He reached up and helped me off the horse.

"So they're your enemies?"

"Likely," he replied, even quieter than before. Pressing a finger to his lips, he silently shushed me before reaching up and taking the bags off our horse's back. "We'll return for her later. If we take her any farther, she'll lead others tae us. Won't ye, ye wee clumsy oaf?" he added adoringly, patting her on the neck as she bent to eat. "Follow me, Elizabeth."

The Highlander took off through the brush, leaving me to hike up my dress and attempt to follow. Between the skirts and the weird shoes, our trek took forever. He'd stopped and turned back for me about three times before finally stopping altogether. And it was about time, too. Any farther and I would have turned back for the horse myself and taken off in search of freedom.

"This should be far enough." He bent, setting the bag on the ground and peering up at me in the afternoon light.

I found a spot to sit down and unbound one of my shoes, barely glancing at our tiny picnic area. "God, that feels good," I moaned at the first circle of my thumb over my foot. Cailen's eyes practically bugged out of their sockets. "What?"

He blinked and looked down at the bag as he opened it. "I've ne'er seen a lass behave so…hae ye nae manners?"

"Oh jeez." I dropped my foot and worked off my other shoe. "Manners have nothing to do with it. The shoes here suck, and my feet are killing me. I'm seriously afraid of what I'm going to see when I get this shoe off since I haven't had a chance to get to a *real* doctor or even put on the "special" medicine your quack job gave me."

The Scot's brows narrowed and he mouthed the words "quack job" to himself as he extracted the tiny vial of medicine. He could just figure out what that meant on his own. "Does it trouble ye so, lass? I wouldn'ae've gone so far had I kent ye were discomforted." Rising to his feet, he stepped toward me and dropped down to the ground. "Would ye mind much if I looked at it?"

I couldn't deny him. Not with the way he'd looked so saddened by the fact I was in pain. Also, because it meant someone else was going to deal with my wound so I didn't have to look at it myself. Lifting my foot, he took it in his hand and gently pushed my skirt up a bit. His hands were rough and gentle at the same time, and tingles ran up my leg and through every limb. When his progress stopped at my knee, I nearly whimpered. That simple touch had been more than welcome, even from a brute like Cailen. It came to a shock to realize that, even with everything that had happened over the last few days, and the fact that I basically hated him at the moment, I needed—and quite possibly craved—more of this Highlander's gentle, hesitant caresses.

His eyes met mine and for the briefest of seconds, I wondered if he'd somehow heard my thoughts. His eyes warmed, and I could have sworn that his breath picked up just as mine did. Then our second was over, and he pulled his hand from my knee.

"Ye can uh…" The Scot's throat cleared. "Ye may want tae get comfortable, Elizabeth. I'll rub the medicine in."

"Are you sure? I mean, you don't really—"

"Oh, aye. I can get a better look at it than ye can. Make yerself comfortable."

After eyeing him for a few more seconds, I did what

he'd said. "Alright, that looks a lot more comfortable down there in the grass." Scrambling off my perch, I laid in the grass and rested my head on my hands. Cailen's touch returned. Warm hands moved over my foot, his thumbs working in roaming circles from my heel to my toes. My breathing quickened again and I let out another moan as the pleasure shot up my leg and settled at my core. If he kept this up, he was going to witness a lot more than just moaning. The Highlander's hands froze and I sat up, leaning on my elbows. "I'm sorry, I just—"

"Nae. Nae need tae apologize." he interrupted, and looked sheepishly at me. "I shouldn'ae've spoken so rash earlier. It isn'ae yer fault yer no' from ma time."

"I thought you were just going to apply the medicine." I fell back again and stared up at the branches above my head.

"I was goin' tae." He cleared his throat again. "But I can see why ye've been in such pain, yer shoes dinna fit as well as I'd hoped."

"Yeah." I almost chuckled thinking of just how much didn't fit. My shoes were only the beginning. My dress didn't fit me, and neither did the time and place I was stuck in. The entire time we'd been sneaking through the forest, my feet had slipped back and forth on the leather.

"Dinna fash. I think I ken how tae fix it. Ye may just need more holes along the top so we can strap them on tighter." He set once more to rubbing my foot, and I laid back, doing whatever I could to keep from making the sounds that threatened to escape my mouth. For someone who'd probably never given anyone a massage in his life, he was masterful at it. I relaxed, staring at the backs of my eyelids, letting the soothing touch of Cailen's hands rub one foot, and then the other.

My eyes flashed open when an unexpected scent hit my

nose, and I sat up to see the Highlander sitting over a small fire, cooking some sort of meat.

"Awake then?" he asked.

I yawned and rubbed my eyes. "I fell asleep?"

"Aye o'er an hour ago. I was able tae catch us somethin' tae eat and build a fire." He grinned as though my nap had lasted a millennium.

I wasn't about to ask him what tiny creature he was roasting over the fire. I'd learned my lesson from that poor little bunny rabbit we'd had that first night. If I didn't know what died or what I was eating, I couldn't imagine it running around, enjoying its life until it was brutally taken from it.

That was me: Scarlett Michaelson—Animal Lover.

I got to my feet and made my way over to him, careful to avoid anything that looked hard or sharp. My feet were still bare, but I was thrilled that they weren't hurting either. At least, not other than a gentle throb in my one toe.

"Ye'll want tae keep off o' it," the Highlander said, pointing at my foot. "I put some salve on it, but it looked like it needed tae breathe."

"Thanks." I peered at him as he hunched over the meat, testing its doneness with his fingers. I stepped toward him. "How's your arm?"

"Oh." He peered down at his bandaged arm. "It's well. The doctor gave me some salve for it as well."

"I haven't seen you put any on."

"I haven'ae."

I chuckled. "You've got to put it on. Where is it?" As he reached into his sporran, I pulled on the ties and started unwrapping his arm, revealing the long slash from the boar's tusk. Cailen tensed, and my pulse quickened.

"I thought he was a 'quack job'," he said quietly.

Dashing some salve on his arm, I started rubbing it in,

careful not to put too much pressure on his red, angry cut. I peered up, meeting his eyes. "Something is better than nothing, don't you think?"

The Highlander stilled my hand, his gaze traveling from my eyes down to my lips and back up again. "I'm startin' tae."

The meat's juices hissed and spit as they dropped into the fire. He bent quickly, turning it over so the other side could cook.

I stepped away, shaking my head at my own foolish thoughts. What had just happened? Letting out a silent breath, I sat on a moss covered boulder surrounded by thick bushes. "Do you want any help?"

Cailen grunted, focusing on the cooking meat. "Just rest. We've still more journey ahead o' us."

He finished cooking and we ate in silence, with only minor comments on how tasty our meal was. The food in the past—in this current time—was so different than that of my own time. I'd been camping with my dad and brother enough times to know that tinfoil dinners and Dutch Oven Mountain Dew Chicken were staples in the wilderness. But here, we only had the land around us to survive on. Toilet paper didn't exist, but leaves did. Dutch ovens weren't around yet—or at least, I didn't think they were. Coolers, tents, sleeping bags, motor homes: none of those luxuries were even invented yet.

As soon as the meat was gone, I rubbed the last of my hand sanitizer on and reapplied Cailen's bandage, doing my best to avoid his stare, and hopefully, avoid the tension we'd shared earlier.

He peered at the wrap just like he'd done before and smirked at me. "That's a tidy dressin'. Dae ye often take care o' savage boar injuries?"

I laughed. "No. Never."

The Scot chuckled and kicked dirt onto the fire, extinguishing the flames after his first few kicks. "We should get back tae our mare—"

"Bud," I interrupted.

"Eh?"

"I named her Bud." I'd thought long and hard about what to name her during our ride today, as well as during lunch. And though there were certainly more feminine names, it just seemed fitting to name her after the beer that would, one day, be responsible for her breed's popularity.

"Ye shouldn'ae get attached tae her," he said. "We've only purchased her tae ease our trip tae Kilninver. I ken some men there that we can barter wi' for a boat tae Mull." Cailen picked up his satchel and tossed it over his shoulder. "We've only a few hours' time before we lose our light, and I'd like tae reach the loch before it gets too late."

I hobbled over to where my shoes were and carefully threaded the ties and wrapped my feet. Cailen had added a few extra holes, making the shoes fit tighter against my toes. Hopefully that would keep them from slipping.

"Wow. Thanks," I said. When he looked at me questioningly, I gestured to the shoes.

"Och, dinna thank me yet. We've a long way tae go still."

Scooping up my purse, I made sure my heels and regular clothes were still securely bound to it, and then slid it over my head so it laid across my body.

Our trip back to Bud seemed to go a bit faster than before, and once her white nose came into view, I sighed and sped up to reach her. "Hello, sweetheart. Did you have a nice lunch break?" I petted her soft, velvety nose and scrambled back as she tried to nibble at my hair. I turned then, laughing as she made another play for my hair, only to see Cailen approaching slowly, his face sullen. "What's wrong?"

His eyes were locked on to something behind me and I peeked over my shoulder. There was another man there, another Scot wearing a kilt and a filthy sweat-soaked shirt. His gaze flicked back and forth between us, but his pistol was trained on me.

"If ye'd like tae see the lass get shot point blank," he said to Cailen. "Then by all means, keep walkin'."

He stopped.

"Now there's a good lad. Drop yer weapons and nae one will get hurt."

"Says ye, Angus." Another man said as he stepped from the surrounding trees. "I'll be makin' nae such promises." I tried to turn, to react to his voice, but something went over my head and cinched around my neck, and I was plunged into darkness.

"I told ye someone would happen by," the first one said.

The two Scots laughed and an arm wound around my waist, and up past my stomach to cup my breast.

"And what a braw lass she is."

CHAPTER EIGHT

I hated Scotland. The place was riddled with thieves and kidnappers, and as I'd learned over the last while, perverts.

I could hardly move as I was held, bound and blindfolded, to one of the Scots. It may have been the one who'd bagged my head that gripped me, but since I couldn't see a thing, it was really hard to tell. All I knew was that he was pretty hard up, thrusting against me as we rode toward wherever it was we were going. It terrified me to the core, especially considering the vulgar remarks I'd heard since our capture.

Cailen was somewhere nearby. That was the only beacon of light in my otherwise black abyss. He was the sole reason I was riding on Bud, even if it was with a Scottish piece of crap degenerate who thought me nothing more than a moving object he could mount.

If he tried anything more than he had already, he'd be losing his favorite appendage.

Every once in a while we stopped, either to allow Bud to drink, or because the walking Highlanders grew tired. My bag hadn't been removed from my head even once. As far as I could tell, neither had Cailen's. It was his voice that kept me from hysterics. I thought maybe he was purposely talking a lot—and doing a great job at annoying our kidnappers—to make sure I knew he was there. I tried to do the same. Whenever I had the chance, I'd say something loudly, just so he'd know I was alright.

Or at least, I hoped I was. I hoped we both were.

The sounds of the forest gave way to the soft swishing

of grass dancing in the wind, and then to voices of men, women, and children. Quiet at first, they grew louder with each passing minute until we were surrounded. I'd only heard a few muttered words in English. Most of the people spoke Gaelic, and even though I couldn't understand them, I guessed at the general gist of what was said. Those in this town—or wherever we were—asked who I was, who Cailen was. The men who held us captive gave short, clipped answers, invoking no other questions. I wished I knew what they'd said.

Bud's gentle trot came to a halt and the bastard behind me dropped to the ground, pulling me with him. Once on my feet, I stretch my legs and back, nearly groaning from the ache in my body. "Cailen?" I yelled through the bag.

"Aye, I'm here." He wasn't very close.

One of the Scottish thugs wrenched on my arm, and I tried to pull free. "Let go of me, you stupid bastard!"

"Shut yer gob. Yer comin' wi'me."

"No! Let me go!"

Even Cailen began yelling and through the sounds of my attempts at fighting, I heard grunts as my friend probably tried to escape his guards.

I fought, but he dragged me to a place I didn't know and couldn't see. My feet skidded over dirt and rocks, and then up two stairs and over a rough, creaky floor.

"That'll dae, Finlay," a rough voice barked. "Ye'll no' harm a lady under ma roof."

"But she's a trespasser," the one holding me argued. "She was on our land, wi'out so much as an invitation or permission tae pass through."

"That may be, but I will'nae see her hurt until we get things sorted."

Until?

Someone stepped closer, their shoes thudding on the

wood floor and echoing around the room. The bag over my head was loosened at the neck, and then pulled gently free. It wasn't bright inside, but I still blinked at the sudden change from pitch black. My gaze met the steel gray eyes of a man who was probably in his late thirties. My first thoughts were that his nose was a bit too big, and his eyes were a bit too small. He was dressed well—for what I'd gleaned of this time—and his salt and pepper hair was pulled back at the nape.

"She's nae more than a lass. Where did ye find her?"

"Just off the road, no' far from Bhearraidh."

"Alone?"

Finlay remained quiet for a second or two. "She was wi'a man."

"Did ye capture him as well?"

"We did."

The man flicked his gaze at me before returning it to Finlay. "And where is he?"

"Angus, Gordon and Ranald are takin' him tae Neil's tae be...held, for now."

"Nae." He'd barely taken his eyes off me. "Bring him tae me. We must learn who they are before we dae anythin' rash."

"Aye." Finlay's hold on me released and he shuffled out the door, slamming it behind him. Once I was alone with the other man, he finally spoke again.

"Gi'us yer name then, hen."

I lifted my chin. Might as well stick to the lie I'd been feeding Cailen since day one. "Elizabeth."

"No' a Scot then?" he said, surprised. "And where might ye be from?"

"A place you've never heard of."

His eyes sparkled with amusement as a wide grin spread across his face. "Verra well. I'm Donnan

MacDougall." He bowed. "'Tis a pleasure tae make yer acquaintance."

I couldn't put my finger on what wigged me out about Donnan MacDougall, but there was definitely something there. Maybe it was that look in his eyes that put me on edge, or maybe it was something else. No matter what it was, I didn't trust him.

Footsteps sounded outside, and the door swung open, admitting three Highlanders and Cailen, who was no longer blinded by a bag.

"Ah," Donnan said. "Our other guest. Please, Elizabeth, would ye kindly hae a seat? There's some business we men must discuss."

My eyes met Cailen's, and he gave me a single, almost imperceptible nod. Crossing to the nearest wooden bench, I sat down and watched as Donnan circled Cailen, his hands behind his back as he eyed my Highlander. Cailen merely stood there, his chin high as he returned Donnan's glare. He couldn't have really done anything else, not with the way the others kept their grasps on his arms and shoulders.

I couldn't help but notice how impressive Cailen was. It took three other men to hold him there, almost as though they knew that if there were any less, that my Highlander would overpower them and break free. Not that he tried anyway. Our entire journey here, I hadn't heard any evidence of him trying to escape. Not until I'd tried to fight just outside this house.

"Now, ye're a Scot," Donnan said, halting just in front of him.

Cailen lifted his chin, and I smiled. Funny how he did the same thing I had.

"No' on yer clan lands?"

"Nae."

"I suspect ye ken what happens when ye cross intae

other clan lands, wi'out permission."

Even from the bench, and being half-blocked by Donnan MacDougall, I could see Cailen's jaw tighten. "I dae. And I ken the borders well enough tae ken that yer men nabbed ma lady and me from Argyll land."

The other man peered over his shoulder, his brows raised as his gaze met mine. I couldn't believe Cailen had just said I was his. I kind of liked it. Donnan faced my Highlander again. "Yer lady, is it?"

"Aye, she is."

Wow. My heart started to hammer. How could such a simple statement make me want to run him and let him take me into his arms? Why hadn't I realized until then that I'd been desperate to hear it?

"What's yer name, MacKinnon?"

"Ma name is o' nae concern o' yers."

MacDougall stepped back, and one of his gofers punched my Highlander in the stomach. Cailen doubled over, but was quickly righted at the insistence of his guards.

"I had hoped this would be a *civil* meeting—"

"Any hope o' that vanished the minute yer baheided numpty bagged ma lady and strangled her," my Scot interrupted.

That stopped Donnan, and he peered over at Finlay, who shrugged. "And for that, I dae apologize. Nae harm should'ae come tae anyone, especially a wee hen such as Elizabeth."

At hearing my name, Cailen's eyes turned dark as he glowered menacingly, his lips tightening into a hard line.

"And from what ma men hae told me, ye were on our land. Isn'ae that right?"

"Aye," the three lackeys barked.

I still couldn't see the expression on Donnan's face, but there was no doubt in my mind Cailen would have sent the man to an early grave if looks alone could kill.

"Take him tae Neil's and make sure he's secure. I'll let ye decide on yer own who's tae watch him."

"And what o' her?" one of his men asked.

"The lass will be stayin' wi'me. Dinna fash, MacKinnon, I'll be sure tae keep her warm." Donnan turned his back on Cailen, a big smile on his face as my Highlander spat a bunch of words I couldn't understand, and tried to wrench his arms out of their grasps.

His desperation to break free sent a shot of panic through me. "I really think I should stay with him."

MacDougall approached me as the three other men hauled Cailen from the building. "Nae, ye'll be stayin' right here wi'me."

"Ye dinna hae a husband o' yer own?"

"No," I replied, shaking my head. I'd remained in the same spot I'd been in when Cailen was escorted from MacDougall's cabin. One of the lackeys returned minutes later, placing Cailen's sporran, knives, and sword just inside the door.

My Highlander was weaponless.

Donnan had tried talking to me over the last couple hours, but I'd only given him short answers. He didn't seem to get the hint that I wanted nothing to do with him. His cabin was more or less empty of furnishings. The place had two benches, a table, and a fireplace with a cauldron in it, and lastly, a bed. Other than the benefit of having a roof over his head, I was starting to see why Cailen chose to rough it in the woods.

"What is MacKinnon tae ye?"

"That's not really any of your business." I had no idea.

I wanted Cailen, my desire for him grew more and more every day. Did he want me the same way? Or had that whole *mine* business just been for Donnan? No matter the answer, I wanted a chance to talk to him about it. What if he'd meant to be my husband?

MacDougall took a sip of his soup and eyed me as he set his spoon back into the bowl. "I wish I could interest ye in some broth."

"I'm not hungry." I replied. "I just want to get back to...MacKinnon."

"Ye ken, I've ma own quarters at Dunollie House."

"That's nice." What the crap was he getting at?

"I used tae share them wi'ma wife, Sara, but she died earlier this year."

I glanced at Donnan at the sound of his voice. He didn't sound saddened by his wife's death in the slightest. "I'm sorry to hear that."

"She died in child birth. Neither she nor our bairn survived."

I remained silent, my hackles rising at the deadpan tone in his voice. He seriously didn't care about Sara or their baby. What a prick!

"We're goin' tae Dunollie in the morn. MacKinnon is tae be tried by ma brither for trespassin'. He's the chieftain, ye ken."

Okay, Donnan was clearly trying to impress me. Was it working? Not even a little bit.

"Ma clan has somethin' o' an issue wi'the Clan MacKinnon. One made an attempt on ma nephew's life. 'Tis no' verra likely that ma brither will let yer friend live. But...there may be somethin' I can dae tae save him." He leaned forward, his elbows resting on his knees as he reached out and touched my knee. "An arrangement, perhaps."

I slapped his hand and yanked my knee out of his reach.

Undaunted, he leaned forward again. "I could make ye ma wife. I've plenty o' money tae provide for ye."

"No thanks. Seriously."

"If no' ma wife, then why no' be mine this night?" He stood and took the space next to me on the bench. He gripped my thigh and I bolted upward, dashing toward the door.

Donnan caught me quickly and yanked me away from the only exit I'd spotted in this shack.

"Ye dinna need tae run," he grunted, still pulling me farther into the room. I tried to throw my elbows at him, but he'd pinned my arms against my body. "I'll be gentle wi'ye."

"I'm not a whore! And I will never marry someone like you!"

"Oh, ye will, hen. Ma brither is the chieftain. We'll be mairrit in the morn, whether ye like it or no'."

I stilled, breathing heavily as Donnan's hand skimmed up my skirt. He tried to pull off my purse, but I kept my hand on it, refusing to let him take it off of me. Giving up on that, he grabbed my breast and nuzzled my neck. "Look at me."

I turned slowly, meeting his gaze dead on. My heart was beating so wildly that I felt my blood thrum through my body. If he loosened his hold for even a second, I was taking a crotch shot.

"There's a good lass. Now, gi'us a smile."

I sighed and shook my head, our gazes still locked as I let a small smile curve my lips.

He grinned back just before I kneed him in the balls.

Cailen kept his eyes closed, waiting until his guard's footfalls fell silent. This was the third sentinel this night, and so far, the one who'd checked on him with the least frequency. He estimated nearly a half hour between visits the last two times.

Plenty of time for him to break free.

In fact, he'd already started working on the ropes that bound his wrists. The cask behind him had proved to be handy indeed. Backing once more to the barrel, he placed the rope against the hard wood, rubbing the two together. He thought he'd already broken through some of the threads, and it was only a matter of time before the others would follow suit.

Cailen had long since analyzed his surroundings, finding the room to be no more than a small one meant solely to store whisky and other brews the owner had concocted. There were no windows, and no doors other than the one leading to the tavern.

He couldn't believe he'd allowed Elizabeth and himself to get caught. Especially by the bloody MacDougalls. He should have kent though. No doubt it was the men who'd tried to sneak up on them that last night in his camp. Likely been tracking them ever since, scouring the land for any trace.

It's exactly what he would have done on his own land.

The owner had closed the tavern a while ago, though he still remained. He was talking to Cailen's guard, their voices carrying through the wall so loudly he could have guessed they were in the same room. It was the break in their discussion that had alerted him to his guard's approach, and had given him ample time to return to his sleeping form on the floor. He'd managed to position himself the exact way he'd been earlier, and to his surprise, the wallaper hadn't bothered to check his binds.

It'd be a mistake he'd have to take up with Donnan MacDougall long after he and Elizabeth were gone. One of the guards had told him they were to travel to Dunollie in the morn, and Cailen would do anything to avoid that. He and the chieftain's son had gotten into a bit of a stramash over a year ago. Cailen had lost part of an ear. MacDougall had lost a hand.

They'd been searching for him ever since, though he suspected that none of them kent who he was.

Cailen continued to rub his wrists back and forth, feeling the rope threads shred and give way. Oh aye, any minute now, so long as he wasn't interrupted. The conversation in the pub died down, the two men going their separate ways. One went into an adjoining room, his door slamming shut before the rustling of hay reached his ears. Alright, that was the tavern's keeper, off to bed. The other had likely walked outside.

Aye, he had. The front door opened and closed, the man's pounding footsteps growing louder.

Gotcha.

The rope snapped and Cailen launched himself forward, lying on the ground once more. MacDougall's cur stepped into the storage room, but Cailen didn't move a muscle. Not even a minute later, the man left the room, returning to the front, where he very loudly sat his arse on a chair or bench.

Cailen silently rose to his feet and approached the door. It hadn't closed completely, so he was able to see quite easily into the other room. The guard sat on a stool near the kettle, a bottle of whisky in his hand.

He pushed the door open, allowing just enough room to sneak out. He had to do this quietly otherwise every Scotsman within earshot would come straight for him. Inching ever closer to the bastard, he grabbed the rope still

116

attached to his wrist and shot both hands and the rope over the man's head. Yanking backward, he caught him by the neck, and held him there. The stool tipped over, but Cailen paid it no heed. The direct threat was before him, trying to loosen the strangling choke around his neck.

Cailen held the rope for only as long as it would take for the man to be out cold, and then he released it, letting the guard tumble to the floor. It took him four steps before he was out the door and into the shadows.

It was about time he go see Donnan MacDougall.

I yawned, tensing my stomach muscles so no noise escaped my mouth. I couldn't let myself fall asleep, and up until the last hour or so, there hadn't been any chance of that happening. But now, I was exhausted, and the hunger pangs made we want to fall asleep just so I couldn't feel my stomach cramping.

I'd learned easy enough that Cailen either didn't sleep, or that he had a remarkable way of coming to at the first blip of sound or movement; and I had no way of knowing if Donnan shared that same irritating quality.

Then again, I'd been operating on the *safe than sorry* model since I'd stepped foot inside this man's shack.

Even when I'd kicked the asshole in the balls, it'd been out self-preservation, and it had worked like a charm. Donnan had fallen to the ground, holding himself and gasping. He'd gripped one of my ankles otherwise I would have gotten the hell out of there. As I'd hoped, his aggressiveness had ebbed, for the most part, and he'd apologized for his behavior.

I still didn't trust him.

The fire in his little fireplace *popped* and *whizzed*, the flames jumping up to meet the kettle that was suspended above it. Whatever was inside smelled awful. And burned. So very burned. The man had nothing on my Highlander in that department, not with Cailen's knack for finding and cooking *good* food. Actually, he had nothing on my Highlander in any department.

"Get in ma bed," Donnan had ordered before he shoved me onto his bed and joined me.

"I'm not tired," I'd replied, trying to push my way back up. "I'll watch the fire for a bit, and when I get tired, I'll sleep over there."

"Nae, ye willn'ae. I'm goin' tae sleep and ye're no' goin' anywhere."

I was still lying in his bed, with his arm thrown over my stomach as he snored away. I was so freakin' tired, and as hard as I'd tried not to, I thought that I'd fallen asleep for a while. Until a really loud *pop* came from the fire and scared the crap out of me. I sighed, closing my eyes again and focusing on the sound of the fire. There was no way I'd be able to stay awake all night. And if I did, then what? It'd be impossible to stay awake all day tomorrow, or tomorrow night, or however long it took me to get away from Donnan MacDougall.

I needed a plan, I knew that. But I was completely out of my element. This wasn't home, where I knew that the window at the end of the hall made absolutely no sound when opened, and that I could tiptoe along the roof just over the garage and slide down the tire swing rope that hung from the big old tree on the side of the house. There wasn't a car I could hot wire and speed away from these crazies—not that I knew how to anyway. There was no one I could call. No friends, no police, no family. I had me. And for now, I had Cailen.

If I even knew where he was.

The fire popped again and Donnan twitched, hugging me closer to him before rolling away. Holy crap, I was free! I slid off the bed and snuck across the room, grabbing my purse, which he'd forced off of me, and snuck toward the door. There was a gentle scuffling outside the house, and I froze next to the door.

Please don't be a minion, please don't be a minion, please don't be a minion.

It'd be my luck that one of Donnan's goons was patrolling just outside the house.

The door opened and I backed against the wall, not daring to move or breath. As though my thoughts conjured him, Cailen snuck inside, jumping in surprise as he caught sight of me. My heart leapt into my throat and we met halfway. His hands gripped my arms and he checked me over. I did the same to him.

"Are ye well?" he mouthed.

I nodded. "You?"

"Fine," he replied silently.

Another crack from the fire had us both looking at it as a hot ember shot out of the fireplace and landed on the bed.

"Elizabeth?" Donnan shot up suddenly, patting at the flames until they died. "Eliza—" He pushed to his feet, his gaze angrily locked onto Cailen as he barreled toward us. "The lass is mine, MacKinnon!"

I glanced at my Highlander, wanting nothing more than to leave. Cailen didn't take the hint though. He'd gotten a really pissed off look on his face and stepped past me. The two Scots met and limbs started flailing. I kept my spot against the wall, but closed the door so no one else would hear.

Fists hit faces and stomachs, and the two men grunted as they pounded each other. They were slamming into walls and rolling on the floor, each man trying to take control.

Cailen stepped back for a brief second before lunging at Donnan, covering the man's mouth with his palm. He flipped him around and wrenched his arm behind his back.

"Get me somethin' tae gag him."

I looked around the tiny house, finding a pair of socks in a satchel. As soon as Cailen's hand left Donnan's mouth, I shoved the wadded socks inside. Cailen bit down on the rope around his wrist and untied the knot. "Cut this in half."

I bolted for his things and gripped his knife before rushing to his side and cutting the rope into two. My Highlander shoved Donnan to the floor and knelt on his back. "Sit on his legs, lass."

MacDougall continued to thrash, even after I put all my weight on his legs, and he yelled through the gag.

Wrists and ankles were bound.

"That's just in case ye get any ideas," Cailen remarked darkly. "I'll take it personally if ye decide tae follow us. Oh, and give yer nephew ma regards." He stood as Donnan yelled even louder through the socks. Grabbing my hand, he led me from the house, only stopping to grab his belongings.

Once outside, I peered around the surrounding homes. "Where are we going?" I whispered.

"We must get tae Kilninver as fast as may be."

"What about Bud? Did you find her already?" My feet rushed over rocks, dirt, and grass as Cailen pulled me at a fast clip.

"We canna risk it. She'll make too much noise and alert MacDougall's men."

I didn't say anything more until he released his hold on my hand and turned to face me. With every step we'd taken getting us farther from those guys, I'd felt a little better. Apparently the Highlander hadn't felt the same way. He still looked angry and worried, like maybe he needed to punch something.

Cailen looked me over again, inspecting my arms for damage, and then lifting my chin with his fingers so he could study my face. "Did he harm ye?"

My heart thudded again at the look in his eyes. "No. He didn't touch me that way."

"*That way?*"

I turned my face away, and he dropped his hand to my shoulder.

"Did he say what he wanted wi'ye? Wi'us?"

"He's lonely and looking for a wife. He…sorta figured I should be his."

"After I told him…" Cailen practically growled, releasing a loud breath. "I told him ye were *mine.*"

Yes, you did. Thud. Thud. Thud. How could something so primitive cause this reaction in me? Did he really think of me as his?

Did I?

Cailen's face relaxed somewhat, but there was still an angry edge to it. "Would ye hae accepted him? As yer husband, I mean?"

I laughed. "No. I'm against marriage right now, remember?"

"Good." He dropped his hands and stepped away from me before looking over his shoulder. "Stay that way until ye find a good man, aye?"

I'm looking at one. While lying in bed with Donnan, it never once occurred to me that Cailen would leave me behind. I didn't know him well, but I believed in him enough to know he wouldn't strand me with his enemy.

I blinked, shaking free of my thoughts, when I realized he was leaving. Rushing ahead, I caught up with him and walked by his side.

"Why did he call you 'MacKinnon'? Does that mean something in Gaelic?"

He snorted, but never slowed his steps. "MacKinnon is ma family name. It just means he kent the clan I belong tae."

We reached a small patch of trees and bushes, and I stepped around one, taking the opposite side from what Cailen did. "So, your name is Cailen MacKinnon?"

"Aye."

He offered nothing more than that, and I felt a little dumb for asking. "What's with the secrecy of your name?"

"Eh?" He looked at me this time, his eyes narrowing into slits. Oh yeah, he knew what I meant. But, if he was going to make me explain...

"When we met a few days ago, you didn't want to tell me your whole name, and a few hours ago you avoided telling Donnan your first name. Why keep it a secret?"

"Must I remind ye that I've yet tae learn yer surname? Why no' tell me that?"

Oh.

I shrugged, hoping he didn't see me stumble over my thoughts. "Well, for me it's obvious. When we met, I was alone, in a strange place, and for all I knew you were connected to my kidnapping."

My Highlander slowed his forward progress and peered down at me. "What dae ye think now?"

I chuckled. "I really don't know what to think. I now know you weren't responsible for kidnapping me, but I have no idea how I ended up two hundred and forty years in the past."

"So why no' tell me yer family name?"

His piercing gaze met mine and I held it. "Michaelson. My last name is Michaelson."

The Highlander's mouth twitched and he bowed low.

"Well then, 'tis a great pleasure tae make yer acquaintance, Miss Michaelson."

"You don't have to do that." I laughed nervously. He really didn't need to add to his long list of ways to make me blush. "We've already met."

"Aye, but we didnae really ken each other."

Cailen turned away from me and continued on as the small patch of forest opened up into a huge field of grass and weeds. I followed him numbly, lost in the feelings and thoughts racing through me. He was right. We hadn't known each other in the beginning, but it seemed that with every minute that passed, I liked that rugged, chivalrous Highlander more and more.

He'd fought and killed a boar to protect me, he'd saved me from being forced into a marriage with a psychopath who hadn't deserved one to begin with, and he'd done nothing these last few days but take the time to put me first.

For the first time, I could imagine what it would be like to be this strong, fearless man's wife, and I liked it.

CHAPTER NINE

The sun was just starting to rise when we spotted the first tell-tale signs of an eighteenth century town. Kilninver came into view not long after we rounded the base of a hill, and I sighed at Cailen's confirmation of what I'd hoped we'd found.

We'd stayed within a certain distance of Loch Feochan, which, as Cailen had explained, broke off from the Firth of Lorne. I had no clue what he was talking about, but latched onto the fact that whatever this Firth thing was, it shared the name of the pub I'd gone to with Shannon.

That thought had brought me to tears, and also somehow excited that hopeful part that still resided in me. Did that mean we were somewhere near what would someday be Oban?

"At last," Cailen said, slowing his pace as we passed a single house on the outskirts of town. "I was prayin' we would reach Kilninver before the MacDougalls found us."

"Do you think they're actually after us?" I couldn't imagine them putting that much effort into trying to find Cailen and me. They really had no reason to. Unless... "Did you attack Donnan's nephew?"

"*Eh?* Oh, nae, I didnae. He came after me, and I finished the fight. He gave me this." My Highlander pulled back the hair on the side of his head.

Oh my... The top third of his ear was missing, and just behind it was a diagonal scar. Donnan's nephew had actually sliced at Cailen's head! "Does it hurt? Or did it, I mean?"

"It did when it first happened, but I got him a bit better. I didnae mean tae, ye ken, but durin' the stramash, I…well, I sort o'…cut off his hand."

I gasped.

"It wasn'ae ma fault. MacDougall attacked me o'er the color o' ma tartan. If he hadn'ae, he'd likely still hae his hand."

"So that's why they'd hunt us."

"They may. But it doesn'ae matter now. We'll find a place tae stay until the sun leaves the sky. We'll leave during the night."

We passed sheep and long-haired cows that he called "heelin' coos" as they grazed in the grass. The sky brightened as we neared the small clump of buildings. "Don't we have to worry about being seen? If the MacDougalls come here, what's to keep us from being found?"

"We dinna need tae concern ourselves wi'that here. These are good folk, Elizabeth."

I flinched a little at hearing my middle name. It was the first time he'd said it since we'd been "properly introduced". Why hadn't I just told him my real name? Why couldn't I now?

"They're mainly cotters and fisher folk. They dae hae a new distillery," he added, with a wide grin. "Which is why they hae means o' transportation that comes in verra handy for a Scot like myself." I narrowed my eyes and he continued, "They are kent among a precious few tae be rather…discreet about certain visitors, if it is so wished."

"And it would be wished?"

"Aye. It would."

We were nearing the clump of buildings now, close enough that I saw an older guy step out of his home and stretch as he peered out over the water. "Is the ocean what you called the Firth of Lorne?"

"Nae. Close though, I suppose. That right there is the Firth o' Lorne. It's a channel o' water that runs between the mainland and the Isle o' Mull." He stopped walking and turned away from me, pointing at the land across the loch. "Dae ye see that wee spot o' land out there in the distance?"

I peered in the direction he was pointing, seeing blue hills rise up from the water. "Yeah."

"That's the island I saw in the painting on yer cell phone. I ken the island well, and that's no' far from the mainland where I found ye."

"*Really?*" Holy crap! I *was* close to where this had all started!

He grinned, pointing in another direction. "Aye, and just o'er that hill is the Firth o' Lorne. If we were tae hike up tae the top, ye'd see Mull." Cailen gazed at the hill with longing. The base of the hill itself was still a good distance away, otherwise we'd probably have already started hiking it.

"So where do you think we'll stay today?" I asked, breaking the silence we had fallen into.

"I dinna suppose ye'd like tae sleep on the beach off the loch, would ye? We'd be able tae fish for our supper."

"Ugh." I shuddered. "Not really. I *hate* fish."

The Highlander snorted, his smile lighting his entire face as he shook his head at me. The smile began to fade. "Surely ye're jokin'."

I lifted one brow and shook my head slowly.

"How can ye hate fish? It isn'ae possible."

"Oh, I promise, it is. I can't *stand* fish. The way they look and smell, and how they wiggle around and gape at you when you catch them. They taste nasty and you have to worry about their stupid bones. Oh, and their eyes. *Ugh.*

Especially when they're dead, and they have those gross dead fish eyes." I shuddered again.

"Ye're serious," he gaped, looking horrified. "I've ne'er met anyone who has such a dislike for *fish*."

I hiked my thumb at myself. "Well, you're looking at her."

"Well, get ready tae enjoy ev'ra meal then lass, because they serve salmon for breakfast, dinner, and supper."

I groaned as he stepped around me, laughing. He nodded his head in greeting and spoke Gaelic to the man I'd seen stretching outside his house. Passing him by, my Highlander led me directly to one of the houses, and knocked on the door.

A woman answered, her eyes coming into view as she barely opened the door enough to peer out at us. "Eh?" She glanced at me first and then up at Cailen, her face relaxing into an easy smile. The door opened wide and the old woman allowed us to go inside. "Oh, it's good tae see ye lad, good tae see ye." She turned toward me. "And who's the lass?"

I couldn't help but smile at her. She was just so warm and bubbly. Nothing like Mrs. Ferguson's distrustful glare. "I'm Scar—Elizabeth. My name's Elizabeth."

"Oh, wonderful tae meet ye. I'm Mary Paterson."

"How are things, Mrs. Paterson?" Cailen asked as he shut the door behind us.

"Oh, ye ken how things are. The whisky business is daein' quite well. We haven'ae had any tenants for a spell though."

"Nae?"

"Nae. It's prob'ly been three…no, four weeks since anyone's passed through and needed tae lay their heads for a night."

"If ye'll hae us, we'd like tae stay for the day."

She grinned up at him again before flicking her gaze at me. "I'd hoped so. Old Uilleam will be pleased when he hears o' it. Ye ken he's right fond o' ye, laddie."

The thin, old woman whisked her way down the tiny hall and turned, facing the wall. To my surprise, she pushed on the wall, and a thin doorway appeared.

"Ye ken where tae go," she said. "Would ye dae an old lady a favor and show yer lass where tae sleep? I'll fetch some blankets for ye."

"Aye, I will."

"Will ye be needin' any food or drink?"

Cailen and I glanced at each other, and I nodded. "Yes, please."

Mrs. Paterson blinked, her eyes widening. "Where did ye find a wee lassie wi'such an accent?" I might have thought she was offended somehow, if it weren't for that wide grin that spread across her face. "We ladies may hae tae talk for a bit, if old Uilleam and wee Cailen give us a chance, aye?"

Wee Cailen? I smirked, purposely not looking at my Highlander. If I did, I'd probably laugh. There was nothing wee about him. Everything I've seen and felt on the man definitely wasn't wee.

She stepped away from the hidden door and started shuffling toward the big room in the front. "Awa wi'ye then. I'll get started on breakfast."

I watched after her, only turning to face Cailen when his hand wrapped around mine.

"I'll hae ye follow me doon. It's a bit tricky unless ye ken where ye're goin'." He gently pulled me into the hidden alcove and we shut the door behind us. After a few more steps into the pitch black room, he stopped. "There's a big step doon here." In illustration, I felt the jarring of his hand as he lowered himself to a lower stair. "Then there are two more. Come on and step doon. I'll keep hold o' yer hand."

I slid my left foot forward, toeing the floor until I couldn't feel any more of it there. Very carefully, I stepped, waiting for my right foot to actually touch the landing. *Not yet, not yet. Holy crap!* I pitched forward, careening into Cailen, who cursed and gripped me as his other arm wound around my back. My face had landed against his shoulder. I knew, because it fit, perfectly cradled in that spot between shoulder and neck. I had an overwhelming desire to just lay my head there, resting it against the man who'd risked everything for me. But I didn't.

"Sorry." I pushed onto my feet again, but Cailen hadn't removed his tight hold on my arm. "I guess I just didn't realize how far down the step was."

"Dinna fash. It's happened tae me before. Twice while I was sober, and I canna e'en count how many times while I was blootered." He chuckled. "Are ye well enough tae try the next step?"

"Yeah. I think I'll hold onto your shoulder this time, though."

We made it to the bottom without any other incidents.

"Stay here." Cailen's feet shuffled through dirt. There was a scraping sound, and then light filtered into the room from a tiny, open block that he'd removed from the wall up near the ceiling. "This hole comes in handy durin' the day. By nightfall, Uilleam or Mrs. Paterson will gi'us a candle so that we might see where we're goin'."

I made my way toward him, ducking in the tiny crawl space. Now that he'd opened up the small window, I could see that there were ten beds inside, meaning that there was hay thrown in piles with a single sheet and blanket spread over the top. "This is supposed to keep us safe from the MacDougalls?" I asked, sitting on the bed next to the one

Cailen stood by.

"Aye. I dinna think they would hae cause tae ken about this safe house. Mostly it's just clansmen o' the clans on Mull that might hae need for a place like this. Normally there aren'ae rooms like this underneath homes, so anytime someone must hide, they'd crawl tae the top o' the house and lay in the heather. If the MacDougalls come, they'll no' think tae search under their feet."

"So we have to stay down here all day?"

A small chuckle escaped him. "Nae. We can go up whene'er ye wish. I wanted tae make sure ye kent yer way around doon here first, and tae let ye put yer satchel in here as well."

I'd forgotten my purse was still around me. I drew it off slowly so it wouldn't catch my hair, and set it on the bed. "I'd really like to go upstairs. I feel a little claustrophobic down here."

"What's that?"

"It's when you get nervous from being enclosed in tight spaces. Like this dark basement. It makes you feel trapped." There was only one escape route in sight, and it was up the stairs and through a hidden door in the wall. All around us, there were slabs of rock—granite, maybe— except under our feet was dirt, and above our heads were planks of wood.

"I've heard o' folks wi'a fear o' that. I didnae ken it actually had a name." Cailen stood and walked past my bed toward the stairs. "I dinna want ye tae be nervous needlessly. Let's go up and see if Mrs. Paterson's finished wi'our breakfast."

"So, tell me where yer from, dear." Mrs. Paterson smiled

brightly at me, her eyes sparkling with anticipation.

She was a beautiful older lady with blonde hair like mine, which was pulled up into a tight bun. Only a few strands fell around her face. No way had she accidentally let them loose. The woman was meticulous with absolutely everything she did. From head to toe, the woman was perfectly coiffed, and she strove to actually clean her house—enough that I even felt comfortable. Even better, she was so easy to hang out with, that I'd found myself relaxing around her. For just a little while, I was able to forget that I was two and a half centuries in the past. They had nicer furniture than I'd seen in other homes, and took pride in what they had.

I'd learned during breakfast that old Uilleam was actually her husband, and was solely responsible for building the hideout underneath their house, as well as crafting most of their furnishings. It seemed he'd been a wanted man a long time ago, just after he and the Mrs.—Mary—had met. He'd been lucky to have survived, and the two had been even more fortunate to have married each other after their trials. Of course, it'd been Mrs. Paterson who'd told us about their story, since Uilleam had been out working at the distillery.

I thought it was sweet, just how much the woman loved her husband even after all these years. I envied that sparkle in her eyes, and the way the mere thought of the man made her smile. It made me wonder if I'd ever love my Highlander as much. I thought I might someday. It felt like I was already well on my way to being enamored with him.

Once Uilleam had returned home and spotted Cailen, the old man permanently removed him from me for most of the day. Even now, the two of them were hunched over their table, playing cards and drinking whiskey. Mrs. Paterson and I were sitting in two hand-carved chairs next to the fireplace, where we sipped on hot coffee, and I frequently checked on what the men were up to. Hours ago, Cailen had disappeared, only to return cleanly shaven. I'd been almost unable to look away from him; his strong, square chin clearly visible now that the scruff was gone. I was surprised to see that he had a cleft chin, which just made him that much sexier.

"I'm from the U.S.—the Colonies. I grew up there."

"Oh? Where from?"

I shrugged. "Probably a place you haven't heard of. It's, uh...new." Ahead of the times, in fact. *And*...we were already treading in dangerous waters.

"Isn'ae ev'ra town new in the Colonies?" Mrs. Paterson laughed. Her wide, doe eyes never left mine as she seemed to be patiently waiting for more.

"Yeah, I guess so. It's near Salt Lake City, which is the biggest city in that area."

"What about yer mither and faither? Where are they from?"

"They're from there too." My smile faded as my thoughts turned to my family. What were they doing right now? Or, what would they be doing, if I were in my own time? Right now, they weren't even born yet. *I* wasn't even born yet. And if I wasn't born yet, then how was I here?

"I'm sure yer mam and da miss ye as well." Mrs. Paterson reached across the small coffee table, grabbing my hand. Her sympathetic expression morphed at first contact, her brows lowering as she concentrated on my face. I stared back, not really sure what was going on. Was she about to have a heart attack or something?

"Ye really are no' from here, are ye?"

I shook my head. I'd just told her that.

Her gaze narrowed as she lowered her voice. "And ye're no' from this time either, are ye lass?"

Someone might as well have dumped a bucket of ice water on me with the way my entire body chilled. I glanced over the old woman's shoulder at Cailen, who was fully engrossed in the card game he was playing with Uilleam. When my eyes met Mrs. Paterson's again, I shook my head. "How did you know that?"

Mary peered down at my hand and turned my palm upward. "Legions."

Holy crap! "What are Legions?"

She shushed me quietly and flicked her gaze over her shoulder at the men. "I must keep ma gifts a secret. Folk dinna take kindly tae witches."

Witches? She was a witch? *Mrs. Paterson* was a witch? A part of me had written that possibility off, thinking Cailen was probably the only person who thought they actually existed. Besides, she didn't seem like the type. She didn't have warts or wear a pointy hat, and the only thing I'd seen her do with a broom was sweep. My brain couldn't get passed it, even though I knew she was still talking.

"Are ye all right?" she asked suddenly, hesitantly touching my hand again.

I shook free of my thoughts and peered back at her. *She's a witch. Mary is a witch. How else would she know I wasn't from here and now?* "Can you send me back? Can you put me back into my own time?"

Mrs. Paterson shook her head. "I'm afraid no'. The spell is a verra powerful one indeed. There isn'ae anythin' I could dae tae counteract what the Legions hae done. And it wouldn'ae be so wise tae anyway."

My heart sank with every word she spoke. What did that even mean? "Do you think I'll ever go back?"

"I dinna ken. I canna say why ye've been brought tae this time, or what must be done." She looked excited suddenly and leaned in closer. "What year?"

"2013."

The old woman chuckled silently, her lips curving into grin. "Oh, what I wouldn'ae give tae see what ye've seen." She sighed, and stood up before patting me on the shoulder. "I think this old lady might go get some rest. I'll be seein' ye in the morn."

"Goodnight, Mrs. Paterson."

"Call me Mary," she sang as she made her way over to the men's table and talked to them in a quieted voice. The old woman touched Cailen's shoulder, patting it gently as she wished him goodnight. I might have missed that slight stiffening of her body, if it weren't for the fact that I was watching her like a hawk. Mary flicked her gaze toward me as she whisked from the room. What had she sensed from touching Cailen?

She disappeared down the tiny hall and I sat in my chair, feeling more than astonished. Only days ago, I'd begged Cailen to take me to a witch in hopes that one could send me back to my family. And now that I'd stumbled on my best chance to get home, she couldn't—or wouldn't—try. Maybe I really was under some sort of curse. She'd said the witch was powerful—or had she said the spell was? Did it matter?

Who the hell had sent me here? And why? Why go through all the trouble of sending me so far into the past without taking credit?

Mary's reaction had been enough to scare me. She said there was no way around it. I had no way to get home. I felt dizzy and numb, and had somehow made it to the hidden door when Cailen's hand gently gripped my elbow.

"Are ye all right?" he asked. His eyes wandered over me, the concern reflecting back at me making me feel even worse.

"I just need to go to bed," I replied, stepping away from

him and pushing open the door.

Impossibly, I made it down into the basement without falling on my face or my ass. A small blessing since I felt so separated from myself that I couldn't tell what was up, and what was down. Plopping down on the hay bed, I yanked my cell phone from my purse and turned it on. I didn't look for a signal, I didn't hit the buttons for the internet, email, or text like what I normally would have done.

I pulled up my pictures and scrolled through shots I'd taken of my family and friends, doing my best to memorize every line on their faces through the tears blurring my eyes. I'd already feared days ago that I would never see them again, but I'd been hoping and praying that I'd find a witch and she'd snap her fingers or chant a rhyme and send me back. Now, that couldn't happen. My only ticket home was gone forever.

I only spent a few minutes looking over the pics of my friends, knowing who I really wanted and needed to study. There were 1,136 pictures on my phone, and only a few of them were of my mom, dad, and Jason. It was the videos that I spent most of my time on. Watching and listening to my quirky little brother ride his skateboard through the house. I couldn't count how many times I'd yelled at him to knock it off, but now I wished for just one more chance to try it with him. There were a few of my dad, on the days that he actually took a break from work to hang out with us.

No videos of Mom, though.

I talked to her as I gazed at her pictures. She was maybe the only one who could actually hear me right now. As with every time I needed to talk to my mom, I stared at her eyes, wishing that she could respond in some way. I wished all of them could respond.

My tears continued to fall and I rolled onto my side,

letting the videos loop. This is all I had left of them. The only piece of my past that I had to latch on to.

I'd never see my family again.

"Och, ye've won again, lad. Ye've gotten good in yer old age."

"Old age, Uilleam?" Cailen smiled and focused on stacking the cards after what must have been their tenth game of Penneech. "I'm barely two and twenty."

"Aye, and ye haven'ae taken a wife. Unless…" He puckered his lips and drew his fingers through his wiry beard.

"Nae. Elizabeth is no' ma wife. I've barely kent the woman for three days now, and she doesn'ae want anythin' tae dae wi'me."

Old Uilleam guffawed, which turned into a retched hacking. "That lass doesn'ae want anythin' tae dae wi'ye? I've seen the way she looks at ye, and ye've only been here since this morn. *And* ye've had three days tae figure it out? Dae ye hae any sense a'tall?"

Cailen laid the perfectly stacked cards face down on the table. He really should go talk to the lass. She'd looked upset earlier, and he'd desperately wanted to follow her then. But it would have been rude of him to leave Uilleam, especially since he and the older man had grown close over the years. Besides, he'd won Elizabeth's stay for free, so he only owed Mr. and Mrs. Patterson money for himself.

Old Uilleam's eyes narrowed and he stood, sidling up to the wall and pulling back the window cover to peer outside. "Ye may want tae get under the house, lad. And make sure the two o' ye remain quiet."

Cailen stood silently, making sure the feet of his chair

didn't skid along the floor. After giving a nod of thanks to his old friend, he pushed his way through the hidden doorway and slipped down underneath the house.

Elizabeth was lying on one of the pallets, her face awash with light as she stared at her cell phone. He walked briskly past her, sliding the stone piece back into the wall. Other than the light illuminating the lass's face, the room rivaled even the darkest of nights.

She finally looked over at him, and from where he squatted, he could see that her eyes were rimmed with red, her cheeks drenched from fallen tears. What had happened since he'd spoken to her last? He wished he dared ask. Right now, they had to remain quiet to avoid detection from whoever was outside, though he longed to comfort her. Pressing his forefinger to his lips, he pointed at the ceiling above them. Other men were now inside the Paterson's home, their voices echoing through the boards that separated Elizabeth and himself from Uilleam and the newcomers.

The lass nodded slowly, and looked at the wood plank ceiling above them. Her wee light extinguished and they sat there in silence as he listened to the conversation going on overhead. It was the MacDougalls, first asking for Cailen, calling him by his family name. Uilleam had denied seeing him, and that sleekit bastard, Donnan, described Elizabeth as though she belonged to him, telling the old man that Cailen had kidnapped her and made an attempt on his life.

Bloody liar. Now they'd have to be fair careful from now on, with the MacDougalls spreading such untruths. He could kill the dobber now for dragging his family name through the mud.

Cailen still couldn't believe he'd allowed them to be captured; that he'd been so foolish to drag Elizabeth into this mess when she was dealing with her own problems.

Hearing the way MacDougall spoke of her, he kent the man wouldn't stop searching for her. He only hoped they didn't go to Mull, or he'd be forced to come up with a new plan.

A while had passed, neither of them moving other than to shift positions in an attempt to get comfortable. Donnan's men woke Mary while searching the rooms, and she joined the conversation. He'd never needed them to lie for him, but he was never so glad to have their protection now. Both of them behaved as if they were alone in their house, never receiving visitors except for when their sons and daughters came to Kilninver.

The MacDougalls finally left the house, though even through the floorboards, Cailen had heard their doubt at Uilleam and Mary's insistence that there was no one else in their home. His clansmen had even searched the heather, checking to make sure they weren't there.

"Can we move now?" Elizabeth whispered once the loud footfalls disappeared, and the sounds of the men talking now came from outside.

"No' just yet. Keep silent and still lass. They'll pass through soon."

"Can I turn on my phone again?"

"Aye, there should be nae problem wi'that."

Cailen remained where he was, lying on the straw pallet beside Elizabeth's, resting his head on hands. When her cell phone lit up once more, he turned his head to gaze at the wee lass. He still couldn't get over the remarkable particulars of how she'd come to be here. A woman born so far in the future that her grandsire wasn't born yet. Not even her grandsire's grandsire. She was so knowledgeable, kenning words that even he hadn't learned. And he'd been schooled from the time he'd been a young lad up until the day he'd left home. His mam and da ensured he and his wee brothers, Kieran and Cameron, had the best education their wealth and status could buy. But Elizabeth…Lord, he'd never met such a braw and brilliant lassie.

Even now, with her face lit up in the bluish glow that came from her cell phone, she was a stunning creature. Her lovely hair cascaded over the bed as she gazed at her magical device. He often imagined what it would be like to take her to bed, to pleasure her and give her his seed so that she may give him sons and daughters. He actually imagined building a family with her. He'd build her a home that they could share and raise their bairns in until he became Laird of Ardmoir. Then they'd live together in his family's home. She'd want for nothing because he'd give her everything her heart desired.

And he'd be happy and whole, which he hadn't been in a very long time.

As he watched her, a tear slid down her cheek and she reached up to brush it away. "Elizabeth, what's troublin' ye?"

"Nothing," she whispered, her voice shaking from all the tears she'd shed this night.

He didn't buy it. He also didn't say anything in response as her breath hitched in a sob.

"It's just…I'm never going to see my family again."

"How dae ye ken that?"

"I have no way of getting back. I'll never know how my dad and brother are doing, or get to hug them again." Another sob bubbled out of her. "It's just not fair. They'll never know what happened to me. God, they're probably so scared."

"Hey." Cailen rolled off his pallet and made his way over to Elizabeth. He took her free hand between his. "I think they ken ye're well. I'm a firm believer that when ye love someone, ye ken whether they're all right or no'." He rubbed her hand. "Och, ye're shakin', lass."

She gave a small, squeaky cry that she'd tried to cover up by throwing her arm across her face.

Bloody hell, it wrenched his heart in two.

"Can you just hold me?"

His heart sped at her request. He'd do anything for her. Anything. "Hold ye? Lie wi'ye on yer bed?" Like he'd done that night in the woods?

"Yes. Please. Just until I fall asleep."

He nodded, not kenning if she could see him. Releasing her hand, he stood and strode around the other side of her pallet before lying next to her. It was so natural to pull her into him, so close that he was able to look over her shoulder at the images on her cell phone. "Are those pictures *movin'*?"

Did wonders never cease?

"Yeah," the lass breathed. "This is called a video. That's my dad and brother at Lagoon. I was pretty much being a bitch that whole day because I wanted to hang out with my boyfriend. I started to film this because they were trying to cheer me up."

Cailen was mesmerized. It was like he was staring at a wee doorway into another world. It showed such impeccable detail that he could believe he was actually there.

"*Now will you please ride the Colossus with me?*" the young lad in the video asked. He looked quite a lot like his lass, only he was shorter and had less hair. It was fair easy to see the resemblance though.

"*Fine.*" Even without seeing her, he recognized Elizabeth's voice.

"*Oh no, you're leaving your phone with me,*" another man said, his hand reaching out and taking it from her. "*I'll film you two on the ride so maybe we can have proof of you actually enjoying yourself with your old man and brother.*"

Elizabeth walked into view and stuck her tongue out playfully before she and her brother ran toward a steel box. They ran through it, ending up on the other side, where they'd turned left, still racing. The video ended and Elizabeth pressed her finger to her cell phone and started another. She and her brother were sitting in something he'd never seen before and couldn't explain even in his own mind. They sat in a small car as they were taken higher and higher from the ground on some sort of rail. Once they'd reached the top, the machine turned, dropping them at a fast pace.

"Jesus." They were taken through a loop, actually upside down, twice, before the machine twisted in every direction. "That's supposed tae be enjoyable?"

"Yeah." She laughed, her eyes meeting his for a brief second as she peered at him. "It is."

The video ended with the two of them running toward their da with big grins on their faces.

Her phone beeped and went dark as words appeared. "What's that?"

"My phone is almost dead." She tapped it and started another video.

"I didnae see yer mam. Was she no' there wi'ye?"

He shouldn't have asked, and regretted doing so as Elizabeth's entire body stiffened.

"My mom passed away a couple years ago." More flicking of her fingers over her phone, and she pulled up a new picture he hadn't seen before. "This is her."

Cailen studied the woman that smiled brightly as she stood next to Elizabeth. Brown hair, not much lighter than his own, and bright blue eyes, just like the lass that laid next to him. Elizabeth had taken her looks from both her parents, but he could see that same spark of life in mother and daughter.

"What happened tae her?"

"Car accident. A motorcyclist cut off another car on the freeway. They swerved and hit her car. She hit another one, and so on. Three people died during that accident."

She'd explained what cars—among many other things—were days ago during their travels. "I'm sorry. I didnae ken ye lost yer mam."

It was no wonder she wanted to get back to her family. She already kent great loss, and so did her da and brother.

Elizabeth's cell phone beeped again and went dark. The image of her and her mam was burned into his eyes for a time, until it faded away.

"What happened?" he asked into the darkness.

"My phone died."

"Can ye no' just turn it back on like before?"

"No. It's dead. It won't ever be able to turn on again."

Cailen pulled her against him tighter, his heart aching at the hopelessness in her voice. That had been the last tether she'd had to her family, and the line had just snapped.

If only there was some way to help her.

I woke early the next morning to the sounds of our hosts' feet making the wood planks above my head creak and groan. It startled me awake and I jumped, not realizing I was still enfolded in Cailen's arms. I'd actually forgotten I'd fallen asleep with him holding me, and it was probably the best night's sleep I'd gotten since ending up in the past.

"Are you awake?" I whispered.

"Mmm-hmm."

"What time is it?"

"I dinna ken. It's early yet though. Uilleam said he'd wake up early and acquire a boat for us tae take tae Mull."

Cailen's arm left me and he rolled over. Or at least, I thought he did. It was dark inside our tiny crawl space.

I stood up quickly, and smacked my head on the ceiling. "Ow! Son of a motherless goat!" I stooped over, rubbing my head as I scooted over to where I thought the loose stone was. It only took a few minutes of feeling around until I found it. Pulling it free, I expected the room to flood with. It didn't. It was pitch black outside.

I turned, peering down at Cailen, and gasping at the sight I was greeted with. He laid on his stomach with one leg bent out to the side and his kilt lifted high, baring the bottom half of his the most glorious butt I'd ever seen. If I'd moved even one foot to the side, I would have seen a little more of him. I was tempted—boy was I tempted—but I stayed where I was, admiring that beautiful, tight ass of his. Even the muscles on his thighs drew my gaze.

It seemed only seconds passed before Cailen yawned and stretched, and regrettably, pulled his kilt down before rolling over to eye me.

"Good morn."

Coughing into my fist, I gave him a little smile. "Morning. How did you sleep?"

"Verra well."

"Me, too."

"Och, I ken lass. Ye were snorin' louder than Broch and Duff after they've been runnin' through the forest."

"I was not. I don't snore."

"Aye, ye dae."

I wadded up the blanket on the bed and chucked it at the Highlander.

He laughed, holding his arm up and blocking it from smacking him in the head. "If I'd kent gettin' a wee peek at ma arse would make ye this happy, I'd hae done it days ago."

"What?" I gaped. "I didn't..."

He laughed again. "Dinna deny it. I felt the air on ma behind before I e'en rolled o'er. And yer face was redder than I've e'er seen it before." He waggled his brows. "Still is."

I dropped my head into my hands, more embarrassed than I'd ever been in my entire life—including when he'd found my toy and demanded to know what it was used for. When I peeked through my fingers, my gaze fastened on the wall behind him and the dim light that was now streaming down the tiny stairway.

"Are ye decent?" Mrs. Paterson's voice called. "I've started yer breakfast if yer ready tae come and eat."

"Be right up," I yelled, quickly stabbing my feet into the leather shoes and doing up the laces. Out of the corner of my eye, I saw that Cailen was still staring at me. "What?"

"Naethin'." He shook his head. "Well, it's only that I wonder how yer mood might be if ye got a peek at anythin' more."

"*Ughhhhhhh.*" I rushed toward the stairs, my face flaming as I climbed up each one. Pushing through the hidden door, I slammed it behind me and leaned against it. Did that really just happen? And dammit, why was I so turned on now?

"Good mornin' dear," Mary chimed cheerfully. "I trust ye slept well."

"Yeah. Thank you." I nodded, offering her a smile. "Need any help with breakfast?" I was willing to do practically anything to keep away from Cailen and that teasing glint in his eyes. If the man had known I was gawking at that tight, enticing butt of his, why hadn't he put a stop to it earlier? And if he'd liked it, then why hadn't he pulled that damn kilt higher?

Infuriating Highlander.

"Aye, that would be grand," the old woman replied, turning around and stepping into the hallway. I followed closely behind her, shutting the hidden door behind me as I went.

Cooking breakfast had gone by in a blur. Mrs. Paterson and I hadn't mentioned what happened the night before, and quite honestly, I didn't know if I had the energy to. I was seriously curious about what the Legions were, but she wasn't my path home, and I didn't know if another even existed.

Mary, as she'd repeatedly told me to call her, really hadn't needed any help other than when she'd pulled a few small loaves of bread from an oven that looked like it was made entirely out of stone, and sat in their backyard. I'd merely held the candle that lit our way to and from the house, and around the kitchen. Breakfast was the same as it had been the day before, some weird oatmeal or rice cereal that was really thick, only this time there was the added benefit of fresh bread and butter. I'd nearly burned myself trying to stir the pot, standing as far away from the flames as possible as I stirred the food with a wooden spoon. Mrs. Paterson had been acting a little strange today, and so had her husband. I'd caught Uilleam eyeing me a few times with a strange look on his face, and wondered if Mary had told him about the Legion thing.

My thoughts were on Cailen as the old woman whirred around me, grabbing bowls, silverware, and cups. Even when she called the men in to eat, I could only stare at my bowl, trying to avoid my Highlander's gaze. I'd never been shy around men before, but then again, I'd never caught staring at anyone's ass before, either.

Something had happened between the two of us last night. Before I'd gone to sleep or after, I didn't know. In a way, it'd been unexpected, even though we'd shared moments over our last few days together. It had been intimate. Familiar. He'd held me, protected me, and soothed me. And not just until I'd fallen asleep, but long after, until I'd woken this morning. And then there'd been a playful side to him that I'd never seen before. He'd seemed almost excited that I'd seen him partially naked, and relished in the fact that I'd liked it.

And I really liked it.

But could he really fall someone like me? I'd seen a few other women in our travels—women from his own time—and they all had a certain look about them. One being that they were all really thin. I was sure I'd lost some weight the last few days, with smaller meals and a crap ton of walking, but there was no way I could compete with the way those girls looked. They *fit* in this time.

"Did ye hae any luck wi'a boat, Uilleam?" Cailen asked, drawing my attention to him.

"I did. Two o' ma lads were already at the distillery, and I told'em that I'd commissioned someone tae deliver two hogsheads for me."

"Oh? And where are we tae deliver them tae?"

"Anywhere'll dae," Uilleam replied after shoving a spoonful into his mouth. "Ye won them last night, so they're yers."

"I canna thank ye enough. Really, the two o' ye hae done much for us."

I nodded, keeping my mouth shut as I swished the porridge around.

"It's our pleasure. Ye ken we enjoy havin' ye here tae visit." Mary smiled at Cailen, patting him on the shoulder the way she did the night before. I flicked my gaze at her, but didn't notice any of the shock she'd displayed last time.

"When will ye be on yer way then?" Uilleam asked.

"As soon as may be. I'd like tae get a good start before anyone sees us."

"Ye might want tae get ready then. The men that came last night aren'ae camped far from here, and they'll still be searchin' for yer lass."

I choked and coughed, barely keeping my porridge from spray everyone at the table. "They're looking for *me*?" Not us, just me? Had I really missed that when I'd been spacing out last night?

"Aye. Their leader seems tae believe ye belong tae him." Uilleam slid his gaze to Cailen. "Is that so, lad?"

His jaw tightened. "Nae, it isn'ae."

"He spoke o' a stramash inside his home. Claimed ye threatened his life and took Elizabeth out from under his roof."

Cailen leaned against the back of his chair. "Aye, I did. Because he kept her there against her will."

"And ye saved her?" Mary said, her voice taking on a dreamy quality. "Och, so romantic, dinna ye think, dear?"

I shoveled more food into my mouth as Uilleam laughed and shook his head. I'd caught him giving me that curious glance again.

"The rest o' the MacDougall clan isn'ae so bad, it's mostly just the chieftain's brither. The man's no' quite right, so I'd stay awa from him if ye can."

"I'll try. Both of us will." I'd stay as far from Donnan as I could, and I didn't want Cailen anywhere near him either.

My Highlander's gaze went from me to Uilleam. "I think yer right. We should be on our way while the haar is thick."

"Aye. The lads hae prepared ye a boat straight west from here."

Cailen finished eating and eyed me. "Are ye done,

lass?"

I nodded and swallowed the little bit that was in my mouth. "Want me to get my stuff?"

"Aye, we should get our things."

I followed him down into the crawl space, a little surprised that he didn't say anything more about what happened this morning. That playful air about him had completely vanished, replaced by the calm and serious Highlander I was used to.

We returned upstairs to say goodbye to the Patersons.

I gave Mary a hug, and we smiled at each other.

"Take care o' the lass," I heard Uilleam say to Cailen. "She's fair special, that one."

The way he'd said it had me gaping at Mary. "You told him?"

"I did. I wasn'ae sure what Cailen kent o' yer...circumstances, but Uilleam kens well enough what this means." She showed me her palm.

There was a white scar, barely visible, but it was the same design as my own. "You...You're..."

"Aye. I've been in yer shoes. And I wouldn'ae've found ma Uilleam wi'out it."

"Are you a—"

"Legion? Aye. Or, I was. I suppose I was lucky in that regard. I kent what was happenin' when I was brought here. No' many get any explanation."

Holy. Freakin'. Stunned.

Mary Paterson was just full of surprises.

After being forced into a quick goodbye without the time to ask my who, what, where, when, and why's, Cailen and I waded through the heavy fog, heading west as Uilleam had instructed. We reached a row of small wooden boats lined on the shore, with one barely visible farther in the distance. That one had two kegs in it and was out in the

148

water, tied to a wooden post.

Cailen stepped out into the water, and pulled the boat as close to the shore as possible. I got into it with his help, trying my best not to flip the thing over as I balanced on my butt. My Highlander hopped in carefully after he pushed us farther into the water, and we were on our way.

It was silent and uncomfortable. We glanced at each other, and then quickly away. I didn't know what to say to him, and he seemed perfectly fine with not saying a word to me. It was hours into our trip before I spotted land in front of our boat. Cailen rowed expertly, turning us so that we floated parallel to the land, far enough away that I couldn't make out any details of the island we were going to.

"Why aren't we going straight for the Isle?"

He peered over, probably studying the island he knew like the back of his hand. "That there is MacLean land. We'll need tae go a bit farther before we're safe tae travel on foot."

"Can't we just take the boat directly to where we're going?"

"We could, but we risk bein' seen by other clans or ships while we're out in the open water. We'll stay on this so long as the haar doesn'ae clear up. But if it does, we should continue on foot."

I relaxed against the whiskey barrel behind me, and let the sights and sounds around me clear my thoughts. I'd stayed that way for quite a while, our only breaks in silence being when Cailen stopped rowing for a quick bite to eat. Mary had packed a few bottles of whiskey and two loafs of bread for our journey, and we'd gratefully snarfed it down while talking about Scotland weather and how long the fog was sticking around.

My Highlander had returned to rowing, whatever comfort we'd shared the night before having clearly diminished in our silence. And that was okay, I could handle the quiet. It let me think about the people I'd loved my entire life.

"Why didnae ye tell me ye lost yer mither?"

I met his bright blue eyes. "I don't know. I guess I just didn't really think it was something you needed to know before."

"What made ye tell me last night?"

Well, wasn't that a loaded question? We stared at each other as he rowed our boat, and I thought about to respond. "Can I ask you a question?"

He nodded.

"When you said I needed to find a husband, did you have someone in mind?" *Like you, maybe?*

My question seemed to shock him, and he hastily schooled his expression. "Nae, I didnae. It was just the first thought that came tae mind tae protect ye."

"Is that how it works in this time? A woman has to be married or she'll starve to death?"

"Many times, aye. Normally a lass has her own family tae keep her warm and fed. But when one doesn'ae hae family, her best chance o' survival is tae take a husband, or become a whore."

I shuddered. I couldn't believe those were the only two choices for a woman. I mean, I could. I remembered some of what I'd learned in History, but to actually experience it for myself... "Did you ever think of taking me as your wife?"

Again, I'd surprised him. He rowed the boat more before answering. "I'd be lyin' if I said I haven'ae considered it. I've thought a good deal about many things o'er the last few days."

"And what do you think now?" I didn't even want to think about how hard my heart was pounding.

150

Silence stretched as the oars broke the water over and over. And soon, it wasn't only those splashing into the water. It had started to rain.

"*Ugh*," I groaned, cupping my hands over my eyes and peering up into the foggy sky. "*Really?*"

"We should get tae land. This rain will clear out the haar and we could be seen."

And if we were seen, it could lead the MacDougalls right to us.

He turned the boat and rowed fast and hard as we became soaked from millions of raindrops. My hair was soaking wet, and my dress was so drenched that it was growing heavier by the second. Even Cailen's hair was plastered to his face, and his shirt clung to his chest. As soon as I felt and heard the boat scrape against dirt and rocks, I jumped out of the boat, and we both pushed it as far as we could onto shore.

"Now what?" I yelled over the loud drumming of the rain.

He pointed. "We head for those."

I glanced in the direction he pointed and shook my head. There weren't nearly as many trees on the Isle as there had been on the main land. Those bushes weren't going to keep any rain off us. I didn't say anything though, I just followed him up the grassy hill until we were able to sit under our small shelter.

I'd been right. They didn't keep nearly the amount of rain from hitting us as the forest did, but they did at least lessen the onslaught.

"How long are we going to hang out here?" I asked, pulling my purse off over my head and setting it next to me.

"Just until the storm ebbs."

"And if it doesn't?" Yeah, I was getting to know

Scottish weather pretty well now.

"Then we'll move on until we find dry ground."

I pulled my knees up to my chest and rubbed at the goose bumps on my arms. "Kinda cramped in here, huh?"

Cailen looked sideways at me and cocked a half grin. "Aye. Dae ye mind much?"

"No. At least we can keep each other warm."

"Aye. We can." My Highlander's arm wound around me, and I felt the heat of him along both my shoulders and back. Somehow even a small movement like that could send my heart into hysterics. My eyes met his, and he gently pushed a lock of wet hair from my face, his hand lingering before it dropped slowly to my shoulder.

"What exactly have you been thinking of the last few days?" I sputtered, recalling what he'd said on the boat.

Cailen's gaze dropped to my mouth, a small smile curling his lips. "I've thought a lot about ye, lass. There are a fair many things I've longed tae dae tae ye."

Gulp. Heart pounding. "Oh? Like what?"

"This." His eyes focused on my mouth, and he dipped slowly, barely touching his lips to mine.

Pound. Pound. Pound. Pound.

I opened up to him and deepened the kiss, feeling the effects from head to toe as he tugged me closer to him. His lips were soft and warm, and he tasted of whiskey. I moaned against him as we explored each other. He was like a drug I never wanted to get off of.

My hands roamed down his wet shoulders and back before I pulled his shirt up and over his head, only breaking our kiss long enough to rid him of it. Our mouths collided once more, greedily taking each other's mouths forcefully. His hands were all over me, cupping my ass as he lifted me onto his lap. I yanked my dress up so I could wrap my legs around him, and a fresh wave of excitement coursed through me at feeling the heat of his body against my legs. He felt so good, so strong, so powerful. I needed him to take me. Needed it more than I needed to breathe. Needed him more than I'd needed or wanted anything my entire life. Cailen had said earlier that he'd thought of a lot of things over the last few days, and I'd had my fair share of imagining all the wicked things my Highlander and I could do to each other. I'd dreamed of this very moment, and the real deal was so much better than anything I'd even hoped for.

"Cailen," I moaned between kisses. "Undo my dress." I rocked my hips against him, feeling the very long, very hard proof of his excitement just under his kilt.

"I canna. It's no' right." He set to kissing me again.

"*Please*, just do it. I want to feel you against me." I smiled against his mouth as it met mine again. "They say that's the best way to get warm."

"Well then, who am I tae argue?" His fingers brushed over my back as the laces loosened inch by slow inch. The dress fell to my waist, leaving my top half in nothing but a thin slip and bra. My Highlander hesitated then, his gaze falling to my breasts, my bra visible through the damp cloth.

"Don't stop," I whispered, causing his gaze to meet mine. "I get cold when you stop."

"Elizabeth." He wiped at some of the rain falling down his face. "I dinna want tae stop. If ye only kent how much I want ye. But we shouldn'ae be daein' this. It's wrong."

My heart slumped, feeling like it fell into my belly. "Does it *feel* wrong?"

"*Nae!* Ye dinna ken how hard it is for me tae say this." My Scot shook his head as his hands roamed down my back. "If I'd nae manners a'tall I wouldn'ae hae said anythin'."

I drew my hands up his chest and rested them on his shoulders. "What if I asked you not to stop?"

His brows shot up. "Ye...like it?"

"*Aye*," I said, imitating his accent. "*I love this, and I doona want you to quit.*"

The most miraculous expression came over his face and he chuckled before pressing his forehead against mine. "I think yer wantin' us tae go farther than I can allow."

"I'm just planning to go as far as this takes us." I wanted him. And on top of that, my own rule of sex before marriage was niggling in the back of my mind. That, and the fact that only days ago, this sexy Highlander had told me he'd probably never get married.

I guess things changed.

"We canna. Dae ye ken what it would dae tae yer reputation?"

"I don't see anyone here but us."

"And we're no' mairrit."

"Yet."

He pulled back, blinking at me as different expressions crossed his face. "A man and a woman canna just hae relations wi'out bein' wed. It's no' like that here, Elizabeth."

"I know that," I said, a little sharply. I didn't like that angry tone in his voice. "It's just, that's something I can control, right here, right now. I can't control anything else going on in my life, except for this *one* thing." I laughed bitterly. "Do you really not want to do this?"

"It's no' that I dinna *want* tae."

He clearly did want to, if that hard length pressing against me was any indication.

"It looks like the weather's clearin'," he said suddenly, his gaze drawn to the sky.

The moment was over.

I peered out of our tiny shelter and saw a break in the rain clouds, bright sunlight shining down on the green hills of Mull.

"We should travel as far as we can. There's nae tellin' how long until it storms again." Cailen pushed me slowly off of him so we could crawl out of our hiding spot. As soon as we were standing, he silently did up the laces of my dress and handed me my bag.

I felt hot, and really, really bothered at what just happened. I'd been ready to actually have *sex* with him, and he'd passed. I'd never felt strongly enough for anyone to give it up, and when I finally did, the guy *passed*.

I fought back tears as embarrassment crushed me. *Keep breathing, Scar.* Not being wanted wasn't new to me, but it had been years since I'd experienced it. Memories of junior high came flooding back. I hadn't been good enough for anyone then either.

I followed a few feet behind Cailen as he strode through the light green grass that covered the hillside. It looked like I was going to be a virgin bride after all.

CHAPTER TEN

I was pretty much fed up with walking everywhere. For days, we'd done nothing but walk and hide. And now we were on an island that had a lot more fields of grass and a lot less shade. I was sunburned and my heart ached from the Highlander's rejection. At least the sun was about to set.

For most of our walk, he'd remained a good distance in front of me. It was only during the last hour or so that he'd held back, making sure that we walked side by side.

"Ye've been quiet. Are ye feelin' well?" Cailen asked, peering down at me.

"I'm fine." *I'm freakin' pissed off, that's what I am.* If he didn't want me, then why in the hell drag me all this way to marry me?

"Mayhap I've upset ye?"

"Oh? And why would you think that? Why would getting rejected *upset* me?" I could handle it if he just didn't like me that way. I'd turned down guys I wasn't interested in—it was what it was. But the Highlander had given me those smoldering looks. He'd held me, and taken care of me. If he hadn't been falling for me, then why do all that?

"I've been worried that had done it."

I sighed and picked up my pace as we got closer and closer to a small patch of trees. With so few places to remain hidden from other Scots, Cailen was constantly on watch, waiting for any sign of movement.

"In a hurry?"

"To get away from you." I flicked my gaze at him from over my shoulder. He'd sped up as well, and was only a few steps behind me.

"Och, lass. I didnae mean tae anger ye."

I ducked under the low branches of a tree, making my way into the miniature forest until he said we were far enough inside to avoid detection. I dropped my purse onto the ground and sat down next to it. "I think we're done talking about it."

"Nae, we're no'." Cailen sat down, far enough away that we weren't touching this time. "Ye and I are verra different," he added. "Perhaps in yer time, it's common for a man tae take a woman wi'nae regard for her. But I was no' raised that way. I was taught tae respect lasses, and that beddin' one was a gift meant only tae be shared wi' the woman I wed."

"There's another difference between us," I said, brushing at my dress that still hadn't dried. Ugh, I just wanted to take the damn thing off. I couldn't stand it. I couldn't stand anything about this place—about this time. "You have a choice of who you want to marry. I'm being forced into it."

"Dae I? And here I thought I was in the same boat as ye in that regard."

Our gazes clashed and I looked away quickly, feeling a blush crawl up my neck and flame my face. So he did plan on marrying me. He just didn't want to. I groaned and stood up as much as I could, scurrying away from him with my purse in hand. Reaching behind my back, I yanked on the laces and pulled open the two sides of the dress until I was able to shimmy it off.

"What dae ye think yer daein'?" Cailen asked,

following me again.

"I'm taking off this damn dress. I need to feel like *me* right now, because I don't feel like me anymore. Uh oh, you better turn around. I'm about to get naked and we both know you don't want to see that." I turned, peering over my shoulder and saw that he had actually stopped stalking toward me. There was a mixed expression on his face: shock, for sure; anger, maybe; and something else. I glared and dropped the slip, the fabric pooling at my feet as Cailen gaped at me. He squeezed his eyes shut and turned away with a long growl.

Yanking my shirt and skirt from my bag, I drew them on with a *humph* and stomped away from the bastard. I'd never felt so ugly—so unwanted. And the Highlander was following me again. Whirling around, I pegged him with another angry glare. "Am I really that repulsive in this time? Because Donnan MacDougall didn't think—"

"Dinna e'er say that man's name again, woman," Cailen warned, his voice lower than I'd heard since that night in Donnan's house. He bolted toward me, bending as he lifted me in his arms and held the back of my head so I couldn't look away. "And ye are far from *repulsive*. I didnae take ye because I'm a gentleman. I've tried tae ignore what I feel, but ye've tested ma patience long enough."

Oh. I couldn't breathe suddenly, the desire in his voice rolling through me like a caress.

He laid me down on the ground, his hand running up my body. "Dinna expect me tae be so well-mannered anymore."

His words, along with that menacing growl in his voice, stoked a fire in me. I was useless except to peer up at him as he laid his body on top of me and melded his mouth with mine. I closed my eyes, relishing in the feel of him. He was rough and angry, and very, very ready for sex. Maybe as much as I was.

Wait, he hadn't wanted this. He'd turned me down. Forcing my lips from his, I breathed, "I don't want this from you out of pity."

"Shhh." He kissed me again. "Pity has naethin' tae dae wi'this. We both ken I've wanted ye. I'll no' deny us any longer."

My Highlander's hands rubbed and grasped at me, and I did the same. He was all muscle. All strength. All male. Running my palms up his arms, I stopped every few inches to just enjoy every flex of muscle I felt: across his shoulders, along his back, and down his chest and stomach.

He was beautiful. And he was all mine.

My fingers wrapped around his cock, and he jumped, a groan escaping him as he pulled back from me. "Easy lass," he breathed, holding something in front of my face. "Now, exactly how does this work?"

I focused on the shiny silver vibrator in his hand, and moaned. "It doesn't matter. Just keep doing what you're doing. It's good." *So good.* I wanted more. I needed more.

"Hmm." Cailen peered down, holding his weight on one fist, with only his hips and legs still lying against me. "Maybe we should stop."

"No! No, no, no!"

"Will ye tell me then?"

"Ugh. Fine. You just twist it."

"Show me."

"Cailen, *please*?"

"Show me, or I'll stop now."

I groaned, snatching the bullet from him and turning half of it, making it vibrate.

He nabbed it back from me, and gaped at it before narrowing his eyes on me. "How?"

How did it vibrate or how did it help? My head fell back against the ground and I sighed. I reached up and guided Cailen's hand to the junction of my legs, pressing the silver bullet against me. I'd tried not to, but the feel of it had me squirming like crazy. My Highlander was motionless with the most miraculous expression on his face.

He caught me looking, and cleared his throat. "This really…It really *pleases* ye?"

"Mmm." I smiled. "What do you think?"

"I think I've ne'er seen anythin' like this."

"Like this?" I asked, pointing to the bullet. "Or like me?"

"Neither."

The toy hit a particularly sensitive spot, and I moaned and wiggled again.

"What am I tae dae wi'it?"

"Just what you're doing. Oh God, *Cailen.* I want more." I was already breathing rapidly. My entire body started quaking and I arched up to kiss him. "Let me touch you."

The Scot's eyes widened slowly. "Ye want tae touch me?"

"Like I did before. Please."

He changed positions and I reached up his kilt, gripping his shaft. At the first pump, Cailen arched and the vibrator left my skin. "Sorry. Och, dae it again."

Oh *really*? "You like that?"

"Aye. Dae it again."

His barked command nearly sent me over, but I reined it in, fascinated by this rugged Highlander who, until now, had been so strong and sure of himself. I wielded that power over him in this moment. I didn't want to give it up, and I didn't want him to know that he held the same over me. I'd never allowed myself to get this close to any man;

vowed that I wouldn't until I was sure of one that I could give up everything for. The freedom to choose the man I wanted to share my life with was gone now, but surprisingly, our lives had intertwined in this incredible way, and my feelings for him only grew every day. Even during the times I hated him, I'd wanted him and berated myself over it. He was a victim of circumstance every bit as much as I was, but finally he was seeing my way in this. If we were about to be wed—whether we were ready to or not—why not see if we enjoyed each other before taking that plunge?

"Take off your shirt. I want to feel your skin. I want to touch all of you."

He did as I said, untying the laces at the top of his shirt and loosening them one-handed, just enough to yank it off over his head.

I stroked him once more, up and down, his body trembling with every inch. I could watch every muscle in his body flex all day. As it was, with every pump of my fist on his shaft, he grew more excited—more primal. More commanding. Soon, he was on top of me as he pressed the vibrating toy against my core, sending me closer and closer to that cliff I'd been holding myself from.

"Does this feel as good as what yer daein' tae me?" he groaned, his eyes desperate.

I nodded, and gave him a faster pump.

"Oh God, lass. I dinna want ye tae stop. I want ye tae feel this way. Tell me what tae dae."

I could barely think anymore, and I didn't realize I'd reached up and brought his free hand to the apex of my legs until I'd already guided him there. With the first touch of his fingers, I moaned again. "Inside."

Seconds passed before I felt a finger press inside me. It was incredible. And it was all I'd needed. My entire body spasmed and I cried out as wave after wave of bliss rocked me. I came back down from my crest, still stroking Cailen's cock as he came, his semen jetting from his shaft as he groaned and clutched me to him. I was rapt again, and kept at it until he halted my hand.

"I dinna think I can take anymore," he breathed. Cailen pressed his forehead to mine and our gazes locked just before he kissed me. He rolled, pulling me in close to his side and guiding my head onto his chest. His breathing slowed and we both started to relax into sleep. "Ma braw, wee Elizabeth."

I couldn't stop smiling after our encounter. There was only one thing that could've made it better: Cailen going inside me. If I'd been able to think clearly at the time, I would have guided him there.

We still hadn't technically had sex, but it was a lot further than I'd ever gone before. And it left me wanting more.

I thought my sweet Highlander might have been thinking the same thing. Ever since we'd woken in the night and continued our trek over the island, he'd been so attentive, holding limbs out of my way, or lifting me over prickly patches that would've poked through the leather straps around my feet. I'd caught him glancing at me and smiling more times than I could count. He even caved and let me spend the day in my own clothes, which helped tremendously. They really did make me feel like my normal self again.

My thoughts constantly drifted to him: the way he looked in the throes of passion, the way his lips felt against mine, the weight of his body on top of me, the velvety softness of his penis.

He'd also turned playful during our travels today, only growing serious at the threat of other people nearby, which were possibly the MacDougalls. I still didn't understand how people who lived so close to each other could war, but it seemed like such an important thing to him, that I couldn't doubt its validity.

For the last while now, we'd been mostly out in the open, navigating the grassy hills by moonlight. The grass was broken up sometimes by houses, rock pillars, and standing stones. He'd called some of them cairns. I brightened, seeing a new clump of trees in the distance. Trees meant privacy. "How much longer do you think?"

"Until we reach ma clan? Och, we'll reach it on the morrow, I should think. We may need tae stop for the rest o' the night." He peered over at me. "Unless ye'd like tae continue?"

No, I didn't want to keep walking. I wanted to stop for a bit and put more medicine on my foot since the last dose had been early that morning. Not to mention the other things we could do to keep us busy. "Actually, I had something else in mind. You'll just have to catch me to find out exactly what."

I yanked my Juicy tee off over my head and flung it at him before dashing into the trees. He made a sound that made my entire body tingle in anticipation of another match with my Highlander. I looked back only once, long enough to see that he'd bent to grab my shirt from the ground before he'd set off after me.

I ran as fast as I could, dodging trees and bushes, and trying not to laugh at the mere thought of what Cailen might do when he found me. Rounding a tree I knew I could hide behind, I whirled around, peeking around it in case he was already that close. My breath left me in excited rushes and I had to force my breathing to slow.

"Lass," he called playfully. "Where are ye?"

Oh, that teasing lilt in his voice.

"Nuh uh uh…You have to find me," I sang back. I'd barely spotted movement between trees. He wasn't that close yet.

"Ye're in a fair amount o' trouble. I dinna think ye want tae ken what'll be done tae ye when I find ye."

"Ooh." I laughed. "Are you going to punish me?" He was closer now, so I took off at a dead run, knowing that if I'd stayed put he would have found me in seconds.

I gasped as an arm came out in front of me and I clotheslined into it before falling to the ground.

"Nae need tae run, woman. In fact, I wouldn'ae try it if I were ye."

I peered up into the dark eyes of the stranger, and a scream bubbled out of me as cold steel pressed against my neck.

Cailen held back from finding his lass. For one, he'd been shocked to see so much bare skin as she'd lobbed her shirt at him and ran, leaving her only in her tight wee skirt and small patch of black that covered her pert breasts. He'd get a peek at them this night if it killed him.

The woman wanted him to look at her, wanted him to touch her. Any reservations he'd previously had vanished the moment her soft fingers had worked his cock to a frenzy. His seed had never come so hard as it had when her hand had clutched it.

He caught sight of her rushing through the trees as she tried to get away from him. He turned as well, following her trail, kenning that if she slowed at all again that he would catch her. Perhaps it was time to capture the wee lass, after all.

Cailen opened his mouth to tease her once more, to gather her location from her voice alone, but a bloodcurdling scream echoed through the forest, choking off anything he'd been about to say.

He lunged forward, passing tree after tree, watching for any sign of her. His heart pounded rapidly, his worry for her overwhelming every other sense. Was it the bloody MacDougalls? Had they found her already? No, he couldn't accept it. He needed her. She was a part of him now.

Another muffled scream had him changing course, and he barreled through the forest in search of his wee Elizabeth. Remaining silent was his only course of action, hoping to take whoever—or whatever—had her, by surprise. There was a shuffling of leaves up ahead and he slowed, listening.

"Ye may as well come out," a man yelled. "We ken ye're there."

Cailen's jaw clenched as he reached into the sheath under his plaid, and extracted his dirk. There was no sneaking up on the bastard that held his woman, but he refused to walk into a possible massacre without at least one weapon in hand. There was one thing for certain: If Donnan MacDougall had Elizabeth, he'd fight the bawbag to the death before he'd ever leave her to a scullion like him.

"Out wi'ye, man. Ye're woman hasn'ae come tae any harm."

"Is that so?" Cailen replied, searching for any movement as he strode ever closer. If a single hair on her head was harmed, he'd tear the man apart. "Are ye well, lass?"

"Y-yes," she replied, her voice quiet and shaken.

He stepped into a small clearing in the middle of the forest. A camp, he realized a second later. Elizabeth was standing next to someone, her arm being clutched by his tight fist. He gaped at the man responsible for nabbing her, hardly believing his eyes. "Grant? Is that *ye*?"

"Cailen." Grant Ferguson laughed. He released Elizabeth's arm and stepped forward, slugging him on the shoulder. "I didnae think we'd see ye any time soon."

"Aye. I hadn'ae planned tae return yet." Other members of his clan stepped out from the surrounding woods, and he met the eyes of more than one of them. "What are ye all daein' here?"

"Huntin'," Grant supplied. "We've run low on meat at home, so we came out here on a huntin' raid."

"So far from home?"

"Aye. Huntin's been scarce. If we're tae catch anythin' off guard, it must be where they're no' used tae us."

Scarce? Already? It was one of their warmest months. There was still time yet before winter overtook the land.

"We also need a good deal for tradin'," a familiar voice said from behind him.

Cailen turned and saw the ugly mug of none other than Gregor McIntosh, his oldest friend. "Gregor," he greeted, unable to keep the smile from spreading across his face. "It's good tae see ye. How's yer wifey then?"

"Flora? Och, she's about tae give me another son or daughter. Any day now."

"Another?" That was a surprise. He hadn't even known there was one.

"Aye. She's already blessed me wi'a son. Wee Hamish."

Cailen strode over to his friend and gave the man a quick hug. "Congratulations, ma brither. I canna wait tae meet yer bairn." He peered over at Grant as the man apologized in great detail to Elizabeth, who still looked pale from her ordeal—and, he realized, very nearly naked. He approached her, quickly handing her the shirt and placing a tender hand on her shoulder once she'd stabbed her arms and head through the tiny openings.

"Ye'll return tae Ardmoir wi'us then?" Grant asked.

Glancing down at Elizabeth and then returning his gaze to his clansmen, he nodded. "When dae ye plan tae return?"

"Half o' us are plannin' tae leave on the morrow. The other half will stay in search o' more food for trade."

"All right then. The lass and I will return tae Ardmoir wi'ye."

This time Gregory stepped forward, folding his arms as he stood by Grant's side. "And who is the lass, Cailen? Ye've yet tae make introductions."

"Oh." He coughed. "This is Elizabeth Michaelson. Elizabeth, these are ma clansmen."

"That's a…that's great." She hugged her arms around herself as a chorus of quiet "Good e'en's" and nods came from his men. Elizabeth merely eyed them, blinking as she stepped closer to him. Damn them for scaring her. Damn them for scaring *him*.

"Well it's settled then. We'll leave at first light. Welcome, Miss Michaelson." Grant bent low in a bow, giving her the smile that had felled more lassies in Ardmoir than any other lad's. Elizabeth returned his smile.

He didn't much care for her looking at another man.

People stopped and stared as we entered the little village Cailen had grown up in, but I got the feeling that was more due to my Highlander than because of the presence of a stranger. I received friendly welcomes, but he'd gotten pats on the back and outright awe as he passed.

Every single adult in sight was wearing tartan, only the children and young girls wore other colors. I wondered what kind of welcome I would have received if I'd shown up in my T-shirt and skirt. Cailen forced me into it after seeing some of the other men gawk at me.

Probably a good thing he did. After the whole *"Ooh, sorry I held a knife to your throat. Gotta keep an eye out for enemy clans, you know,"* thing, I'd gotten uncomfortable within seconds from their stares alone. Being that close to so many strange men kept me up all night, and I was seriously feeling the effects.

"We should go tae ma home directly," Cailen said, inching close so he could speak quietly in my ear. "Ye can rest there and I'm sure we can hae a doctor see tae yer foot."

"That'd be great." I smiled up and let him take me by the elbow as he led me away from the mini parade of hunters who'd been hauling dead carcasses the entire way to Ardmoir. "This is where you grew up?"

"Aye."

There were a few homes and businesses there, they were mostly older homes like the ones I'd seen along the way. They all seemed to be surrounding a much bigger one, that had a rock fence that ran around the perimeter. Inside the small rock wall, there was a stable housing three horses, and just next to that was a large area where two "heelin' coos" grazed. At least a dozen chickens scurried around, flapping their wings in irritation as a small boy ran back and forth wherever they tried to rest. In the distance there was another building, nowhere near the size of the main house, but I couldn't tell exactly what it was used for.

The main house was a good deal bigger than every other home in sight, with the exception of the church just up the hill. The home was two levels, with open windows on both floors. The yard itself wasn't much to speak of, except it had big, bushy plants with vibrant red and purple flowers at the entrance. That was more than what I'd seen of other homes so far.

Before we even reached the house, a girl about my age scurried inside, slamming the door behind her. We were only a few feet away when a man yanked open the door, peering out at us with disbelief. He was as tall and well-built as Cailen, only his hair had a reddish tint to it, and he sported a thick beard. Yep, definitely my Highlander's dad.

A woman peeked out from around his side, and pushed her way through the door as she saw us approach.

"Cailen! Och, ma wee Cailen! Come here, lad!" Her arms spread wide and she gripped him in a hug as he lifted her off the ground. Tears streaked down her cheeks, but she laughed through them. "We didnae ken if ye were alive or deed. I'm so glad ye're all right."

"Mam," he said, grinning at the woman as he set her down. "'Tis good tae see ye."

I teared up at seeing their excitement, and brushed them from my cheeks. That used to be me and Mom, and I'd never have that again.

I stood by, uncomfortable as I played absolutely no part in this family reunion. I smiled though, in case anyone actually did look my way. I also focused on his mom, comparing her to the towering son she'd somehow created. It was a bit harder to make out her features since she was covered in a big dress and her hair was mostly covered with a hat.

"Hello, son."

Cailen glanced past his mom and nodded. "Da."

The older man approached, holding his hand out for Cailen to shake. "Ye've been gone a long while."

"I needed time."

"A bit too much, maybe," his mom replied. "Och, who's *this*?"

All eyes fastened on me and I knotted my fingers together.

"This is why I've come." Cailen stepped toward me. "Elizabeth, this is ma mam, Ailsa MacKinnon, Lady o' Ardmoir; and ma da, Conall MacKinnon, Laird o' Ardmoir. Mam, Da, this is Elizabeth Michaelson."

"Hi." I waved lamely. Seeing his parents lit something within me, and I no longer felt exhausted. I just wanted to learn more about these people since I was about to be incorporated into their family. And I really hoped they'd like me.

"Welcome tae Ardmoir, Elizabeth," his dad said, offering me a bow just like the ones I'd received from the Highland hunters the night before.

Cailen touched my elbow. "Come, lass. I think we've much tae discuss wi'ma mam and da."

As soon as we were inside, I was given a tour of their living room, dining room, and kitchen, and then upstairs where all of the bedrooms were. The inside of their home was beautiful, with paintings on the walls and cabinets filled with beautiful dishes and silverware. This was unlike anything I'd expected. I'd thought Mary and Uilleam's home was nice, and they were a close second, but this was incredible. Over the fireplace hung a shield and two swords—Conall's, apparently—and over each of the chairs and benches were pillows and blankets. Cailen's mom had painstakingly made this the most comfortable home she could.

Servants had already gotten to work on making up bedrooms for us. Ailsa had pulled one of the servants aside and instructed the girl to fetch Cailen's little brother,

Cameron, while I was being toured around their home. The furniture inside our rooms didn't disappoint. There was a mirror and vanity, and even a small tub that I assumed was for bathing. It was more than twice the size of the room at the inn in Kilchrenan.

"Are ye sure ye dinna want tae rest, dear?" Ailsa asked. "Ye seem a bit knackered."

I stole a glimpse at Cailen, giving him a look that I'd hoped would tell him I had no idea what she'd just said.

"Actually," he replied. "She needs a doctor tae look at her foot. She was injured days ago and we've been keepin' a salve on it that another doctor gave us."

"And don't forget your arm," I added.

"I'd wondered what happened tae yer arm. What hae ye done now, Cailen?"

"Mam." My Highlander rolled his yes. "We were attacked by a boar. I had tae keep it awa from her."

"Boars." She tsked. "Ye've still no' learned, I see."

"Ailsa," Conall drawled. "Dinna give him grief. He did it tae protect the lass."

"Ye ken how Cailen is, he prob'ly angered it on purpose. *Emily!*" Ailsa barked, looking at the woman who made my bed. "Go fetch Stewart McCrary. Tell him tae bring his bag."

The servant bobbed a curtsy and scurried out of the room without a sound.

"Ye should prob'ly hae a seat, dear," his mom added, more or less pushing me down onto the partially made bed. She sat down next to me and glanced up at her son.

"Now," Conall said, folding his arms as he, too, eyed Cailen. "Since we've some privacy at the present, what was it ye wanted tae speak wi'us about then?"

"Dae ye bring news o' Kieran?" Ailsa asked, her voice hopeful.

Cailen's face hardened and he shook his head. "Nae. I've no' seen him. I've come home because o' Elizabeth."

Again, his parents' eyes fell on me, both with mixed expressions of uncertainty and hope. I wanted to sink into the bed, not really knowing exactly how Cailen was about to tell them that he and I had to get married because I had no family, no money, and nothing to my name. Oh, and why not add in the bit about how I wouldn't be born for over two hundred years and see how his parents took it all?

My Highlander peered at his dad, the two of them standing in identical poses with their arms folded and their feet shoulder-width apart. "Ye ken the clan better than anyone, so ye may ken who might be willin' tae help her."

I narrowed my eyes, wondering just where he was going with this. It definitely didn't sound like anything I'd imagined.

Conall snorted. "Yer mam has more knowledge o' ev'ra clan member in Ardmoir in one finger than I dae." He smiled, winking at his wife. "What does the lass need our help wi'?"

Cailen glanced at me, his gaze falling to the floor for a brief second before he returned it to his dad. "She nae longer has family."

Ailsa's hand immediately covered my own. I couldn't take my eyes off my Scot though, not with the rock forming in my gut. This really didn't sound anything like "Hey, Mom and Dad, we're getting hitched".

"Okay," Conall replied slowly.

"I need ye tae find her a husband."

CHAPTER ELEVEN

I was stunned. And so freakin' pissed off.

I could have spit on that Highlander, and punched him in the face, and kicked him in the balls.

After Cailen had dropped the bomb about me needing to find a husband—because apparently he wasn't going to marry me—the doctor had shown up, so he and his parents had left the room. I knew they could see how pissed off I was. They might have even tried to talk to me, but I was so dazed that I couldn't even care enough to listen. The doctor checked out my foot and gave me something else to keep on it, but he thought it was likely healing since it itched like crazy. He'd left quite a while ago, and I'd been in the room by myself ever since.

A knock sounded at the door, but I ignored it, just like I had the two times before.

"Elizabeth," Cailen's voice boomed through the door. "Open the door. I'll break it doon if I must."

I stood and paced by the bed. Damn him. Damn that man for everything: for making me want him, for making me crave his touch and his kiss, and for making it so that even the sound of his voice was enough to bring tears to my eyes. And to make my heart simultaneously flutter with desire and rip into two.

"Elizabeth," he barked again. "I'm no' jokin'. Ye hae three seconds tae open the door, or I'm comin' in."

I gritted my teeth and stared into the fireless fireplace. He counted to three and must have punched the door, because it rebounded off the wall with a *crack*.

"What dae ye think yer daein' in here, holed up like some sort o' prisoner?" he growled. "We've come all this way tae find ye a husband. How dae ye expect tae find one if ye're locked in here?" There was a brief second of silence. "And when did ye put yer clothes back on? Ye canna wear those here."

"Fuck my clothes, and fuck you, too." Yeah, there was no more holding back what I was feeling.

"I dinna ken what ye meant by that, but I gather yer feelings behind it."

Still, I didn't look at him. "Oh, you gather my feelings, hmm? About time, I guess. Too bad it's a bit too late for that."

"Elizabeth." He sighed.

"Stop *calling* me that!" I yelled, turning toward him.

I thought he'd step back, but he didn't. He swallowed though, as his eyes searched mine. "What would ye hae me call ye?"

"How about 'that girl you once knew', or 'that one girl, who somehow got thrown two hundred years into the past, fell into your lap, and you threw her away', or better yet, 'that girl that you made fall in love with you, the one that you gave hope to, only to rip it away'. Yeah, any of those would do."

He squeezed his eyes shut as his fists clenched repeatedly.

"The stupid thing is, I normally wouldn't let this get to me, but I let my guard down because you made me think you were falling in love with me." All of the anger and frustration I'd been accumulating over the last week hit me at once, and I let it fuel me. "Where I'm from, it's well known that most men are pigs. Women are raised knowing that we're bound to get hurt by guys who think they're King Shit, and that they have every right to go after however many girls they want. I expect guys from my own time to act like pricks, but you...You make the guys I'm used to look like amateurs. I've *never* been played like what you did to me."

"Played?" he gaped. "I didnae play—"

"Why didn't you tell me you weren't going to marry me?" I interrupted.

"God, woman. It's because I couldn'ae say it!" he yelled, darting in and taking my mouth roughly as he held me to him.

I pushed him off of me, wiping the back of my hand across my mouth. "You don't get to do that! You don't get to reject me and think you can still kiss me!" A tear fell down my cheek and I flicked it away with my hand. "I loved you."

"I ken," he said quietly. "Or, at least, I'd thought ye might. I should'ae done somethin' tae keep it from happenin', but...I couldn'ae tell ye that we couldn'ae be taegether." His face morphed to one of pain and sadness as he gripped my arms. "I couldn'ae e'en say the words tae ye."

I tried to look away from him, but he angled his head so he was always in my direct view.

Searching my eyes, he continued, "I didnae want them tae be true. Ye made me feel like a man, a good one. One that could take care o' ye and build a life. I let myself believe that we could make it work, but I was just kiddin' myself. Ye ken I want ye, but I canna hae ye. Nae matter how I wish it were different."

"You won't marry me because of who I am."

His face had hardened, some of that sadness being replaced by irritation. "I canna marry ye because o' who ye are not."

The 'T' rang out with finality, and I stepped back,

feeling like he'd slapped me. *Because of who I'm not?*

"You have someone else," I breathed, feeling the truth of it. "All along, you've had someone else. You said it wasn't likely you were going to get married, but you were just buttering me up to get me here and marry me off to one of your hard-up friends. Let me guess, it's for the same reasons that Donnan wanted me: I look well fed and healthy, and let's not forget that I'm not related to any of you. I know how pesky blood relatives can get when matchmaking. Well, good job, Barbarian, you've done your duty to your clan."

Cailen's jaw tightened, his eyes dark and ominous.

"I don't even know why you bothered to bring me all the way here. I wish you would have just let me get shot that first day. It would have saved me a hell of a lot of pain. Kinda surprised you didn't find what out Donnan MacDougall was willing to pay."

The second I saw his mouth open to speak, I lifted my hand, stopping him.

"You know what, Cailen. I think you should just leave." He didn't move, so I took a step toward him. "I'm serious. Get. Out. Of. Here. I don't want to see your face for another second. I don't even want to waste another thought on you."

It felt like an eternity—an eternity that I was forced to stand there, holding back from letting anymore tears fall, and getting a sore throat from the effort—but he finally backed away and left through the door. I sat down on the chair in front of the fireplace and started to cry as I listened to the sound of his boots *clomping* down the stairs.

"I'm verra sorry Cailen broke yer door," Ailsa said. She

stood by the fractured door, peering at me from a safe distance. When I didn't say anything, she stepped inside and clasped her hands together. "We've planned a banquet in yer honor. I dae hope ye'll join us for supper. Cailen mentioned that ye dinna much care for fish, so our cook has been preparin' a lamb."

"Thanks, but I don't really feel like eating."

"But ye haven'ae eaten a thing since ye arrived. Surely ye must be starvin'."

Not for what she was offering. No, I had to stop thinking that way. I couldn't let myself think about him anymore.

I blinked hard, trying to keep tears from pooling in my eyes.

"Oh dear." Ailsa frowned and sat beside me on the bed. "I ken how ye're feelin'. The men in this family are verra stubborn. I'm afraid Cailen takes after his da in that regard." She chuckled and fell silent before adding, "I heard the two o' ye arguin' earlier. I dae hope ye realize that he is tryin' tae dae right by ye. He's no' had the easiest life the last few years, and I believe wi'all ma heart that he feels he's daein' what he must for ye."

Alright, so not thinking about him wasn't working. I refused to cry in front of Cailen's mom, I just couldn't break down in front of her. Instead, I rubbed a hand down my face.

"Ye're in love wi' him."

I peered over at Ailsa, blinking as I took in the features that seemed so vaguely familiar. Probably because I could see a part of Cailen in her. "I thought I was. Seems I was wrong."

"The heart is rarely wrong, lass. Sometimes it just falls for someone we canna hae."

But why didn't he love me? And how had I fallen into

this rut where I just felt like giving up? I'd never given up on anything in my life, always refusing to be one of those girls who thought their life was over because their boyfriend broke up with them.

"Why dinna we get ye ready for supper?"

I chuckled. "I'm surprised you're not asking me where I got these highly inappropriate clothes. Everyone else who's seen me in them has asked."

"It's no' ma business. Cailen spent a good deal o' time today tellin' us about how special ye are, forby. I've ne'er heard him regard a lass the way he does ye." She patted my knee. "But, we should prob'ly get ye dressed in a proper gown. I've had ma seamstress preparin' somethin' special for ye for the banquet."

"Oh, you really don't have to do that. We bought that one just a couple days ago." I hiked my thumb at the brown dress that was tossed over the edge of the bed.

"And it's filthy." She tsked. "Ye've traveled a great distance in that poor dress wi'out so much as a break tae care for it."

Yeah, like I even knew how to take care of it without the help of Tide and Downy.

"Mum?" a servant said from the hall. "I've boiled some water for Miss Elizabeth's bath. Will she be acceptin' one?"

"Aye." Ailsa stood and approached the servant as she squeezed through with two buckets of water. "I think a warm bath is just what ye need, dinna ye?"

I met Cailen's mom's light blue eyes, and smiled. "I think you're right. A bath is exactly what I need."

A while later, I was clean, dry, and wearing a brand new dress that actually fit me. The hot soak washed away some of my tribulation, which opened me up to actually talking with Ailsa MacKinnon. As far as moms went, she was pretty cool. She carefully avoided mentioning Cailen's name. Instead, whenever she talked about her family, she referred to them as her husband and sons. Mostly, she talked about their home and their clan. Conall and Ailsa were the Laird and Lady of Ardmoir, which meant that they maintained their small village and surrounding area, and collected taxes from clan members who were sworn to the MacKinnon Chieftain, who was now with the majority of the MacKinnon Clan on a different isle.

We'd left their home a short time later, me in my cream and green dress, and Ailsa wearing one that was equally beautiful, which was trimmed with tartan. By luck, they had planned an outdoor banquet under a sky that was cloud-free and just starting to show a few stars in the waning light.

I guessed that every member of their village was in attendance, working hastily to bring chairs and tables from their homes and placing them in a big square around the spit that held the body of a lamb as it cooked over the flames. Women buzzed around, placing food and drink, plates, bowls, and cups on each table.

"Is there anything I can help with?" I asked, stepping out of the way as a speedy woman rushed past me.

"Nae," Ailsa replied. "As one o' our honored guests, we'd like ye tae hae the opportunity tae speak wi'different members o' our clan." She steered me toward Conall, who was among five other men, all of which were decked out in their matching kilts.

"What do you mean 'one of' your honored guests?"

"Oh. Well," she said uncomfortably. "We're also celebratin' Cailen's return. I hope ye can find it in yer heart tae forgive him, at least for supper, since the two o' ye will be sittin' next tae each other."

I gritted my teeth, only forcing myself to lessen the

pressure as a twinge of pain worked through my mouth. Did I really have to spend an entire meal sitting next to the man who threw me away? "Fine. I won't say anything mean to him, but don't expect me to play nice."

Ailsa's mouth twitched. "Right then. Why dinna ye meet some o' the men Conall is talkin' tae? They're verra nice, and quite excited tae make yer acquaintance."

It turned out that I'd already met two of the five men standing around Cailen's dad. They'd been in the hunting party that had returned with us earlier that morning, and all five were friendly, bowing formally to me.

I spotted Cailen out of the corner of my eye. He stood probably thirty feet away from me, conversing with Gregor, his best friend and one of the men I recognized from the hunting party, as well as a few other men I didn't. He glanced over, his eyes meeting mine and holding. I hastily turned away, pretending to be completely engrossed in the man who was talking about herring. Ailsa gave me an apologetic look, and I smiled in return. No brownie points for herring boy. I hated fish, and based on the way he lit up while talking about all the ways to fillet them, I knew there was zero chance I was marrying that guy. If I was signing my life away to a loveless marriage, I wasn't also going to get stuck eating fish every day.

Damn Cailen for putting me in this position.

After a few more minutes of talk on how to cook herring, I was gratefully whisked off to a seat at a table, right next to Ailsa. Cailen strode over as well and sat right next to me, and despite my promise to his mom, I tensed.

"Ye look verra bonny, lass," the Highlander said, leaning in close to me.

"Well I should, I guess. Apparently my future husband is here right now." I peered down at my plate as a woman plopped meat and bread on my plate. Another followed right after, spooning some sort of soup into my bowl. Cailen still eyed me.

"Why are you staring?" I snapped, earning a few shocked glances from other clansmen and women.

"I wasn'ae. I mean, I was. I just…" He sighed. "Elizabeth—"

"I told you not to call me that," I growled, keeping a smile on my face as people glanced my way.

"I thought that we might still be friends."

"Friends? Are you freakin' kidding me? I bare my feelings for you, and you not only shut me down, but work on selling me off to the highest bidder…and you want us to be friends? If you wanted that to happen you probably shouldn't have made me think we felt the same way about each other."

"Ye two," Ailsa whispered. "Mind both yer promises tae me. Behave."

We were all silent for a second before Cailen flicked his gaze from his mom to me. "Ye're no' being *sold*, so I dinna ken why ye keep labelin' me as some sort o' monster. And aye, ye did tell me o' yer feelings, but there isn'ae a damn thing—"

"Cailen!" his mom barked.

"—I can dae about it. I've already told ye, I would if I could."

"I don't see anything stopping you," I countered, before turning to face his parents and brother. "I really want to thank you for everything you've done, but I think it's time that I go to bed."

Standing, I walked away from the table, attempting to smile at a few late stragglers who made their way to the banquet. Once inside my room, I shut the splintered door behind me and pushed a heavy chest in front of it, locking out the rest of the world.

"What did ye dae tae her?" his mam snapped. "And what hae ye done tae yer hand?"

Cailen peered over his shoulder at her, shrugging as he bent to grab a pan from the chest. "Naethin'." Of course his mother would blame him. He wouldn't tell her he'd gone outside and slammed his fists against the dyke until he bled. It was none of her business why he'd done so, and he didn't wish to invoke questioning.

Una shrank away from them and silently slipped out of the kitchen.

"Ye've done somethin'. She willn'ae come out o' her room. I've tried, yer da has tried, e'en Emily and Una hae tried tae get her tae open the door, but she refuses, e'en for food!"

"What dae ye want me tae dae about it?" Cailen asked as he shoved the pan inside a new satchel, along with fruit and bread.

"I want ye tae go upstairs and talk tae her." His mam stopped talking suddenly, her eyes narrowing on what he was doing as his father stepped up behind her.

"What dae ye think ye're daein'?"

Cailen eyed his da. "What does it look like? I'm leavin'."

"Ye canna just leave again," his da argued. "Ye're no' a young lad anymore. Ye're a man. Ye've brought a lass tae our door. 'Tis yer duty tae make sure she finds a good husband."

"Nae, it isn'ae. I brought her tae ye. Ye are the leader here, ye can make that decision far better than I could."

"Ye'd really leave her?" his mam asked, shaking her head as she put her hands on her hips. Great, he was in trouble. "She doesn'ae ken anyone here but ye, and ye'd just leave her?"

He threw the bag over his shoulder and glared at his parents. Sighing, he strode up the stairs and to Elizabeth's door, banging his fist against the wood. "Elizabeth," he barked. "Come out. Ye canna stay in there. Ye must come out."

When there was no sound on the other side of the door, Cailen stomped down the stairs, passing his parents. "There, I've tried. The woman wants naethin' tae dae wi'me."

"Ye ken as well as I dae that's no' true," his mam replied. "I think she truly does. Yer faither and I ken ye hae feelings for her as well."

His forward progression stopped and he turned. "What does it matter if I dae? When hae ma feelings mattered? O' course I want Elizabeth. I love her! But I hae a duty tae ma family, and we all want Kieran back."

"Cailen," his mam replied softly. "Ye canna still believe in the curse. It's been years and we've no' heard from Kieran."

"He prob'ly took off like ye've done," his da added.

They still didn't believe him. After all this time, they really thought Kieran just ran away? "Ye haven'ae heard from him because that witch took him, and I've spent the last two years searchin' for the one who could bring him back. I dinna get tae stop searchin' and take the woman I want as ma wife or none o' us will e'er see Kieran again. And it wouldn'ae matter if I could marry her, because the woman hates me!"

What else was he to do? He'd tried to speak to her, to apologize for everything, but she wouldn't have it, and she'd stormed away from him.

It was his mam that spoke. "So ye'll leave the only

woman who might make ye happy?"

"I need tae leave. I canna stay here." He gave his mam a hug and went tae dae the same wi'his dad. "Just...find her a good man. Make sure she'll be taken care o'."

The good Lord in Heaven kent the lass deserved to have something good in her life.

He left his home without another word, stopping only to give Cameron a hug, and to say goodbye to Gregor.

CHAPTER TWELVE

I sat down, leaning my back against the small tower of rock I'd found days ago, and peered out at the sea. So far, this was my favorite hideout from the day-to-day life I'd been planted in. The sea called to me. I could've watched it any part of the day, from sun-up to after the sun had gone down. Many times I could see ships in the distance, some even closer as they crept into the channel between this isle and the next, stopping at random places along both sides. The MacKinnons taxed those ships for passage, and used that opportunity to trade goods with sailors from all over the world. Even yesterday, a few of the MacKinnon boys had happily skipped into town, carting baskets of chickens for the farms.

Down on the beach not too far from my tower, there were three shipwrecks. Spanish vessels, from what Conall had told me during one of our excursions. He'd taken me down to see one of them, carefully leading me down into the hull, where I'd been able to see where the Spanish sailors had slept and ate. From the beach, he'd pointed out a few more sunken ships farther out, only visible by their masts barely sticking out of the water. He'd mentioned how his sons had taught themselves to swim so they could extract gold and precious stones from the vessels. They'd built quite a family fortune from that alone.

Hugging my knees to my chest, I couldn't help but think of the man who'd brought me here, only to abandon me.

At first, I hadn't believed Ailsa when she'd told me that

Cailen had left. I'd assumed she'd just been trying to convince me to leave my room and join her, Conall, or Cameron on one of the adventures they'd been upselling. But for days now, I'd been out in the village, talking to people, and I'd learned that he really had left. It'd been two weeks since the night of that banquet, and two weeks since I'd seen or heard from Cailen. The ache that left in my heart alone compelled me to stay in my bed all day, to live in my own solitary bubble and mourn what could have been. At other times, I gave myself a mental ass-kicking. I knew my life would go on, and I'd done my best to not allow everything I saw or heard remind me of him. It would just take time.

It was obvious that Conall, Ailsa, and Cameron were sad he left, and even though they should have blamed me for it, they didn't. They'd all been nothing but nice to me, letting me share in their family meals, and including me as one of them throughout each day.

Conall took me on horse rides, while Ailsa preferred showing me around their village, where I met women of all ages and sizes, and witnessed firsthand the jobs they did day in and day out. Cameron reminded me of Jason. He just wanted to hang out, and seemed to like taking me to meet other teenagers his age. Cameron was the reason I heard all the clan gossip. He snuck extra treats to me when no one was looking, and he sat silently with me whenever I needed to get away from everything.

It hadn't taken long for me to realize that no matter where I was or what I was doing, I was on show for the eligible bachelors of Ardmoir. I received gifts of homemade trinkets and jewelry, and was invited to go on walks around the outskirts of the village.

"Elizabeth."

I turned my head, peering around the tower as Cameron

hiked up the hill, his red tartan kilt whipping in the wind. "Hi." I smiled and patted the grass next to me before he sat down. I'd come to admire the boy over the last few days. Even though he was only fourteen, he seemed mature compared to the teenage boys I'd gone to school with. Maybe it was because times were so different, which made people grow up so much faster than in my own time. He was still in an awkward stage, where his muscles from his long days of work hadn't quite caught up to his height. He was already taller than me, which had been the cause of constant teasing, but he hadn't filled out like Cailen yet. He had his mom's eyes and his dad's hair, only it fell into his face, not quite long enough to tie at his nape like his older brother. "I really wish you'd stop calling me that."

"I would, but ye haven'ae given me another option," he said, a little breathless.

I rolled my eyes. "I'll let you pick what you want to call me."

"Elizabeth it is, then." He grinned, shoving his shoulder into mine and making me laugh. "I'm surprised tae find ye up here."

"It's my favorite place." I shrugged. "I like how far out I can see. How I can spot travelers even though they probably can't see me. And, I dunno, I guess I really like to watch the fog roll in and out around the isle." That part reminded me of *him*.

"I see. Hae ye started tae settle then? Ye seem more comfortable now."

"Yeah, I think so." I reached down and played with my dress, not wanting him to see whatever pain might be showing in my face. How could I tell someone I really wanted to go home, even though that wouldn't exist for hundreds of years?

"Yer thinkin' o' Cailen," he said suddenly, turning a

sad smile toward me.

"Why do you think that?"

"I've seen it often enough on yer face. I wasn'ae sure what troubled ye at first, but I realized ye hae a certain...expression whene'er yer thinkin' o' him."

I swallowed, hard. "What does it look like?"

"Like ye wish he were here wi' ye, rather than runnin' off like a bloody coward."

"Hey," I snapped. "Cailen is not a coward. He just doesn't want me." *And I hadn't handled it all that well.*

Cameron snorted, shaking his head. "Daft lass," he muttered, reminding me way too much of his brother. "He wants ye. He's just afraid tae go after what he wants rather than what he was told."

"What do you mean?"

"Oh." His face reddened and he plucked a blade of grass out of the ground. "It's naethin'. Just forget I said anythin'."

I leaned against the tower and stared out at the ocean, wondering exactly what it was Cameron wasn't telling me.

"I'm grateful ye were willin' tae join me for a ride," Conall said as he steered his horse through one of the many wide, open fields on the outskirts of Ardmoir.

I nodded, bumping my heel against my horse's side, urging him to follow. "Yeah. Thanks for inviting me."

I'd been introduced to the MacKinnon's horses a few days ago, my favorite being the one that looked exactly like my little Bud. This one was a male though, but no less beautiful in my eyes, and maybe even more fitting for my own version of his name.

"There is somethin' I've been meanin' tae speak wi'ye

about. Dae ye ken a man by the name o' Donnan MacDougall?"

I gaped at him. "Yeah, that's the guy who tried to force me into marrying him. Why?"

"That's what I thought. Cailen told me o' yer troubles wi'someone from another clan, but he didnae mention any specifics. One o' ma clansmen came tae me early this morn, and he said the MacDougalls are on Mull, searchin' ev'ra town for ye."

Crap. I'd been afraid that would happen sooner or later, and Cailen and I had even discussed the possibility of it happening, especially since Donnan had recognized Cailen's clan tartan.

"It seems he means tae make ye his bride. He claims that one o' our clansmen kidnapped ye, and he aims tae rectify it."

"Does he know where I am?"

"I dinna believe so. He's searched other towns and villages on MacKinnon land, but none o' them ken ye. It willn'ae be so easy tae keep ye hidden from him if he comes tae Ardmoir though. Too many folk ken ye."

And the last thing I wanted to do was to bring trouble to Conall and Ailsa's door. "What should I do? Should I leave?"

He grunted. "I'd no' turn ye out, lass. But as far as what ye should dae, that depends. Dae ye want tae marry MacDougall?"

"No." I shook my head. There was no question about that. I didn't want anything to do with him.

"Good. That's what I'd prayed ye'd say. I've thought hard on what might be done tae help ye, and I ken yer no' so pleased wi'Cailen for bringing ye here, but I think he was right tae dae so. We can only hope that ye'll be mairrit before MacDougall comes. If ye're another man's wife, then he canna exactly stake any claim on ye, aye?"

I knew he was going to say something like that. But really? Stake a claim, like I was some kind of property? The eighteenth century was so effed up.

"Liam Black came tae see me today," Conall continued after a few seconds' silence. "And verra timely, I might add. He's asked ma permission tae marry ye."

I blinked, trying hard not to show any emotion as I stared straight ahead of me, doing my best to focus on where Bud the Second was taking me. *Breathe, Scar. You knew this was going to happen sooner or later.* But why had I been waiting for Cailen to come back home and profess his love to me?

Liam was one of the guys I'd hung out with a little bit over the last couple of weeks. He was nice, around my age, and he was good looking. My problem was that, whether I'd meant to or not, every man I met was automatically compared to the way Cailen had been before he betrayed me, and not one of them stacked up.

"What did you say to him?"

"I've agreed tae the match. I'd been ponderin' on what tae dae wi'yer predicament, and I didnae believe ye wanted tae marry Donnan MacDougall, so I accepted on yer behalf." He shrugged, giving me a half-smile that looked so much like Cailen's that my heart lurched. "I've seen the two o' ye talkin'. Ye seem comfortable wi'the lad, and he'd make a fine husband. He comes from a good family, ye ken, and he's plenty o' money tae support ye and any bairns that'll come."

Ice prickled up my spine and through my limbs. I couldn't do anything more than nod as Conall listed all the reasons I should be happy to be engaged to a man I hardly knew. And what was worse, if I didn't go through with it, then I was going to be forcefully married to a man who

190

scared me.

"…one week's time."

"I'm sorry, what?" I asked, focusing on him.

"He's chosen one week from today. He wanted tae speak wi'ye himself, tae make ye a proper proposal, but he and his da left early this morn tae find a pastor. If one might be found before then, then ye'll be mairrit as soon as may be. If ye really dinna want Donnan MacDougall, then we must act fast."

Holy. Freakin'. Shit.

I couldn't tell which I felt more now, the blistering heat that erupted through my body, or the prickly icicles that scraped slowly through my veins, iceberging it toward my heart. I knew the lesser of the two evils. Liam seemed nice and gentle. I hadn't seen even a glimpse of that pushy, chauvinistic dominance that Donnan had shown me from the get-go.

"Ailsa asked Emily tae start mending a dress for ye," he added when I said nothing in response. "I dinna ken why she's taken such an interest, but she wants tae make sure yer gown is perfect. I think ye've made quite an impression on ma wife."

"Umm, okay." I pulled on Bud the Second, bringing him to a halt. "Do you mind if we just stop for a minute?"

"No' at all. Are ye all right?"

"Yeah, I'm just…Yeah." I was sick and breathless. The feeling washed through my body and took me down before I had a chance to slide off of the horse. The ground rose up to greet me, and pain erupted on the side of my head as the entire world began to spin.

"Lass!"

Conall's face came into view, his eyes darting over my face just before everything went hazy and darkness overtook me.

"...dear. Oh, Elizabeth, dear. Can ye hear me? It's Ailsa. Dearie, can ye hear me?"

I groaned and pressed my palms over my eyes, blocking out the light I could see through my eyelids. "What happened?"

"Och, thank the Lord. *Conall!*"

Lifting my hands from my face, I blinked up at Ailsa. The second I got a good look at her, I realized I was in my own bed at their house. "How did I get here?"

"Ye're verra lucky Conall was wi'ye. Who kens what might hae happened if ye'd been out there on yer own." She shook her head and patted my hand. "I take it yer upcomin' marriage came as quite a shock?"

I chuckled and sat up, earning a glare from the doctor as he felt my forehead. "You could say that." When Doctor McCrary finally stepped away from me, I glanced at Ailsa. "Where I'm from, women get to choose who they marry."

Cailen's dad chose that minute to stroll through the door, and breathed a sigh of relief. "Glad tae see ye're up."

"Yeah. Thanks for bringing me back." Or maybe not. Why couldn't I have woken up in 2013, after traveling while unconscious? Just like last time. Being back in Ardmoir meant that I was getting married in less than a week. "Do you know what happened?"

"Conall said ye stopped breathin'," Ailsa replied. She pressed a cold, wet cloth to my face and I hissed in a breath as she pressed it to the left side of my head.

"Aye, and ye didnae start again until ye were out. I couldn'ae wake ye."

"As soon as ye were home, Cameron kent what happened. Cailen told him o' it before he left." Ailsa leaned in closer. "Cameron's doonstairs waitin' for news o' ye. He's been fair worried."

"We've sent someone for Liam," Conall added. "He'd

192

want tae be here wi'ye. Wi'any luck he should arrive shortly."

Oh, God. Breath in, two, three, four. Breath out, two, three, four.

"Would the two o' ye excuse us? I'd like tae speak wi'Elizabeth alone."

My eyelids popped open at Ailsa's voice as Conall glanced at the doctor. "Aye, dear," he said before the two men left the room, talking in hushed voices.

"I like ye, Elizabeth—"

I cringed, not for the first time, at hearing that name. "Please don't call me that."

"That's one thing I wanted tae talk tae ye about. I ken there's somethin' ye're no' tellin' me. Why dae ye no' want us tae call ye Elizabeth?"

"Because that's what he called me." It was our thing. He called me Elizabeth, and I didn't want anyone else to.

Ailsa studied me for a little while, opening her mouth to talk only closing it again, until she finally said, "What name dae ye want us tae use?"

"I haven't decided yet. My name belongs to my old life. It has nothing to do with this one."

"Cailen told us ye dinna hae family anymore. What happened?"

I picked at the blanket that rested on my lap as she pulled her legs up onto the bed and sat Indian style. "I can't really tell you. Cailen made me promise."

"Why would he make ye dae that?"

"He said people wouldn't believe me, and that bad things could happen if I told anybody."

"Well, that's prob'ly ma fault. He came tae us about somethin' years ago, and neither Conall nor I believed him. I think that's why he left. I may no' believe things happened the way he says they did, but I'll ne'er again dismiss anyone the way I did him."

"I don't know." I shook my head. "It sounds completely insane. I think Cailen's right, I should just shut up and leave the past in the past." Or the future in the past. That was confusing.

I'd never seen that expression on Ailsa's before, but I suddenly felt six years old again, gaping up at my mom when she'd caught me coloring all over my bedroom walls with her Sharpies.

"Talk. Now."

"Please just don't think I'm crazy, okay?" After she nodded, I continued, "I know I'm different than everyone here. I don't sound anything like you or dress or act like you. I'm not used to your customs, and I'm used to sitting on my butt all day unless there's something fun to do." In the last two weeks, I'd helped milk cows, sheer sheep, witnessed two babies' births, learned how to make bread by hand, and discovered the art of catching fish—which I hated. The days of going for long drives, playing video games, flirting with guys at the mall, and bathing daily were long gone. "And it's because I'm not from here."

"Aye, I ken that. Ye're from the Colonies."

"Yeah, only where I'm from, we call it the United States, and the state I live in isn't even a state yet. I'm from the year 2013."

Ailsa's eyes bugged momentarily before she closed her eyes and mouthed some words before looking at me again. "Ye think ye're from the future?"

"Yes, because I am. Where I'm from, there are big cities with paved roads and hardly any trees. We have cars that can go a hundred miles an hour with a press of a foot. We buy all our food at big grocery stores that have more food stocked in them than everyone in Ardmoir could eat in a month. I came to Scotland by flying in a huge airplane

194

that had over a hundred people on it, and I made it from where I live in the U.S. to Glasgow in less than a day."

She shook her head. "It isn'ae possible."

"It is," I insisted, grabbing her hands. "I don't know why I've been sent to this time, but I promise you that I'm telling you the truth. The clothes that I had on that one day were what I was wearing the day I got dumped here…now."

"Ye told Cailen o' this?"

I nodded. "That's why he brought me here. I showed him proof that I don't belong in this century, and that was when he decided that my only chance was if I found a husband. I can tell you don't believe me, and I don't have any proof anymore other than a dead cell phone and a few things in my purse."

I slid off the bed and bent down next to my bag, pulling out my phone and the pocket watch that started this whole mess. Sitting down again, I offered my phone to her, which she inspected.

"It's my cell phone. It's how I proved everything to Cailen. And then there's this." I handed over the pocket watch. "This is what I was holding when I got sent back over two hundred and forty years."

Ailsa's face stiffened and she took it from me, studying the design on the outer case before opening it and peering at the face. "Where did ye get this?"

"Some guy in a pub. I was having lunch with my friend and he freaked out before practically throwing that thing at me. Next thing I knew, I was here."

"What did he look like?" Her eyes were wide, desperate.

"I don't know. He was wearing a cloak so he was mostly covered, but at the end, I did get a glimpse of his eyes." I met her gaze. "They looked a lot like yours.

Actually, he kinda looked…like you."

Ailsa gripped the pocket watch so tightly that her knuckles had gone white, her face was almost equally as pale.

"Ailsa," I said slowly. "Are you okay?"

A tear slid down her cheek. "What is yer name, dear?"

"What?"

"Yer name. What is yer real name." She gripped my wrist with one of her hands, and I felt the trembling of her body. "E'en if ye dinna want tae go by it now, I must ken it."

"Scarlett. My name is Scarlett"

"Scarlett," she whispered to herself. "Michaelson?"

I nodded.

She slumped on the bed, exhaling with relief.

"Ailsa?"

She launched forward and pulled me into an embrace. "Oh, Scarlett. I'll ne'er be able tae repay ye for this. For two years he's been lost, wi'nae word on where he is."

"Cailen?"

"Nae." She pulled back, meeting my eyes. "I bought this watch for ma son for his birthday. I gave it tae him the morn he disappeared. Dinna ye see? This is Kieran's." She held up the pocket watch as more tears welled in her eyes. "Kieran's gone tae yer time tae send ye tae Cailen."

CHAPTER THIRTEEN

Liam had returned to Ardmoir a lot sooner than anyone expected, and his arrival had sent the entire village into an excited frenzy—everyone but me, and surprisingly, Conall and Ailsa.

I hadn't learned anything new about what Cailen's mom had been mumbling about in my bedroom, and Cameron's sudden disappearance meant I had no one to give me intel. I missed the boy and his shy smile and quick wit, and wished that I knew where he'd gone. I'd asked his parents, but neither of them had told me, immediately changing the subject to village business. Their excitement over the wedding had diminished noticeably, now seeming to match my own. Now if I could only get everyone else on board with not wanting my forced wedding. The entire village of Ardmoir was buzzing about Liam's return with one of their favorite reverends, who I'd met one of my first days here when Ailsa had hauled me to "kirk".

Even now, I knelt behind the sheep that Merna MacKinnon sheered, hoping Liam and Reverend Astor wouldn't spot me as I held the sheep still for her. I'd seen them strolling through the village, visiting with clansmen and women, and—as I'd feared—searching for me. One of the older men they'd spoken to pointed in my direction and I ducked down low, smiling up at Merna as she narrowed her eyes on me.

"Just thought I'd get more comfortable." I grinned, hoping I didn't look guilty.

I wasn't sure what type of response I was about to get

from her, because she turned suddenly, brightening at the sight of the two men strolling toward us. "Och, if it isn'ae Reverend Astor and Liam Black," she chimed. "I'm certain they've come tae discuss yer marriage, aye?"

"That's what I'm afraid of," I mumbled as I peered to my left and right. Damn, there was nowhere else I could hide.

"Miss Michaelson. How nice tae see ye again," Reverend Astor said, his red, round face smiling down at me from over the sheep's back. "Mr. Black and I were hopin' tae hae a wee chat wi'ya. If ye've the time."

"Umm." I cleared my throat. "Do you think we could meet later? I'm helping Merna with the sheep."

"I will'nae hear o' it," Merna grunted. "Go chat wi'yer man and the nice reverend. I can manage on ma own."

Liam rushed around the sheep and offered a hand, helping me to my feet. "Good day tae ye, Elizabeth."

Seriously. Did I have to tell every person in Ardmoir individually? I didn't want people to call me that! "Uh, hi Liam."

"Would ye join the reverend and me? We've much tae discuss."

"Sure." I stared at the ground as I fell into step beside him.

Astor walked on the other side of me so I was between the two men. "I understand the two o' ye would like tae marry as soon as may be?"

"Aye," Liam answered.

"I don't know," I said at the same time. "I'm not sure we really have to rush."

"Oh, but we dae. Conall told me o' yer wee problem wi'the MacDougalls." Liam pulled me in close, wrapping his arm around my shoulder as if he were consoling me. We walked in silence for a few steps before he faced the reverend. "Would ye mind terribly if Elizabeth and I speak in private?"

"Nae. I hear the Smytt's had a wee baby they'd like me tae visit. I'll be wi'them. Good day, Elizabeth. Good day, Liam."

We both nodded and he took off down the hill, on his way to the Smytt's house. I mostly kept my eyes on his retreating form, but finally glanced up at my fiancé as Liam turned toward me.

He sighed. "Dae ye mind if I speak frankly?"

"No."

"Good...I like ye. Verra much so. That's why I spoke wi'Conall MacKinnon about makin' ye ma bride." He shrugged slightly. "I ken I should'ae talked tae ye first, but, well...ye dinna hae a faither for me tae ask first, so I went tae Conall. I've watched ye since ye came tae town wi'us that day, and I ken that yer thoughts are wi'Cailen."

I blinked, unable to keep the flush from creeping up my neck to my cheeks. Was it that obvious to everyone?

"I think I could make ye happy if ye'd just give me a chance. I may no' be as learned as he is, or be in line for the lairdship o' Ardmoir, but I hae a good family, and I'm a hard worker. I'll spend ma days providin' for ye and our bairns, and I'll dae everythin' in ma power tae please ye. If ye'll give me the chance."

"I—"

"I ken ye dinna love me. All I ask is that ye give me a chance. E'en if it's only tae keep ye from the MacDougalls."

Bloody hell. It'd been weeks since he'd seen Elizabeth, and he'd spent every waking—and sleeping—moment thinking about her. At times, it was her feistiness that occupied his mind, while other times, he'd lose himself just thinking of the way she'd reacted to that wee toy in her bag. He'd spend the rest of his days dreaming about that, and didn't much want to regret leaving her behind. He'd left her in capable hands, kenning well enough that his mam and da would take care of her and see her to a good husband. But the thought of her married to someone else sent him into fits of rage. Sometimes he felt sick over it.

Which is why he'd never left Mull, and why he'd spent every day scouring the land for the bloody witch who cursed him.

In times past, he'd searched for her with an entirely different plan in mind, but this time, he'd meant only to speak to her, to learn more about the curse that had destroyed his family.

Ducking down low in the heather, he trained his eyes on a group of men and women traveling on horseback over the hills. They could be MacLeans, but he was too far away to tell for certain.

Once they passed, he set back into motion, approaching a small cave he'd stumbled on years ago, not far from where he and Kieran found the witch. Dropping into the cave from the upper ledge, his feet smacked against the small rocks, the sound echoing off the cave walls. He ducked inside, following it as silently as possible, listening for signs of anyone, or anything, inside.

No one was there, nor had they been for quite some time.

Sitting down on the cold rock, he leaned his back against the wall and pulled a bit of dried seaweed from his sporran. A few bites into it, he put it back. He just didn't have an appetite. Not when every thought was with Elizabeth. He'd not only left his mind with her, but his heart, too.

What was he doing? He couldn't leave her to another man. *He* wanted her. *He* needed to spend his life loving her and caring for her. Be damned to that witch and her curse. Kieran wouldn't fault him for following his heart, if he was even alive. And certainly his mam, da, and Cameron would celebrate that he'd finally found happiness. If he cursed his family further, then they'd deal with it then.

He refused to run from life any longer. It was time to embrace it, and to win Elizabeth back.

Standing, he rushed from the cave and lowered himself to the rocks below the opening. If he took a direct path north, he could reach Ardmoir within a day. Besides, that close to the sea meant more opportunities to squat inside caves for the night. As far as he kent, nearby clans didn't frequent them, so it should make for faster travel back home.

More time passed, and so did more thoughts of his lass. The sun had set before he'd seen another soul on the beach. The orange glow of a fire flickered from a slight indent in the rock, and Cailen sped up his pace, sneaking up on the lone traveler. Whoever it was, he wasn't careful to remain hidden....

"Cameron," he gaped. "What dae ye think yer daein' all the way out here?"

His wee brother whirled around with his dirk in hand as he let out a terrified breath. "Cailen! Ye should ken better than tae sneak up on me. I could'ae killed ye." He took another breath and re-sheathed his dirk. "I've been searchin' for ye. Mam sent me tae fetch ye. Ye're needed at home presently. It's about Elizabeth."

Cailen's heart sank and he sat down, waiting to hear what was amiss.

"She's gettin' mairrit," Cameron continued. "Tae Liam

Black."

"*Liam*? Nae, no' *him*." Surely his da wouldn't marry Elizabeth off to the blundering gowk who'd been solely responsible for setting the kirk on fire. The man had been nothing but a mess since he could mind.

"Aye. But she shouldn'ae be marryin' him. She should be marryin' ye. We all feel that the two o' ye belong taegether."

He'd been about to tell his brother to mind his own business, but that last part quieted him. "Truly? But what about the curse?"

"Mam says we dinna need tae fash about that anymore. She—"

"Shhh…" Cailen held up a hand, silencing his brother. He'd heard movement up on the rocky hill above them. "Snuff the fire and hide. We're no' alone."

He stood and jumped onto a boulder, pulling himself up onto another one higher up. The entire area was nothing but crags, and every move he made sent small rocks tumbling down to where his brother had killed the flames, and hid somewhere nearby. He'd been only thirty feet away from where he'd left Cameron when a man's arm came into view. Cailen moved to pull the man from his hiding place, but came face-to-face with a gun pointed between his eyes.

"Well, it's ma lucky day. Donnan's been lookin' all o'er for ye, MacKinnon"

"Is that so?"

"Aye, yer wanted for attackin' him in his own home, and he's offered a nice reward for yer heed."

I felt cold with sweat as Emily and Una finished dressing me in the red tartan dress they'd made for the wedding.

Ailsa had been in the room the entire time, but she'd been distracted, pulling back the window covering and checking outside every few minutes.

"She's ready, mum," Emily said, causing Cailen's mom to look at me for the first time.

"Oh lass, ye look just beautiful." She drummed her fingers on her lap and stood up nervously before taking my hand. "I guess it's time for us tae go tae the kirk."

"I guess so." I squeezed her hand, wondering why she was so twitchy as we walked from my room. "What's wrong?"

"Naethin'. It's just that…well, we've received word that MacDougall and his men reached the village closest tae us last night. I fear we've run out o' time."

Which meant I couldn't stall anymore without running the risk of Donnan finding out. "I understand."

We'd made it out of Ailsa and Conall's house, and followed the dirt path past the dyke and out into the village.

"I hope ye ken how much I'd love tae hae ye for a daughter, Scarlett," Ailsa said sadly. "I've prayed Cailen would come in time, that he'd see that the two o' ye belong taegether."

I inhaled, flicking my gaze at her as we neared the church where every man and woman in Ardmoir were already gathering. "Wh…I mean you…You think we should be together?"

"Aye. So dae Conall and Cameron. That's where Cameron's gone, tae tell Cailen tae come back."

And he hadn't. Cameron left days ago. If he'd even had enough time to reach him and come back, then that would've meant that Cailen had chosen not to come for me.

Unless he hadn't had enough time.

"I'm afraid it's too late now though," Ailsa continued. "We just canna risk leavin' ye free for Donnan MacDougall tae claim ye as his own."

"What right would he have to take me?"

"He's the brither o' a chieftain. The entire MacDougall clan could descend on us if he asked it o' them. We'd fight for ye, lass, but I dinna ken that our whole clan would be inclined tae. Ye're no' part o' our clan until yer mairrit tae one."

I pulled her to a stop just as three women rushed toward us, gushing over my dress—which probably looked the exact same as each of theirs had, since it seemed every bride wore a tartan dress on her wedding day—and tittered over how stunning Liam Black looked in his freshly washed kilt. They shoved a bundle of flowers into my hands and tugged my hair into place before rushing me through the door of the church. It felt like everyone inside went silent, and I glanced at Ailsa, who was still by my side.

Conall approached and bowed. "Ye look bonny, hen." He flicked his gaze at his wife and even I could tell that there'd been a short, silent conversation between them. He stepped in closer, bending over to speak to me quietly. "I ken I'm no' yer da, and I'd ne'er mean tae replace him, but I would be greatly honored if ye'd allow me tae give ye awa."

I hadn't realized I'd gripped Ailsa's hand even tighter until she'd yelped and yanked her hand from my own.

"Breathe lass. Dinna faint. Keep breathin'," she whispered.

I sucked in a breath and let it out slowly before turning my gaze on her. "Do you think he loves me?"

"Liam?" Conall asked, flicking his gaze between the two of us.

"Cailen," Ailsa replied, shaking her head in exasperation. "And yes. I dae."

His mom believed it. I had to, too.

"I can't marry Liam. I have to see if he comes for me. We don't know anything until Cameron comes back."

"There's nae time," Gregor McIntosh said, stepping up from behind Ailsa. "There are men on horses ridin' toward Ardmoir e'en now."

"MacDougall?"

"I dinna ken. I couldn'ae see their tartan."

Conall's brows lowered and he walked to the door of the church. "How far?"

"We'll be able tae see them any second. I saw them in the distance while on ma way here."

Cailen's dad peered out the door and shut it tight before whirling around to face me. "Nae time. We must start now."

"Can't we just tell them I'm already married or something? They don't have to know if I really am or not."

"We'd need someone tae claim ye, and nae one would dae that unless ye're his wife." Conall gripped my elbow and led me toward the altar where reverend Astor and Liam Black stood. "If the man is that intent on havin' ye, then he'll require proof. He'll demand tae meet yer husband. I wish it were different, lass." He made eye contact with the reverend. "We must begin. Now."

Now? We had to start now? My mind scrambled, desperate to find any other option. Cameron had gone after Cailen. I'd never forget how he had rejected me before, but my heart had to know if he still felt that way.

Liam took my hands so that we faced each other, and everyone in the church quieted once more with a quick command from Conall.

Reverend Astor started speaking, but every word he said didn't register. I only heard his voice, only saw the smile on Liam's face, only felt the beat of my heart. Liam spoke now, his voice shaking as his hands tightened around mine. *Breathe in. Breathe out.* And now it was Astor again. His voice echoed through church, fading away as every eye focused on me. There was only silence, and a few uncomfortable coughs coming from the pews.

"Elizabeth?"

Liam's voice reached me through the haze and I concentrated on him, feeling as though everything was going in slow motion. I couldn't go through with this. Even if Donnan was outside with all his men, I couldn't just give in and marry another man to save my own ass. I wanted the man I loved.

"I'll lie for ye. I'll tell'em yer ma wife. Ye dinna have tae go through wi'this."

I blinked at him, running his words over in my mind. *Oh my God. He's stepping down?*

The door to the church crashed open and the sound of someone running drew my attention. "It's the MacDougalls," Cameron yelled, saying the words I'd feared. "They've taken Cailen."

He reached me just as Conall and Ailsa did, the four of us standing in a circle. "What's happened?" his dad asked.

"I found him out there. He was still on Mull," the boy replied. "Someone took him, and I o'er heard him say that the MacDougalls put a price on his heed."

Ailsa gasped and gripped Conall's hand. "What can we dae?"

"I have to go for him," I said.

"Yer no' goin' after Cailen." Liam shook his head. "I'm willin' tae lie for ye, but I draw the line at lettin' ye risk yerself for him. Right Conall?"

Cailen's dad opened his mouth and shut it again.

I peered at Liam from over my shoulder. "I'm sorry, but I have to try. I refuse to let him die for protecting me from that asshole." I faced Cailen's parents and brother again, meeting each of their eyes. "I love him. If there's anything I can do to save his life, I'm going to do it."

Conall released Ailsa's hand as I stalked past them, down the aisle toward the door. "Gi'us a minute, lass. Yer no' goin' alone."

Donnan's voice boomed throughout the barn, the sound mixing with the shuffling of the nearby animals. The scent of his own blood burned his nose as it mixed with the overwhelming tang of cow and horse shit.

The MacDougalls had holed him up in there, chasing off the property owners so no one was nearby to hear him. He hadn't kent how long he'd been there—days, likely— nor did he ken where Cameron was. He prayed the lad made it safely away. The last thing Cailen needed was to be responsible for another brother's disappearance, nor yet another reason to be a disappointment to his mam and da— or that of Ardmoir.

There were two horses, three sheep—including one lamb that couldn't be much older than a few weeks—one cow, three chickens, and rooster. He'd counted the animals over and over again, using them as a distraction to escape what was happening. He was in a great deal of pain, and had lost more blood than he cared to consider. The owners had quite a collection of animals, considering how far inland they must be. He couldn't even hear the sounds of the ocean, nor that of ships passing by. And he'd listened.

A hard fist pounded against his face, and his entire body spun as the rope wrapping his wrists twisted ever tighter. That was Angus's fist. The man had been at it at Donnan MacDougall's behest, delivering blow after blow whenever Cailen refused to answer—or when he gave an answer Donnan didn't like. Another punch, and he spit his blood onto the straw below him, which was now covered in bright and dark blood.

"I'm no' lyin'." He was. "Elizabeth is long gone. I was tasked wi'seein' her awa'." Donnan's eyes grew heated again, and so he continued. "I helped her tae Tabbor Moire. She caught the first ship that would take her home."

"And where would that be?"

"She's gone tae the Colonies."

MacDougall narrowed his eyes and leaned against the back of the chair. "Angus?"

This one landed square in Cailen's stomach, and he coughed, spitting out more blood. Every drop was worth it, so long as it meant Elizabeth didn't fall into this bastard's hands. He groaned, opening his mouth. It was all he could do to breathe through his mouth. His nose had long since swollen up to the point he could hardly get air.

Donnan continued to eye him from the comfort his chair—one which he'd taken from the owners home and placed a few feet in front of Cailen. Far enough he didn't get splattered with blood, but close enough he could see every speck of damage.

"I've sent half ma men tae search Mull. I hae it in mind tae kill ye either way, but I would like ye tae see when they bring her tae me."

"And what good would it dae tae be killin' me?"

Donnan scoffed. "I've a price on yer heed, MacKinnon. Ye attacked ma nephew, the son o' our chieftain. And ye entered ma home wi'out consent, and attacked me. I had tae fight for ma life, and lost ma bonny wee lass in the process."

"She's ne'er been yer lass, nor will she e'er be," Cailen gritted.

"She will be mine!"

"And what is it ye want wi'her? Why dae ye want her so?"

"Same reasons ye dae, I expect. I'm no' a fool. I saw the way ye looked at her. It's no' often men like us come across a lass like her, is it?"

He had no idea.

Donnan continued, "She's unlike any other woman I've met. And best o' all, she's no' tied tae any clan. Nae one will fight for her—'cept for ye, it seems—and nae clans will be at odds for me takin' her. A lass like Elizabeth demands power. Any who meet her desire her, respect her—"

"And ye think that forcin' her intae marriage wi'a man she doesn'ae want is *respecting* her?"

Cailen gritted his teeth as the words he spoke caught up with him. It was the very thing he'd done to her. *He* had forced her into a marriage she hadn't wanted. When she'd asked him for any other option, he'd refused to even discuss it, and told her she had to marry. Bile rose into his throat. For the first time, he felt like he and Donnan MacDougall were very much alike in that sense. And it rankled.

There was one difference though: Cailen wanted to correct his mistake.

Donnan stood and stalked over to him, glaring into his eyes. "Aye. Makin' her ma wife will mean she'll ne'er want for anythin'. She'll be a woman o' status and respect tae all her ken her. What could ye possibly offer her more than that?"

If she were mine, she'd one day be the Lady o' Ardmoir. And she'd hae the man who would love her more than any other could. And I'll spend the rest o' ma days provin' it tae her.

Elizabeth was his lass, and though she was about to become another Scot's wife, she'd forever be his. She'd staked her claim on his heart, and he'd keep it for her. Until his last breath and beyond.

"That's what I thought," Donnan spat, evidently taking Cailen's silence as having no reply, and forcing his thoughts from the one place they wanted to be. He stepped back from him, returning to the chair he'd spent most of his time on. "I've grown tired o' yer lies. For two days, ye've done naethin' but deceive me about her whereabouts." Crossing his ankle over his knee, he peered up at Cailen. "I've warred wi'myself on what's tae be done wi'ya, but I ken now that ye'll ne'er give the lass up. I'll no' waste another minute on ye. Angus, string him up."

"If there is a price on ma head, then I should be tried before yer chieftain."

MacDougall shrugged. "Ye didnae come wi'us peacefully and we were forced tae take immediate action. Right Angus?"

"Aye."

Cailen's throat sank into his stomach, and he worked fitfully at loosening the ropes that bound his wrists. He was mostly suspended, only the tips of his toes touched the straw stacked on the ground. Twisting his wrists and attempting to wrench them apart made absolutely no difference in the rope. It held as tight as ever, feeling somehow tighter as Cailen watched Angus throw another rope over the truss above him. He made a noose.

No, he couldn't die like this. He couldn't leave this world kenning that the last words between Elizabeth and him had been in anger.

Angus approached, looping the noose around Cailen's neck, not slowing despite his thrashing. The binds around his wrists were slashed and he tried to rush away, only to be stopped by the big bastard.

"I trust ye'll take care o' this," Donnan said. He stepped to the wide door leading outside. "Ye ken I dinna like tae witness such things."

Angus smiled cruelly before Cailen was whipped backwards, his feet leaving the ground as he was raised into the air.

He gasped as the rope dug into his neck, closing off any hope of breath coming in or leaving him. He fought it the only way he could, by forcing his fingers between his skin and the rope, and he inhaled a tiny bit of air before it tightened once more. Angus spoke, but Cailen couldn't see or hear anything clearly any longer. He couldn't even mutter the name he longed to leave his lips before the world faded away, and he felt no more.

CHAPTER FOURTEEN

"Are you sure this is it?" I laid in the grass alongside Conall and Cameron, peering up over the tall grass the same way they did.

Conall lowered himself closer to the ground and flicked his gaze at me. "It must be. They said this is where their farm was. I dinna think they would be mistaken."

"But there's nothing here," I argued. "When we were taken to the MacDougall camp before, they were in a little town with a tavern and small houses."

"There's plenty here. They have more than enough space tae hold someone. And besides, they wouldn'ae want tae take o'er an entire village. Two people are much easier tae o'ercome than a town."

"I still dinna think Scarlett shouldn't go," Cameron said, speaking for the first time since we'd spotted the small farm. He'd voiced his opinion plenty of times on our way.

I lowered myself again so I was eye-to-eye with Cailen's brother. "And I'm not about to let anyone go into this and get more people hurt. Donnan is after me. If I can get Cailen out, then I will." Even if I had to offer myself to him to get Cailen free, then I'd do it. I'd do anything for him.

"But what if Cailen is already deed?" the young Scot asked. "He'll be fair upset wi'us for sendin' his lass tae his enemy for not."

"Dinna assume he's deed," Conall grunted. "Cailen's a smart lad. He'll dae what he must tae survive."

I looked back and forth between the two guys. "We're not discussing this anymore. And no, you're not 'sending' me in. I'm going because I choose to. Just give me a weapon, and let me go and see what the hell is going on."

Both of their mouths gaped open, but Conall reached into his sporran, extracting a small knife very similar to the one Cailen had in his. "Ma sghian dubh. Hae ye e'er used one, lass?"

"No," I replied, shaking my head as I took it from him. "Cailen let me hold his during that boar attack, and my dad made me gut a fish once, so I know my general way around it." Peering at the knife, I ran my fingers over the detail. "This looks just like his."

"Aye, it would. He made them. Put that somewhere ye can reach it easily. And dinna stick yerself," he warned. "One last question for ye then."

I shoved the pointy end of the knife down into my stocking, just above my shoe. "Okay."

Cailen's dad's gaze clashed with mine. "Could ye kill someone if the occasion called for it?"

I didn't look away from him. I simply stared into the man's eyes, weighing his words. He was trying to talk me out of going. "For Cailen, I would." I rolled slightly, putting most of my weight on my elbow. "I can do this. I know I can. I've played video…" *No, wait.* "I've trained for this. I know how to remain hidden. I can be stealthy." *In theory.* "I can stay calm—"

"Can ye keep breathin'?" Cameron asked doubtfully.

"I have to," I replied, rolling again so I was on my stomach, looking back and forth between them. "I have to do this for him. If I need help, I'll find *some way* to let you know."

"I should go."

I looked at Conall. "You're too valuable."

"But he's ma son."

"Your clan needs you. Your family needs you. If something went wrong, what would happen to Ailsa? To Ardmoir? And Cameron, what about you? You're fourteen years old, you haven't even started your life yet. We don't know who saw you on the beach that night? They could kill you just from recognition alone. But they won't kill me. I'm our best bet. I'll search for him, and if I can't find him, I'll come right back. Please, just let me do this."

"All right." The older Scot's eyes saddened. "Just…dinna go for the doors. Ye'll likely be seen, so stick tae the shadows and see if there are other ways inside. And dinna go inside if ye hear anyone."

I nodded. "Got it."

Conall patted me on the back, smiling at me in a way that reminded me of my own dad. I realized in that moment that I really did care about Cailen's family. I wanted to keep them safe, just like I wanted Cailen to be safe. I didn't want anything to happen to Conall or Ailsa, and I wanted Cameron to have a long happy life. Even Kieran's memory was so much a part of the family that I prayed he found his way home, and I thought that, just maybe, I'd forget about the whole ball kicking thing.

"Yer a brave lass, and yer just as stubborn as Ailsa. Ye dae both ma son and yer da proud."

Tears prickled my eyes, and I cleared my throat. I wondered just what my dad would think if he saw me now. He wouldn't let me go for Cailen, that's for sure. And Jason…we'd have to tackle him to the ground to keep him away. But they weren't here. Conall and Cameron were. These men were more than just my friends. I'd grown to love them like family.

"Okay. You guys stay here. I'll flag you down if I need help. Otherwise I'll be right back."

"Scarlett, be careful, aye? We'll be right here, or closer if we can. Ye'll no' be alone."

I gave them a confident smile and crawled through the tall grass, keeping as low to the ground as I could. It was tall enough now that I could have practically sat up without being seen, but there was no telling who was watching the fields. I'd reached a tree before I heard two Scots talking to each other. Keeping as silent and still as possible, I waited until they were far enough away that I dared continue on.

More army crawling, more stopping to listen. Another man spoke now, his commands were short and clipped, and the other men responded, jumping to every command. I popped my head up and saw Donnan standing in the doorway of the house. One of his men stalked from the barn and stepped up to the door beside him. The two spoke for a few seconds before disappearing inside the home. I shuffled forward again, changing course slightly as I crawled toward the barn. I reached the edge of the grass and peered around, searching for any sign of someone who could potentially see me. It felt like an eternity before every Scot in sight either turned away or disappeared around the house.

I ran for it, bolting to the side of the barn, leaning against it as I listened for any sign that someone had seen me. No pissed off Highlanders came barreling around the corner with guns or knives, so I peered at the decrepit building, searching for any way inside. This was built differently than the homes I'd seen since my arrival in this time. I thought it looked a lot more comfortable. The barn was built with slats of wood, and unlike the houses, didn't have a single window. I didn't dare check the side of the barn closest to the house, so I snuck to the front and checked around the corner. Nope, no Scots in sight.

Here goes nothing.

I lifted the skirt of my tartan wedding dress and shot around the corner, dodging through the barn door. I startled the animals inside and skidded to a stop as I turned and shut the door as slowly as possible. It creaked, and I prayed anyone in earshot would assume it closed from the wind.

Resting my forehead against the wood, I released a long breath. Dear God, I hoped no one was inside. I turned, looking around the barn, my heart sinking as I saw that I wasn't so lucky.

And neither was Cailen.

He was hanging by his neck, the rope strung tight between him and the rafters. His head was cantered to the side, his eyes closed and his mouth open. My Highlander's entire face was beaten and bloody, the evidence of his torture ran from head to toe, leaving drops of crimson in the hay below him. His right hand was at his neck, probably from when he'd tried to pry the rope loose.

It was a sight I'd never forget.

I didn't realize I'd moved my feet until hand brushed over his kilt. Tears fell, and my throat felt as though someone had strangled me the way they had my sweetheart. I cried for him. Cried for the mess I'd made of his life. Cried for what could have been. For how I'd treated him.

How could life be so cruel? Why would fate drop me into his lap only to have him die?

I wrapped my arms around his legs, hugging the only part I could reach. This wasn't how it was supposed to be. We should have been together, not apart. I pressed my cheek to his shin as I hugged him, letting all my pain flow into the last connection we'd ever have.

Could angels feel anything like that?

His skin was still warm, and the thought that I'd barely missed him brought on a fresh wave of agony. He'd died at the hands of a monster because of me. And because I'd acted like a child, I hadn't been there to save him. Or to even make sure he hadn't died alone.

His foot twitched, and I scrambled backward, gaping up at him. Holy jeez, his foot twitched again! My gaze shot upward, and I saw the slightest movement of his fingers at his neck.

And then a short, shallow breath.

Oh my God.

"Cailen!" I cried. He was alive. My God, I had to get him down!

I bent and plucked the sghian dubh from my stocking and glanced up at the rope he was dangling from, following it down to where it was tied around a pillar. I sawed at the gigantic rope, each section fraying and popping as I cut as frantically as I could.

"Hold on, baby. I'll get you down." More cutting, more cutting. The final strands broke free.

Cailen crashed to the ground, falling into the bloodstained hay. I was by his side in a second, doing my best to pull the rope away from his throat. He wheezed, desperately dragging in bigger breaths as he gripped the rope, also trying to loosen its hold.

I slid the knife between the rope and his neck, carefully sawing at the noose. "Hold on, Cailen. Please…just hold on, baby. Hold on."

Finally the rope broke and the two halves fell away from him. He rolled, coughing hard as his hands clamped around his neck.

"No, no, don't get up. You can't get up. God, you're alive. I didn't think…I thought you were…But you're…You're alive!" I was laughing and crying. Every emotion washed through me at once.

"I'm so sorry," he breathed. "Shouldn'ae left…Love ye."

Did he just say what I think he did?

I bent down and pressed kiss after kiss all over his face, not caring that my tears were all over him. He'd said he loved me. He was alive. I could have kissed him forever, and would have if it weren't for the fact that we could be killed at any second. I flicked my gaze around the barn, searching for anything I could use to help him. There was no way we were getting out of here undetected, and my Highlander was in too bad of shape to get out under his own steam.

Two voices reached me from outside the barn. The door was still closed, but it might not be for long. The men were talking to each other, and they were getting louder.

We'd run out of time.

I looked down into Cailen's eyes and ran my fingers through his hair. "This might hurt, but I don't know what else to do." I stood and gripped his hands, pulling on him as hard as I could as I backtracked into the corner where the sheep lay. The hay in that corner was the thickest, and as I dragged him toward it, the three sheep stood and scampered away, voicing their irritation at me.

"*Shhhhhut up,*" I hissed. I bent and scooped up clumps of hay and tossed them over him. "Be as quiet as you can," I whispered. "I'll figure something out. Just be as quiet as you can."

I left him there, forcing my feet to take step after step toward the barn door. The voices were even closer now, and I had no way of knowing if the men planned to come inside. There was metal hanging from the wall, and I hurried to it, yanking it to the ground. I'd seen these in movies and TV shows my dad watched.

It was a trap.

Now, how to arm it?

It took me longer than I'd expected to figure it out, but

eventually, I'd wrenched the trap wide open, narrowly missing getting caught in it myself. Tip-toeing with the trap in hand, I set it just in front of the barn door, and gently scattered hay on top so it wouldn't be seen. The men stopped talking and I shuffled over to the wall, gripping a shovel as I waited.

I had barely enough time to come up with a plan as I studied the animals and tools inside. The door creaked open, and a man's shadow fell across the ground. I tightened my hold on the wooden handle, taking a silent breath.

"*What?*" he gaped. "Where did—*AGH!*"

The trap slammed shut with a metallic *clink*, and I leapt into action, slamming the barn door shut and shoving the metal bar into place that would hopefully lock it. I gripped the shovel in both hands and swung, feeling the hit reverberate up the handle and through my arms. The man went down, but he wasn't unconscious like I'd hoped. Face red, he reached out for me as a painful groan escaped him. I jumped back, but he caught my dress and took me to the ground. I struggled against him as he growled unintelligibly at me. He was on top now, and a hard fist slammed into my side. Tears blurred my eyes, and my arms automatically went down as my entire body contracted in pain. I continued to fight him, as useless as it was. I'd lost my shovel when he'd taken me down. I had nothing to inflict damage on him...

Except Conall's sghian dubh.

The asshole was still stuck in the trap, and I shoved my foot down, repeatedly kicking the trap as the man hollered in pain. He rolled off of me and I reached down, feeling for the knife. It wasn't there. It wasn't there! I'd used it to free Cailen.

I panicked, searching around me. The blade was lying

in the hay, maybe three feet from where I was. I brought my knee up again, shoving it into his side before I scrambled backward. My hand wrapped around the hilt, but the guy slammed his fist against my shin and dragged me back under him. There were more growled words I couldn't understand, and more voices coming from the other side of the barn door as fists pounded on the wood. The shaking of the door drew my attention and I glanced at it for a split second to make sure others weren't coming in.

I regretted looking away from the guy on top of me, because he landed a punch on my cheek. My head fell back into the hay, and I stared up at the rafters above, feeling a whole lot of pain throb through half my face.

"I dinna care if Donnan wants ye. Ye're gonna pay, wench."

I wanted to cry. In a ball. Preferably in the hay next to my Highlander. But I couldn't allow myself to give in. Cailen needed me. If I gave up, that could mean his life—or both of ours. Tightening my fist around the hilt of the dagger that still lay in my hand, I threw as much weight into it as I could, and stabbed the asshole in the side.

He yelled again, but his weight was still firmly planted on me. I couldn't get free. The scent of smoke hit my nose, and I peered over, gasping as the walls of the barn had started going up in flames. The animals were all rushing around now, probably as terrified as I was of burning to death.

I fought harder, desperate to get away. That only pissed the Scot off more though, and one of his hands wrapped around my neck, pinning me to the ground as his other hand went to the knife in his side. My hands went to the one around my neck and pushed as hard as I could for air.

No! I hadn't stopped breathing this time! For Cailen, I'd forced myself to keep breathing. I'd promised Cameron

I would keep breathing. And now this bastard was taking it away from me.

I kicked and rolled, trying anything to loosen his hold. He yanked the blade from his side and turned his maddened gaze on me. Flipping the knife around in his hand, he shoved the blade toward me, pressing it just above my breastbone. Panic overtook me as my mind blanked. I'd failed Cailen, and I'd failed his family. For the first time in my life, I wished that I would just pass out.

I didn't want to be awake just to die.

I held the Scot's gaze as the blade pressed into my skin. I pushed on his wrists with all my might, trying one last-ditch effort to save my life. The knife bit in harder and I managed a single squeak through my crushed throat. I couldn't feel much now, other than the pressure at my neck, and the feel of my tears trickling into my hair. I wasn't strong enough. I was a failure. It was no wonder Cailen had walked away from me.

The guy murmured something in in Gaelic, his tone sounded angry with a hint of finality. This was it. I was about to die.

Thwak.

I blinked as he was thrown off of me, his body clearing mine enough that I was able to scramble to my feet and gape at Cailen, who stood with the shovel in hand. Or half the shovel, anyway. It'd broken on impact.

"Ye...all right?" he wheezed, barely able to force the words out as he pressed a hand to his neck. It was barely discernible over the loud *whoosh* of flames all around us.

I nodded, breathing heavily. "You?"

He sort of nodded with a shrug.

"We have to get out of here." The smoke was thick enough that Cailen wasn't clear, even with as close as he was standing to me. My eyes teared as heat waves brushed past me and entered my lungs. The entire barn looked like it was moving from the waves, and it made me dizzy. "Get down to the ground, it'll make it easier to breathe." I dropped to my hands and knees, regretting moving so fast as my side throbbed.

Cailen got down too, only much slower.

"Our only way out is through that door, but Donnan's men are behind it."

My Highlander's gaze met mine, and I focused on his eyes, ignoring the swelling. His entire face wasn't black and blue, but a lot of it was.

"I was going to get you on a horse and get us out of here. Not sure that'll work now with the fire."

He coughed and winced. "Why?"

I guessed we could still escape on horseback, and opening the barn door would mean every animal in here could make it outside. "Okay, yeah. Let's do it."

Cailen swallowed hard and pointed to the smaller horse, which was running around in circles, chuffing and shaking her head side to side. "Can ye get on her? I'll...open the door and ye can ride through."

"What about you?"

"I'll get on that one."

"After I've already ridden out? No way." I shook my head. "We only have the element of surprise once. And if anyone is getting out of here, it's you."

He glared at me.

"You're in worse shape than I am. You're getting on that bigger horse and I'll open the door."

"I'll no' leave ye."

I didn't want him to leave me either, but I refused to

ride out of here without him. "Do you think you can pick me up on your way out?" We really didn't have time to be arguing about this. If we waited much longer, we weren't getting out at all. Cailen gave me a strange look that I couldn't read, so I scooted closer to him. "If I open the door and you start riding toward it, could you pick me up and throw me on there with you?"

He nodded, but didn't look happy about the idea.

"Then we can maybe both get out of here before they realize what's happening. Here, we've got to get you on that horse."

I pushed to my feet, trying not to wince at the pain in my side. We both scrambled over to the bigger horse that was freaking out just as much as the other one, and Cailen worked to calm it down. It finally slowed long enough that he was able to crawl on top with the help of a chair.

I didn't say anything before I darted for the door, coughing from all the smoke I inhaled. I pushed up on the metal bar and pulled the door open, whirling around as Cailen's horse charged toward me. My Scot offered me a hand and I was pulled up with him, latching on from behind as we burst our way out of the barn.

The first thing that hit me was the fresh air. The second, was that there were a lot more Scots than before, and they battled each other with swords, guns, and daggers. Some even had shields. I looked around in amazement as our horse charged through the fray.

"What's going on?" I asked, gripping Cailen around the stomach and doing my best to keep on top of the horse's back. "These guys weren't all here before."

"'Tis ma clan." He coughed.

Our horse slowed, and my gaze landed on two men, just as one of fell lifeless into the grass.

"Cailen," Conall breathed, his eyes bugging at the sight

of his son. "Elizabeth. Och, Lord, I'm glad yer well." He pointed in the direction I'd come from, and said, "Go that way. Others stayed behind tae aid the injured."

"Others?" I gaped.

"Aye, our clansmen followed us here. Good thing, too. More o' MacDougall's men came up behind us."

"Where's Cameron?"

"He should be caring for the injured."

Cailen's gaze flicked around. "Everyone here isn'ae from our clan." His voice was gritty, and he'd spoken slowly.

"The MacLeans heard what Donnan's men did on their land. They've come tae right a wrong done against 'em. Now *go*."

"I'm nae goin'."

"Cailen," I warned. "I don't think you should be talking." Just hearing it reminded me of him hanging from the rafters.

Conall shifted his sword from one hand to the other. "If ye'll no' go for yerself, then go for her. 'Tis nae place for a lass."

My Highlander shook his head in irritation. "Take care, faither." He steered the horse. I held tight as each step nearly jarred me off its back, closing my eyes and trying to block out the gruesome images of battle.

And then, I wasn't holding onto Cailen anymore, and the horse wasn't under me. We were thrown free, the sound of a gunshot ringing in my ears as our horse tumbled to the ground beside us.

"Run, Elizabeth," Cailen said.

There was something urgent in his voice, and I looked up as Donnan tossed a pistol to the ground only to grab another from his waist. He pointed it directly at us. Cailen was already on his feet, and as I struggled to mine, he bent to help me.

Once I'd found my footing, I didn't dare move. No, scratch that, I didn't want to. After everything he and I had been through the last few weeks, there was no way I was leaving his side now. "I'm not going," I said, echoing what he'd said to his dad not a minute before.

"Go," he growled.

"No." I stepped forward, putting myself between MacDougall and Cailen, despite my Scot's attempts to stop me. "You can't just keep hunting me. I'm with him because I want to be."

"Which is exactly why I should hae killed him sooner," Donnan spat, still aiming his gun at us. "Though, I dinna much care tae keep ye alive any longer. No' after the trouble ye've caused" He launched toward me, and Cailen shoved me out of the way. I landed on the ground, rolling back up as fast as I could, gripping my side as the two men fought one another. Donnan, with a pistol and knife; Cailen, bare-fisted. I whirled around, searching for any weapon I could find, and focused on a body lying in the field. I hobbled toward it, pressing my hand to my ribs as I reached the dead man. There was a sghian dubh at his side, lying in the grass next to him.

I scooped it up and sprinted back to the men. They were wrestling now; Cailen was throwing punches and blocking Donnan's blade as much as he could, though there were new cuts spewing blood. He was winded. The other Scot crushed the hilt of his knife against Cailen's head and jumped to his feet, pointing his gun at my Highlander.

"*No!*" I screamed.

Donnan's eyes flicked to me, a wicked smile curving his lips as he pulled the trigger.

Click.

I nearly laughed and cried as the gun misfired, and I

rushed toward Cailen, shoving the knife into his palm. "Here!" Tears streamed from my eyes and I brushed them away. How many times had the love of my life escaped death today? How many times in the last three weeks?

My Highlander had gotten to his feet again, and stood by my side. Breath wheezed in and out of him, and he looked like he'd topple over at any second, but he never let his gaze fall away from Donnan.

From the corner of my eye, I saw the blade that he now held glimmer in the waning sunlight. Now that he held a weapon, Donnan had no chance. My sweetheart battled boars. This piece of crap had nothing on him.

"Yikes. Those misfires can sure be pesky, huh?" I said to Donnan, before smiling. "You are so freakin' screwed now that my sweetie is armed."

MacDougall's eyes flicked from me to Cailen, his brows lowering. "Best silence yer wench, MacKinnon, or someone will shut her mouth for her."

My Highlander let out a sound I'd never heard before and barreled toward the other man. Donnan dropped his gun and the two faced off, each with a single knife in hand. I forced myself to watch as they attacked each other, slicing and jabbing, blocking and punching, until Cailen gained the upper hand.

He slashed the sghian dubh across Donnan's throat, a crimson line forming as the man fell to his knees. Blood gurgled from his neck, spilling down his body as his eyes widened. His gaze danced around as if he couldn't decide what to look at as the life faded from his eyes. His skin grew pale as blood soaked his shirt and kilt. The seconds seemed to take an eternity, but he finally fell face first into the grass, and died.

CHAPTER FIFTEEN

"Oh, shut up," I said, rolling my eyes.

After the battle, most of the MacKinnon clansmen made it back to Ardmoir. A few hadn't walked away from the fight, and even more came home wounded, I thought beyond repair. It was hard to accept that, knowing that they risked their lives for me, and for Cailen.

Cailen had been on strict bed rest. I'd seen firsthand how adamant his mom could be, and I didn't blame her in the slightest. And she'd gotten a taste of my own stubbornness. I hadn't dared leave his side, so I'd demanded I sleep in the same room as him. At least until some of his injuries healed.

I didn't give a damn if everyone on the isle thought it was scandalous, I wasn't letting the man out of my sight.

Cailen laughed. "What dae ye mean, 'shut up'? I can barely speak a'tall."

"Which is exactly my point. You shouldn't be forcing it. Give it time."

"It's been two days," he grumbled. "How long dae ye expect me tae lie here?"

"For as long as it takes. Now if you'll just shut up for a minute, maybe I can get some sleep. I'm freakin' cold."

Damn rain. It was only midday, but I couldn't seem to shake my exhaustion from the last few days. During the times that Cailen wasn't making terrifying breathing sounds that had me sending for the doctor, or when he'd actually stop forcing words through his crushed throat, I'd been able to cuddle up in my blanket and sleep through the chill that was inherently Scotland.

"Yer cold, are ye?" His eyes lit up, and I thought back to our first few nights together. "Ye ken, there is a way tae keep us both warm."

My eyebrows rose. "Are you actually hinting that we should share your bed? Your mom would hand me my ass if she walked in and saw us."

My Highlander chuckled, which turned into a painful sputtering. "Och, lass, the things ye say." He shook his head. "I'm a grown man, and ye're a grown woman. If ma mam is troubled by it, we'll deal wi'it then."

I smiled and crawled off my bed, bringing my blanket along with me. I spread it over the top of his and laid next to him as he held the covers open for me. I rested my head on his arm, facing him. "How bad does it hurt?"

"Ma throat? It's gettin' better. I'll be good as new in a few days' time."

"And then what will you do?"

Cailen's gaze mingled with mine and we laid there, silent, for however long. "I shouldn'ae've left ye. I regretted it e'en before I walked awa."

"Why did you then?"

"Dae ye recall that I mentioned ma wee brither, Kieran?"

"Mmm hmm." I nodded, feeling a prickle of unease at hearing his name. Ailsa thought it was Kieran who'd worn that cloak in Lorne's Pub, and was responsible for sending me here.

"Did I mention that I was cursed?"

"Excuse me?"

"Aye. It was his birthday, and the two o' us were supposed tae be daein' chores. We decided it would be more fun if we just disappeared for a while, and when we were certain our jobs were done by someone else, we'd return in time for supper. So, Kieran and I left Ardmoir. We were messin' around, goin' places we shouldn'ae, when we came across a witch." He shifted and sighed as his throat evidently started to give him fits again.

"You really don't have to do this," I said, even though I was dying to hear what happened. "Your throat is more important."

He kissed me on the forehead. "It's all right. At first we were just teasin', ye ken, bein' ignorant lads, but somehow we angered her. I should've had the sense tae leave her be, but the two o' us kept at it, harassin' her for spells, askin' her tae entrance the lassies in our clan tae fall in love wi'us. She warned us awa, but we didnae listen."

His eyes saddened, and I reached up, touching his chest. "What happened?"

"We were just teasin', as I said, and I told her that Kieran needed her tae dae a spell tae finish his chores, and Kieran told her I needed a spell tae find me a wife. That's when she started laughin'. I'll ne'er forget that woman's cackle, or the look in her eyes. Everything around us changed then, like the sky was afraid o' her, maybe. It got dark and the clouds rolled in. She turned tae me and said there was only one who could be mine. I remember bein' scared and excited at the same time, no' realizin' she was puttin' ma family under a curse. She spoke in riddles so it was hard tae understand, but she said that my one true mate was Red Michael. And if I took any other that ma family would ne'er be whole."

I pushed up, leaning on my elbow as I searched his eyes.

"The next thing I kent, Kieran and the witch were nowhere tae be seen. I searched for them for two years, and I searched for anyone kent as Red Michael. I...I've feared that she cursed me intae fallin' in love wi'a man—which I kent I couldn'ae dae. That's why I told ye I wasn'ae likely tae take a wife. But after all that searchin', I've no' found any o' them, and the closest I've come tae findin' that witch is ye."

"Me?"

"Ye speak the way she did. No' in riddles, I mean. Ye've the same accent."

"Is that why you wanted to keep me away from witches?"

He smiled. "A part o' me still thought ye might be one. I didnae want tae be part o' another curse. And now, I couldn'ae e'er let ye near one." Cailen sat up in bed, facing me as I rolled up as well, sitting beside him. "I meant tae come back for ye, lass. That's when I found Cameron and was taken by Donnan's men. I'd hoped..." He coughed. "Well, I'd hoped ye'd forgive me, and maybe agree tae be ma wife."

I probably looked like an idiot with whatever expression I gave him, but I didn't care. I hadn't really expected Cailen to change his mind. A part of me had feared his confession in the barn was only because he'd thought he was dying.

"Dinna stop breathin'," he added.

"I won't. It's just that...I mean...Are you sure?"

"Aye, I am. I've ne'er been more sure o' anythin'. I'll no' let the curse drive ma actions any longer, and intend tae tell ma family so. If I canna hae ye, then I'll no' take anyone."

Okay. Stunned. Still breathing, but stunned.

"Elizabeth, I've loved ye since the moment I saw ye, wi' that fire in yer eyes and that quick tongue o' yers. I've ne'er met another lass like ye and I'd be a fool tae let ye go when ma heart yearns for ye."

"When you first saw me, hmm?" I shrugged, smiling.

"So my Juicy T and short skirt had nothing to do with it?"

"Och, the sight o' ye in those made ma heart stop. But it was *ye* that made it beat again."

Melting.

"Did ye call me yer 'baby' in the barn?"

"Oh, umm—"

"And in the field wi'MacDougall, ye said I was yer 'sweetie'. Now, that could all be in ma mind, or maybe I'm just hopin' that ye've forgiven me, but—"

"I did say that. Both of them, I mean."

"Ye did then? Oh, I thought so." He nodded, smiling. "At least ye didnae call me a son o' a motherless goat."

The hilarity of him saying that in his accent was enough to bring a bubble of laughter from me. "When did I say that?"

"That day ye got the wee splinter in yer foot."

"That was not a splinter, that was basically a small tree."

Cailen chuckled and pressed his forehead against mine. "We can sort it out later. Right now I must ken if ye'll let me be yer husband."

"If I can't have you, I won't take anyone." I wrapped my arms around him, and we rolled off the bed, laughing and wincing at the same time.

"Is that a yes then?"

"Aye, it is," I said, biting my bottom lip as I placed my fingertip against his cleft chin. "Nothing would make me happier than being yours."

"Ye've always been mine, love. It just took us a while tae realize it."

Our lips met briefly, and we laid there on the floor, staring into each other's eyes.

"There's something I've been meaning to tell you," I said, tracing my fingertips over his lips. "It's something that I should have told you a long time ago, but, well, I was scared I guess. And now I know why your mom got so excited when I told her."

"Oh?"

I got nervous suddenly. What if I was wrong? What if Ailsa and Cameron and Conall were all wrong? "My last name is Michaelson."

"Aye, I ken."

"I think that I'm Red Michael."

Cailen's brows lowered and he eyed me for a few seconds before his face relaxed. "Ye dinna hae red hair, nor is yer name Red."

"Well, that's what I really wanted to tell you. When we first met, I gave you my middle name. My first name is Scarlett."

He quietly stared at me, blinking as he processed what I was telling him. "Yer name is *Scarlett*? Like the color red?"

"I think the witch really was talking in riddles. She was trying to tell you about me."

"Ye're the one I'm meant tae be wi'? I mean, ye *lied* tae me, but...yer ma woman?"

"Of course I'm yours. And I lied to you because I didn't trust you."

He shook his head and kissed me. "Aye, that was smart o' ye. But it could hae saved us a lot o' trouble if ye'd just told me the truth."

We smiled at the same time, laughing again as we held each other. Cailen's hand brushed slowly down my side as he captured my lips. I ran one of my hands down his stomach as the other went up to grip the back of his head, pulling him closer as we explored each other's mouths and bodies. This is what I'd craved since the moment we'd arrived in Ardmoir. His palm brushed up my leg, dragging my skirt higher and higher up my body until he reached under the fabric and cupped my breast.

I moaned against my Highlander's mouth, and he rolled on top of me, pinning my hips with his. "Where's yer wee trinket, Scarlett?"

I shuddered at hearing my name on his lips, and pointed to the wall beside the door. "In my purse."

I didn't want that though, I wanted him.

"Ye might as well toss it out, love. Ye'll ne'er be needin' it again."

Our eyes locked as our foreheads touched. He lightly stroked my bruised cheek with his fingertips, and pressed a tender kiss to it. Everywhere he touched, his lips followed. I closed my eyes, relishing in the moment as he kissed slowly down my body, taking extra care not to hurt my bruised stomach. My eyes flashed open in surprise as Cailen ripped my slip apart, exposing my breasts. His exploration continued, and I gasped as his mouth closed over a nipple, the warm wetness heightening every sense.

"Oh, Cailen. Oh God, oh God." I slapped my hand against the floor, sprawling before him. I felt absolutely everything: the soft press of his lips, the tickle of his hair brushing over my skin, the press of his fingertips as they slid under my thong and petted me where I craved his touch, the pressure of his cock against my leg. I sucked in a breath at another stroke of his finger. "Oh baby, please, I want you inside me."

"Oh, I intend tae be in ye verra shortly."

I lifted my head, meeting his eyes as he latched onto my other nipple. "Even though you don't want to have sex before marriage?"

"We'll be wed on the morrow, love. Right now, I plan tae make love tae ma future bride." He pulled my panties slowly down my legs, tossing them before he wrenched his kilt off. In seconds, he was bare, staring at me with a look in his eyes that had me sitting up, eager to meet him. His hard, chiseled body took my breath away. I'd always admired the way he was built, with his wide, muscle-packed shoulders, arms, chest, and stomach, and the perfection of his face. But now I was starving for him. I allowed my gaze to travel down the light dusting of hair that ran from his belly button to his long, hard length that pointed straight at me. My body quivered with desire to caress every inch of him, to have him inside me, to share something with him that had always been meant for him and him alone. I let the sleeves of my torn slip fall away and I reached up, wrapping my arms around his neck as he lifted me.

We fell onto his bed together, his body pressing against mine, his chest crushing against my breasts. His erection was pressing against my core now, as eager to get inside of me as I was for it. I attempted to reach for it, but he stopped me.

"I dinna ken how long I can dae this before I spill ma seed, and I'd much rather be inside ye for as long as I'm able." He nuzzled the side of my face. "Are ye ready tae accept me?"

"I've always been ready for you," I breathed. I was so very wet. Just the mere thought of him being inside me sent a fresh wave of arousal through my body. Yes, yes, yes, he was actually about do it. I was about to make love to my Highlander.

The head of his cock pressed against my entrance, and I spread my legs wide, angling my hips upward. His hands ran down my thighs, pulling me up as he pushed inside, groaning.

"Och, Eliz—Scarlett. Ye dinna ken how this feels."

"Yes," I moaned. "I do. Keep going slow." He was big,

and the feel of him inside thrilled me, but also created a lot of pressure.

"Tell me if I hurt ye." His hands left my thighs and settled on either side of my body as his cock inched even slower inside. "I dinna think I can go in anymore," he moaned, his body shaking. "Unless it's—"

"You have to push through it. Just be gentle. No…be fast. Do it fast. Please just push inside." I was breathing hard now, as pleasure and pain intermingled.

He caressed my cheek and plunged deep inside me until he could go no farther. We both moaned, and he bent down, muffling our voices by locking our lips together. Our tongues clashed, and Cailen's hips moved back and forth slowly, gaining tempo as I thrashed. What hurt in the beginning now felt indescribably rapturous, and I met him, thrust for thrust, losing myself to him.

Nothing existed outside of this bed, outside of his arms. I touched him everywhere, just as he did to me. His body quaked with desire, making my heart swell.

My Highlander reached down and ran his fingers through the tiny curls at my core as he continued to piston in and out of me. "Yer hair is longer here than last I saw," he remarked, his eyes fastening onto where we were joined.

"Mmm hmm," I responded as my body was pushed up and down the bed. "I haven't found a way to shave here."

"Ye shave there?" he gaped. "Nae, surely no'."

"Mmm hmm." It was the only way I could respond as my body began tightening.

Cailen's thrusts sped up and I peered at him, seeing sweat sticking to his forehead. His muscles were tense as he appeared completely focused. As our eyes met, he slowed and pulled out of me.

"What are you doing?"

"Turn o'er."

I leaned up on my elbows. "What?"

"Turn o'er. There is one thing that must be done before...mmm hmm."

I got up slowly, eyeing him as I turned around so that my back faced him. He positioned me on my knees and spread my legs apart. I cried out as he rammed his cock into me once more. He pumped and pumped, going impossibly deeper inside me. The sudden sting of a slap on my ass had me peering over my shoulder in surprise. "What...was that...for?"

"It's yer punishment for lyin' tae me." He smiled and raised his hand again before I felt another slap against my ass.

I moaned at the feel of it, shocked at the pleasure it caused.

"Tell me ye'll nae lie tae me again."

"Well, if this is my reward."

Slap.

"But I promise I won't lie to you anyway." My body tightened more.

Slap.

Pure euphoria.

The sting, coupled with the pounding of his cock, sent me over the edge. My head went backward as I cried out, and Cailen's hand covered my mouth as he rammed me harder and faster than he had before. He let out a strangled groan as his body convulsed, and I felt his hot, wet seed jetted inside me. His hips slowed, and we collapsed on the bed, enfolded in one another. Neither of us moved other than to hold each other tighter.

I woke the next morning as his door creaked open, and his mom shuffled inside, freezing as she saw us both on the same bed. *"Crivvens, what are ye daein'?"*

"Mam!" Cailen jumped to his feet—still wrapped in

one of the blankets, thank God—and pulled me up with him.

"Oh God, she's about to hand me my ass," I whispered.

Cailen peered down at me, chuckling. "She will'nae."

"I kent it wasn'ae suitable for the two o' ye tae sleep in the same room," she tsked.

"Nae, it's perfectly suitable. Or it will be soon."

Ailsa's gaze flicked back and forth between us. I got the impression that she knew exactly what had happened between us last night, especially since we wrapped in the same blanket, and our clothes were on the floor in front of us. "Oh, and why is that?"

My Highlander grinned at his mom and pulled me into his side. "It's time tae get ma ring. Scarlett and I are tae be mairrit as soon as may be."

"Ye ken as well as I dae that ma mam will, as ye say, hand us our asses if she finds us taegether."

"I don't care," Scarlett replied. "I don't want you to go."

"I dinna want tae either." Cailen brushed his hands through her hair as he studied the way her hair glimmered in the candlelight. "Yer hair is changin'." It seemed everything about his lass was ever changing.

"Hmm? Oh. Yeah, no more trips to the salon for me." She grinned. "That's where people go to change their hair color."

Over the last day the two of them had talked a great deal about the time Scarlett had come from. Her world sounded wondrous, and not that he'd ever tell her, but perhaps a bit frightening. Most of the things she spoke o', she had to define for him, but what made it even more delightful was the *way* she described it. The lass spoke with her hands as though she had so much energy she couldn't help but use her body to help accentuate every word.

He couldn't get enough of her. Every minute of every day, he wanted to spend with her. Which is exactly why he'd snuck into her bedroom tonight. Reverend Astor hadn't been available to perform their marriage ceremony that day, as he'd left for other villages around Mull. Luckily Gregor had gone searching for him, and had brought him back to Ardmoir late into the evening. That man was always looking out for him.

"Are ye ready tae become ma wife?" he asked, causing her to blink her tired eyes again and focus on him. He really should let her sleep, but letting her do so made him feel like it was time lost with his woman.

"Yes," she purred.

The sun had just come up for the day, and the sounds coming through the walls indicated that everyone was busy with their tasks. No doubt his mam had already checked his bedroom to see if Scarlett was inside. He wondered if she kent where he'd spent the night.

Probably, his mother kent everything.

"Dae ye want me tae let ye rest, love?"

"No. We can rest after the wedding. I just want to be with you."

Her words made his chest swell with pride. This was his lass. This was the woman he'd been waiting for and dreaming of since he'd been a young lad.

"I could stare—"

A strange sound cut off her words and she sat up hastily.

"Oh my God." She scrambled out of the covers and off the bed, rushing over to her bag and shoved her hand inside.

"What is that horrible racket?" On and on, it kept making that awful noise.

"That's my cell phone." Scarlett yanked it out and held it to her ear. Her brows drawn low, she slowly said, "Hello?"

Cailen stared at her, unsure of what to make of the expressions on her face.

"Wait I…" When she finally pulled the cell phone away from her ear, she peered at it again. "It's dead again." She'd gone pale.

He was beside her in an instant, helping her to sit on the bed. "What happened?"

"The number was restricted but I…think I know that voice." She peered into his eyes, and unease crept through him. "She wants to meet with me. She wants me to go to our spot."

"Our spot? What is our spot?"

"I think it's that tower thing up on the hill," she replied numbly. "When you were gone, I went up there sometimes, and your mom said it was your favorite place, too."

She hadn't told him that. If he hadn't known, then who did? And how had someone called her? "But ye dinna ken who it was?"

"No, but she said she wanted me to go alone." Scarlett got up and pulled on one of the tartan dresses Una and Emily had made for her.

Over his dead body she was going alone. "Ye're no' goin'. Ye dinna ken who it was."

"I've got to. I swear that I know that voice. And my phone, you know it was dead. They don't just start working like that. It worked for that one phone call, and I have to know why."

Cailen stood and drew on his shirt. He'd never removed

his kilt the night before so, so it was much quicker for him to get dressed than it was for Scarlett. Helping her smooth her dress, he followed her through the door, down the stairs, and outside.

"You shouldn't go with me. She told me to go alone."

"I canna just let ye go. We dinna ken what kind o' trouble there may be."

His lass walked briskly, and he kept up easily, checking the expression on her face as they passed house after house. He felt uneasy about the whole thing, but there was no arguing with her.

They weren't far from the cairn when a woman stepped out from behind it, fully cloaked in a dark blue robe that covered everything but her chin and black lips. Cailen gripped Scarlett's arm. "Stop. It's the witch."

"Ah, how nice," the woman replied. "I'm so glad you remembered me."

"O' course I dae. What hae ye done wi'ma brither?"

"She sent him to my time," Scarlett answered. Cailen gaped at her, but his lass continued to stare at the witch. "That was the guy with the pocket watch, right Shannon?"

The witch cackled suddenly, her bright white teeth gleaming from underneath her hood before she yanked it off her head. "Figured it out, huh? That was a lot faster than I expected. At least that will make this go a lot easier."

Scarlett stepped back, her arm brushing against his again. "What are you doing here? And what are you *wearing*?"

"You know, Scar, you could've let me play the part a little longer. It's not very often I get to be in character, and this guy eats it up like catnip."

Cailen flicked his gaze back and forth between the two women. "Ye ken her? Ye ken the *witch*?"

Scarlett glanced up at him for the first time since they'd

reached the cairn. Her eyes glistened with unshed tears. "Do you remember my cousin? The one I told you about that was getting married?"

"Her?" He pointed in her direction, not feeling any better about this situation. "Nae, she didnae look like that in yer pictures."

"She doesn't normally look like this." She turned toward the witch as her brows lowered. "What's with the goth?"

"I dunno." Shannon shrugged and stepped forward.

Cailen pulled Scarlett behind him, never taking his eyes off the other woman. "Nae. Closer. I dinna hae any qualms wi'murderin' a menacin' witch like ye."

"Oh?" she replied, the corner of her black lips pulling into a smile. "Well you might not, but your *wee lass* would definitely have a problem with it. Do you really think she'd want anything to do with you if you kill her best friend and cousin?"

"Why Shan?" Scarlett asked, peeking around Cailen's side. "Why put us through this?"

"Really? You're going to let your Scottish barbarian keep you from even giving me a hug? I haven't seen you in *weeks*. I've had to lie to your dad and my parents since your little disappearance, and all you want is answers?"

"My little disapp..." She sighed. "Did you orchestrate all of this? Cailen's brother? Me? Me inside the pub at the same time as Kieran? And don't call him a barbarian."

Cailen's mind was whirring. Scarlett had seen Kieran? Why hadn't she told him of this?

"Yes, I 'orchestrated' everything, but not by myself. And before anyone gets their panties or kilts in a wad, I first want to say that I'm not the enemy here. No one is. It's just something that had to be done."

"Why?" Scarlett had beat him to it.

The witch folded her arms, and drummed her fingers. "Do you remember when I went to Scotland during summer break a couple of years ago?"

"Yeah."

"Well, I met a group of people and we really connected, ya know? It turned out that they were witches and warlocks, and their main calling was correcting the balance of life."

Scarlett and Cailen glanced at each other, and she shrugged. "'Kay?"

"So what they do is research the past and find discrepancies. It's their job—well, *our* job—to correct them. I joined them and they hooked me up with a coven in Utah."

His lass shook her head. "I don't get what you're saying, what does this have to do with anything? And how can there be discrepancies in the past?"

"Oh trust me, it has to do with everything. And there are a ton of problems going on...you don't even know. There are dead-ends *everywhere*. Sometimes we just can't find any information about a person." The witch sighed and sat down on the ground, leaning back on her wrists. "So okay...you know I research everything, right? And I totally checked into this group. To prove to me that they were legit, they let me research my own ancestors to see if there was anything screwy going on, and you'll never guess where the trail ended." Her gaze went back and forth between them. "With you."

"This doesn'ae make any sense a'tall. Scarlett, we should get back, the woman is messin' wi'us the way she did wi'Kieran and me."

"I'm not messing with you," Shannon spat. "I'm telling you the truth. One of my ancestors was one of the children of Cailen Conall Grant MacKinnon and Scarlett Elizabeth

Michaelson MacKinnon, and there was zero information about Scarlett's parents."

There was silence all around, with only the sounds of the ocean waves crashing against land, and the gentle squawk of birds overhead.

"History isn't just history. History is the future and the past. It's all one big loop…or a lot of them, I guess. I mean…I know how you feel, Scar," the witch continued, more gently. "I didn't believe it myself at first."

"You don't know how I feel," Scarlett replied. "You weren't dumped in the middle of nowhere, and forced to fend for yourself. Why didn't you just *tell* me?"

"Because you wouldn't have believed me, and because I was so worried that we'd gotten the spell wrong on the pocket watch that I was terrified you wouldn't make it to the right time. I'm not an expert with any of this yet. You were my first traveler."

Cailen placed his hand on Scarlett's shoulder, giving it a gentle squeeze. As much as he wanted to hear of his brother's fate, he kent his lass was hurting. Her dearest friend had been lying to her all along. And he was angry that the witch would put her through this, without even kenning what she was doing.

"Without the two of you hooking up, I wouldn't exist anymore. My mom wouldn't exist anymore, and so on. I *had* to do it, Scar. I didn't want to fade away."

"You wouldn't have just faded away. That doesn't happen."

"It happens all the time. That's what the Legions are trying to prevent. They've worked for centuries searching for those not in their own time, and sending them to where they're supposed to be. Where fate meant them to be."

"Did you just say 'Legions'?"

"Yeah, the Legions of Fate. Kind of a big deal in the

grand scheme of things." Cocky wee bizzom.

"So I'm supposed to be here?"

Shannon's gaze bobbed around, searching the surrounding hills before returning to Scarlett. "In a way. To save *me* you really just needed to be here until yesterday."

"Until yesterday?" Cailen asked. "Why yesterday?" What was so special to Shannon about yesterday? Scarlett had agreed to be his wife, and they'd made love.

"Oh my God," Scarlett said, her hand covering her mouth as her eyes locked with his before moving to Shannon. "We had sex yesterday. Am I *pregnant*?"

The witch nodded, and Cailen barely kept himself from plopping down on his arse.

"So why did I only need to be here until then? Obviously I'd have to stay forever if that's the case."

"That's kinda where I'm breaking the Legion's rules." Scarlett's friend walked toward her and the two girls embraced, though his lass looked numb while the witch grinned happily. He didn't like it in the least, but he was far too stunned to move. "Congratulations on the baby by the way."

"Shan, what did…" Scarlett's voice died away as she pulled something out of her pocket. She gaped at her friend. "What did you do?" There was something in her hand, and she tried to pry it free as she started to panic.

He was beside her as tears trekked down her cheeks. "I can't get it off! It's burning and I can't get it off! Cailen!"

He yanked on the silver pocket watch in her palm, unable to break it free.

"What hae ye done!" he yelled, turning toward the witch.

"I came to take her home."

"I don't want to go," Scarlett cried. "I have to stay! Please, I—"

He whirled around at the sudden silence. No, it couldn't be. Scarlett and that bloody witch were gone.

He was alone.

Cailen slammed a fist against the tower, letting all the pain and rage in his heart fuel him. His knuckles bled, but he couldn't feel it. His Scarlett was gone, never to return. He fell against the rocks, wishing for all the world that he could see his lass again. He didn't ken what he'd do without her. He needed her in his life even more than he needed air.

A long while passed before he made his way back to the kirk. He wasn't sure how he made it, but he'd somehow put one foot in front of the other.

"Cailen! Och, where hae ye been? Everyone's inside waitin' for ye. I feared ye might hae run off again."

He peered up at his mother, trying to form the words. "I…Nae, I didnae leave."

"Where's Scarlett?"

He looked at the ground. "There's no' goin' tae be a wedding, mither. She's gone."

His mam gasped. "Oh no, darlin'. What's happened?'

He stepped past her to open the kirk doors. There wasn't going to be a wedding today, nor ever for him.

I sat up, cupping my hands over my eyes as my head throbbed. I felt like I'd been run over with a steamroller, and my hand tingled from the burn of the pocket watch, which laid in the grass by my side. Peering through my fingertips, my gaze settled on the stone tower. It didn't look the same as it had just minutes ago. Much of it had crumbled apart, it's pieces had fallen to the ground and shattered into gray dust. I was by our tower though. The ocean was just down below, and I recognized the grassy, rolling hills all around me. I ambled to my feet, searching in every direction for Cailen, and feeling panic rise once more as I saw that only Shannon was near.

A plane flew over my head, the loud rumble of its engine drawing my gaze upward as my heart skipped a beat. *No, no, no. This couldn't be happening.* I stomped toward my friend. "What did you do?"

She leaned against the decaying tower, shaking her head. "Whew! I'll never get used to that feeling. Do you feel like crap when you travel, too?"

"*What did you do?*"

"I brought you back," she snapped. "You should be happy."

I wiped at my tears with the back of my hand. She'd taken me away from Cailen, and she thought I should be *happy*? "Send me back."

"*What?* Scar, it's not that easy."

It had to be! It just had to be! I was about to get married to the love of my life. She couldn't have ripped me away from that. "Ugh!" I raced away from her, irritated that tears blurred my eyes as I hauled ass down the hill. My heart was shredding into a million, tiny pieces as every home I'd known in Ardmoir was no more. On and on I ran, ignoring Shannon's pleas as she followed after me. I slowed as I rushed through the decrepit dyke that ran around Conall and Ailsa's home, and fell to my knees as I saw what was left. There were only markers. Stones showing where the outer walls had been. Right there had been the front door, and just in front of me had been Ailsa's flowers. They couldn't be gone.

It couldn't all be gone!

I shoved to my feet again and ran through what used to be Ardmoir, passing more houses that were no more than proof of what had once been. I skidded to a stop as I approached the church where Cailen and I were going to be married. It was gone, too. Only ruins remained.

Everything, everyone, was all gone.

"Scarlett! What the hell is wrong with you?" Shannon said, gripping my shoulders and turning me to face her.

"Let me go."

"No."

"Let me go!"

"No!"

"*What have you done?*" I pulled my fist back and let it fly, feeling the sting in my knuckles as they connected with her face.

She fell back and gaped up at me, clapping a hand over her cheek. "What the hell?"

"I hate you!" I yelled, staring down at her as she sat on the ground. "You just mess with people's lives and do whatever the hell you want. You didn't even care enough to find out what I wanted, or even bother to find out whether or not I love Cailen. Because I do. I love him, and I want to spend the rest of my life with him. I don't want to be here, knowing he's been dead for two hundred years!"

"I thought you'd want to come back home. I mean, God, Scar, look at yourself. You're bruised and you're constantly holding your side. It looks like the eighteenth century was going to kill you instead of doing what it was supposed to." She flashed her puppy-dog eyes my way. "I thought you'd want your family, and me."

"I do want my family. I love Dad and Jason, but I'm not whole without Cailen. He's my family now. He's *everything.*"

Shannon finally stood, wiping small bits of grass from her cloak. "You should probably take some time to think about this. We both know you just jump into things. I'm sure you'll change your mind."

Was she freakin' serious? "I don't get it. Why put me through all of that just to bring me back?"

"Well, I miss you. You don't know what it's been like without you here. Your dad has been searching for you nonstop, and it really would make all of us a lot happier to have you back. I figured that you could raise your baby in our time and eventually my coven could just send your…son or daughter back."

"You'd send my child back there and force them to figure out the past the way I had to? You'd take my baby away from me?"

"No, not your baby. I'd wait until she's older."

She? I was having a girl? "Are you mental? You'd do that to me? You'd do that to *her*? What else are you selfish enough to screw up, besides making it so that I can't be with the man I love, and ensuring my daughter grows up without her dad?"

"No' tae mention other lines wouldn'ae exist."

I turned, only to find probably fifteen people standing there. They were a mix of ages, but there was one that really stood out among them: an old man with silvering hair who looked like he wanted to kill the girl responsible for bringing me back to this time, his expression far more intimidating than the disappointed stares of those behind him.

"Yeah," Shannon said, suddenly quiet as she looked at the ground. "That's why I broke the rules. Any other time someone is dropped into their fate, they're just left there without any explanation. Usually the coven doesn't have a direct tie to the person."

"Legions frequently hae direct ties tae their travelers," the old man spat, his cold gaze fastened on Shannon. "But most o' us are smart enough tae leave things the way they're meant tae be."

"Other lines," I whispered, focusing on the Legions. "Our other children wouldn't be born." I really was pregnant with a girl, and would have more babies with Cailen? I let out a slow breath.

"Nae, they wouldn'ae," another witch replied.

"You don't have to decide now," Shannon said quickly. "It's not like we have to do anything right now. What's done is done."

"There is no choice here," I laughed bitterly. "You think I make hasty decisions, but I've never messed with someone's life before. If I'm really supposed to be in 1770 with Cailen, then that's where I want to be. Even if I'm *not* supposed to be there, he's who I want to be with. And if you think for one second that I would jeopardize the lives of my own children, then you've got another thing coming."

Shannon wrapped her arms around her stomach as tears slid down her cheeks. "I'm sorry."

"You can be sorry all you want, but the only thing I want you to do is send me back." I could only imagine what Cailen must be feeling, and that was enough to wrench my heart in two.

"I can't," she replied. "It takes time to suffuse a watch with magic and get you back to where you're supposed to be. Scar, I can't send you back right now."

The doors opened and the church flooded with light as everyone turned toward Cailen. He strode inside, and his gaze locked with mine as he fell to his knees.

I let out a nervous breath, fighting back the tears I knew would come the second I saw my Highlander. My heart jackhammered in my chest as he rose to his feet once more, and slowly strode toward me. The entire church was utterly silent, his clansmen watching on as he lumbered toward me. His eyes never left mine as he stepped onto the altar. Was he *crying?*

"Scarlett? Are ye an angel before ma eyes?" He lifted his hand slowly, and cupped my cheek, starting as he touched my flesh. "Yer *real?*"

I leaned into his hand, unable to keep my own tears from spilling. "I'm real, baby. And I'm home."

"Ye returned tae me?"

"I wouldn't have stopped fighting until I found my way back to you."

He pulled me to him, gripping the back of my head as our mouths melded together. His tongue darted into my mouth, and I opened up, urging him to take all of me he wanted. Our lips parted, and he pressed his forehead to mine, wiping tears from my cheeks as I wiped his.

"Ye look like an angel?"

"Thanks." I ran my hands over my shimmering white wedding dress the Legions pooled together to buy for me. "Cailen, there's something you need to know."

"Oh?"

"I was gone for two days—in my own time, I mean. And I worked with the Legions to find Kieran."

He lowered his brows as he searched my face.

"I didn't come back alone." I stepped back as Kieran approached us and dropped the hood of his cloak. The two brothers stared at each other as the entire church erupted in chaos.

"Kieran?"

"Cailen."

They hugged each other, speaking in Gaelic as they laughed. Ailsa, Conall, and Cameron rushed up to the altar as well, the entire family hugging each other as happy tears streamed down their cheeks.

I couldn't help but laugh as I watched their elation at having their family whole once more.

They pulled me into their family hug, and though I hardly knew him, I embraced my new soon-to-be brother. "I'm sorry I mentally kicked you in the balls."

Kieran cocked a brow. "Eh?"

"After you sent me here, I mentally kicked you in the balls. Hopefully you didn't feel it since it wasn't *technically* your fault."

He and Cailen laughed, shaking their heads.

The family hug ended and the others sat in the pews.

"Ah lass, ye've given me so much," my Highlander said. "I ne'er thought I should be so lucky tae hae a wife, but now ye've given me ma brither, and soon we'll hae a bairn. I dinna ken what I've done tae deserve ye, but I'm fair grateful. Ye hold ma heart, lass, and I'll spend the rest o' ma life provin' just how much I love ye."

"I love you, too. You're so much a part of me that I can't imagine life without you. I don't want to exist without the other half of my soul." I smiled up at him, memorizing every inch of his face. I planned to do so every day for the rest of my life. "So I was wondering…What do you think about Caylee?"

"Caylee? For what?"

"For our daughter's name."

Cailen's hand went to his heart. "A daughter. We're tae hae a daughter?"

"I have it on good authority."

He took my hands in his as his face split into a huge smile. "I like it, Caylee Elizabeth MacKinnon."

Reverend Astor stepped up beside Cailen and me, facing the members of the clan.

"I didnae ken what I'd dae wi'out ye," Cailen whispered as the reverend's voice echoed through the church in Gaelic.

"You don't have to worry about that," I breathed. "Nothing could drag me away from you again."

"Good, because I dinna want cause tae chase ye, lass. But make nae mistake, I will if ye leave again."

The End.

More by Katalyn Sage:

Angels Incorporated

<u>Primordial Guardians™ series</u>
Dark Seduction
Passion Ignited
Born of Silence
Rapture

For more information, please visit
www.katalynsage.com

www.ingramcontent.com/pod-product-compliance
Lightning Source LLC
Chambersburg PA
CBHW071141170626
46809CB00002B/712